FIREPROOF

Screenplay by
ALEX KENDRICK and STEPHEN KENDRICK

Novelization by ERIC WILSON

THOMAS NELSON
Since 1798

NASHVILLE   DALLAS   MEXICO CITY   RIO DE JANEIRO

Published in Nashville, Tennessee, by Thomas Nelson. Thomas Nelson is a registered trademark of Thomas Nelson, Inc.

Thomas Nelson, Inc., titles may be purchased in bulk for educational, business, fund-raising, or sales promotional use. For information, please e-mail SpecialMarkets@ThomasNelson.com.

ISBN 978-1-4016-8527-0 (repak)

Library of Congress Cataloging-in-Publication Data

Wilson, Eric (Eric P.)
  Fireproof / novelization by Eric Wilson ; screenplay by Alex and Stephen Kendrick.
    p. cm.
  ISBN 978-1-59554-716-3 (softcover)
  1. Fire fighters—Fiction. [1. Fire extinction—Fiction.] I. Kendrick, Alex, 1970– II. Kendrick, Stephen, 1973– III. Title.
  PS3623.I583F57 2008
  813'.6—dc22   2008025922

Printed in the United States of America

13 14 15 QG 9 8

Alex and Stephen dedicate this book to:

Our mother, Rhonwyn Kendrick . . .
Thank you for loving us and Dad these forty-three years.
You are a blessing.
We love you!

Sherwood Baptist Church . . .
May your faith and ministry always remain fireproof.
We thank God for you!

Eric dedicates this book to:

My one and only, Carolyn Rose . . .
Thanks for daring to love me these past eighteen years.
WE H_VE A L_V_ W_RTH F_GH_ING FOR.

PART ONE

SPARKS

MAY 1998

CHAPTER 1

D ense smoke stretched between aisles of canned goods and wrapped its fingers around Captain Campbell's upright body. He tried to remain calm. He could see no farther than his leather gloves as he aimed the fire hose into blackness that pulsed with an eerie glow.

Snaking through aisles and licking along the ceiling, the grocery store's inferno seemed infused with a personal evil. It wasn't the first time Campbell had thought such a thing. Other firefighters had been known to say the same.

He told himself to take steady breaths. To stay focused.

No easy task.

The call had come into the station at 9:49 p.m. The locally owned store was getting ready to close its doors, and most of the shoppers had left. The main concern, as expressed by a cashier, was the safety of an assistant manager last seen heading to the back office.

The conflagration was spreading quickly now, seeming to rise from separate sections of the store and demanding the attention of all emergency personnel. Crews from three different stations had been sent to the scene. Campbell and his partner had entered the fray a half hour ago, with the rescue of human lives priority number one.

Stores could be rebuilt and inventory replaced, but nothing could bring back the dead.

"Tynes," Campbell called out. "Tynes, you there?"

His partner was nowhere to be seen. It was possible the man had followed the hose line back outside, in danger of depleting his composite tank. Or he might've tried skirting the inferno, in search of the missing manager.

Either way, he should have said something, but Tynes was only in his second year and even the best made mistakes.

A fact the captain knew well.

Though Capt. Eddie Campbell had been part of the firefighting brotherhood since the late 1960s, with numerous awards and honors to his name, he had already managed to lose his two-way radio this evening, somewhere between the market's front doors and his present location. Maybe caught it on a shelf. Or dropped it while coupling two hoses.

He was on his own, that's all he knew—cut off from all communication.

The fire, meanwhile, seemed nowhere close to giving up the fight, and the captain stayed firmly planted. Although the quivering hose at his fingertips gave him some reassurance, impenetrable billows continued to close in around him. He felt like a rat in the coils of a boa constrictor.

Steady breaths. Steady.

But he couldn't maintain this position forever.

He called his partner's name a few more times, to no avail. His voice was muted by the mask, and if he called out much more, he would risk losing the precious air in his thirty-five-pound canister.

From his back, several high-pitched beeps sounded in rapid succession.

Could that be right? He peered through the sweat-streaked face guard, squinting to read the dial on his Type 2 SCBA self-contained breathing apparatus.

Was he really that low? The alarm meant he had five minutes max, and then he'd be sucking fumes. The majority of fire fatalities were due to smoke inhalation, and if he didn't find his way out shortly, he would be in deep trouble.

Time to get going. He'd just follow the line back.

He felt his heart rate settle as he eased off the nozzle's water pressure, turned carefully in his gear, and slipped to his knees.

This was routine. He had a plan to follow, a goal in mind.

Campbell started crawling. At fifty-five years of age, he took pride in his physical condition. He moved hand over hand along the hose, knowing that it would guide him back to safety and fresh air. He wasn't done fighting this fire. He'd come back. But he'd be no good to anyone if he were passed out and unconscious on the floor.

His gloved knuckles knocked aside a can of Hormel chili and a box of taco shells. His right knee slipped on a water slick.

How far had he gone—twenty feet, thirty?

A single hose length was fifty feet long, and he and Tynes had been working with two in tandem. That meant it would take another minute or so to get out the door. In all this gear, progress was tedious, but he'd make it if he just kept moving.

Yes, just ahead was his proof. See there? Yellow and red bursts were prying at the smoke, and he realized he must be near the store's front windows. These had to be the fire engine's emergency lights rotating against the glass.

And was that clean air he tasted?

Just in time.

3

Something was wrong, though. Not only was his tank nearly empty, but the temperature was rising. Things were getting hotter with each knee forward.

"Oh no," Campbell said.

The words hung ominously in the mask. He saw now that he was looking at flames, not emergency lights, which meant he had veered off in the wrong direction. How could he have gotten this far off? He'd been following the line, switching from one hand to the other as he shifted along the floor.

The hose—

But no, this wasn't a hose he had gripped in his fingers. It was a pipe.

That couldn't be right. A pipe?

He must've switched over onto an irrigation system that ran along the floor to the produce section. How could he have been so foolish? Despite his tenure as a firefighter, he'd let circumstances blur his focus on the details.

Captain Campbell was breathing heavily as he turned back around. He had to keep his senses about him. The store was shrouded in darkness, and the only safe route was to backtrack to the point where he had erred.

He feared for his life. Would he make it out of here? Would he ever see his wife and daughter again? Joy and Catherine were his world.

Joy . . .

After twenty-six years, they were still together. She was a gentle soul, and she'd spent more than a few restless nights during the course of his career. No doubt about that.

Catherine . . .

She was eighteen, almost nineteen, a bright and vivacious

4

daughter with a streak of independence—some would call it bullheadedness—a trait inherited from her father.

Spurred by these thoughts, Campbell pulled himself onward through the store's suffocating environs. His pulse throbbed in his fingers, but he tried to stay attentive to each change in shape or texture along the pipe.

The hose had to be here somewhere. His only way out.

He kept crawling, even as a memory of three-year-old Catherine played through his mind . . .

CAPTAIN CAMPBELL STANDS just outside her bedroom door and sees shelves of toys and stuffed animals along the wall. A teddy bear has its head and arm wrapped in gauze. A tea set and a wooden fire truck crouch beneath a sign that reads "Daddy's little girl."

He hears giggling as Joy says good night to young Catherine.

"All right, sweet pea," she says at last, "it's time for you to go to bed."

"Mommy, would you ask Daddy to come tuck me in?"

"No, he's at work tonight at the fire station. But he'll be home tomorrow."

Campbell smiles, knowing how surprised his wife will be when she sees that he's come home early—with permission, of course—to celebrate their eleventh anniversary.

"Mommy, I want to marry Daddy."

"You do?" Joy laughs. "Catherine, you can't marry Daddy. He's *my* husband."

"Well, when you're done being married, can I have him?"

Campbell's heart swells. In the moonlight, he catches glimpses of his daughter's drawings tacked up beside her dollhouse. In one picture, blue crayon hearts surround the words "Daddy," "Me," and "Mommy."

"I'm sorry, sweet pea." Joy is chuckling. "We'll never be done. You'll have to marry somebody else."

"Who?"

"We don't know yet. But someday."

"Can I wear a white dress and white gloves?"

"Sure, if you want to."

Campbell edges closer to the doorway. He spots the framed photo of himself, outfitted in his turnout gear and fire helmet, holding his darling, dark-haired girl and kissing her on the cheek while she flashes a grin wider than the pink bow in her hair.

From the bed, Catherine's voice cracks with the hope of every little girl. "Will we live happily after ever?" She mixes the words, but her desire is heartfelt.

"Mm-hmm," Joy says. "If you marry someone who really, really loves you."

"Like Daddy?" Catherine asks.

"Yes. Like Daddy . . ."

IN THE CLAUSTROPHOBIC space of his heavy gear and face mask, Captain Campbell held on to that memory. He was a husband, a father. He did not want to die, not like this. Not here in this store, without the chance to see his family again. Without the chance to walk his daughter down the aisle. And what about being a grandfather? Was that too much to ask for?

He pushed on through the heavy smoke, his knees grinding into the floor. He imagined Joy at home on her knees. He'd never been much of a praying man himself, but he didn't discount the value of a wife who talked to God.

"You're not losing me yet," he whispered. "Not if I can help it."

He couldn't help it, though. Barely able to breathe, he felt disoriented by the blackness.

What was that?

His hand brushed against something slightly larger than the pipe. It was charged with water—*the hose!*

He was back where he'd started, in the middle of the store, but a long trek stretched before him in the opposite direction.

Air. He needed fresh air. He was gulping at nothing, now that the canister on his back had run dry. He knew that to take off his mask would put him at risk of carbon monoxide poisoning. On the other hand, he had only a few breaths left.

How long could he crawl without oxygen?

Forty seconds, sixty? Maybe ninety, if he could force down panic and keep his respiratory system regulated?

He thought again of his wife and his daughter.

One knee forward. *One-one-thousand, two-one-thousand.*

Another knee. *Three-one-thousand, four.*

Five, six, seven . . .

Twenty-two, twenty-three, twenty-four . . .

His eyes were losing focus. His head was swimming. Blood pounded in his ears.

Forty-eight, forty-nine . . .

Movements slowing. Feeling sluggish.

Sixty-one . . .

He peeled off the mask, gasping, finding only toxic fumes that dried out his tongue and seared his throat.

Sixty-two . . .

Three . . .

7

"I love you, Joy," he muttered. "I—"

"Captain!"

Strong hands scooped beneath his arms and jarred him back to the moment. He felt himself dragged along the path of the winding hose, his boots scrambling at the floor. He heard grunts and groans, and then he and his rescuer were exploding through the front doors into the blessed, oxygen-rich atmosphere outside, into swirling lights and cries of relief.

"Caleb found him. Look! The rookie found the captain from Station One!"

"Nice job, kid."

"Captain, are you with me? We thought you were a goner."

EMS personnel swarmed around, their voices smudged by the effects of carbon monoxide and exhaustion. He tried to sit up. He had to get back inside. He was held down, while someone pointed out the store's assistant manager seated on the nearby curb, with minor burns, but safe and sound.

"Tynes pulled him out," another firefighter explained.

"My partner." Campbell looked around. "Is he okay?"

"Man, I'm sorry." Tynes stepped into view. "I thought you were right behind me, Captain. I tried calling over the radio, but you didn't respond."

Captain Campbell nodded his forgiveness and closed his eyes.

A firm hand removed his brush jacket and his boots, letting the cool air work as a balm on his sweat-drenched frame.

Later, as the fire was brought under control and the ruckus quieted, he pulled himself up. Still weak, he felt guilty for not standing by his crew. And where was the man who had pulled him to safety?

On cue, the rookie clapped a hand on his shoulder. "You can relax, sir. We got it under control. We're just glad you're still with us."

8

"Me, too," Campbell admitted.

"We weren't gonna lose you. Not tonight."

"Your name's Caleb? Which station you from?"

"Six. This was only my second real fire."

"You did good, kid. I appreciate you coming after me. I truly do."

"Well, I couldn't let anything happen to you, Captain. If I'm gonna take over your job someday, I need you to stick around to teach me everything you know."

"Is that so?" Campbell raised an eyebrow and looked up into the rookie's soot-stained face. "Tell you right now, Caleb, that might take some time."

"I've got time, sir. And I'm a quick learner."

CHAPTER 2

Caleb Holt, rookie and recent hero, had been given orders to find the hose stretcher. What was a hose stretcher, though? He searched the fire engine high and low for the seemingly non-existent object, ducking his head into compartments and running his hand along every inch of the truck.

That's when Catherine Campbell strolled into the bay, the captain's daughter, his pride and joy.

Eighteen. Brunette, with natural highlights.

Catherine wore a summer dress, with a red mini-sweater tied off above her thin hips. The slight curve of her brown eyes was simultaneously alluring and friendly. "You must be Caleb."

Her voice caused sparks to dance, somewhere deep inside him. "Uh, well . . ."

"Unless you're going under a different name now," she goaded.

"Caleb. Yeah, that's me."

"Thank you for what you did. Saving my dad like that."

He shrugged that off. "You're Catherine, right?"

"Word spreads fast."

"Your father's proud of you. He has a picture of you in his office, but I never realized that you . . . Well, now I guess you're just more . . ."

"More what?"

"Uh, you're older."

She grinned. "Yeah, I wish he'd put up my new picture instead. I was, like, what, fourteen in that one?"

"You looked like you were just a girl."

"*Just* a girl?"

"Well, you know, not all grown up."

"And now look at me." A smile played over her lips. "All grown up."

Caleb tried not to stare and shout a rousing *Amen!*

This was the captain's daughter, and he knew he'd be better off not dwelling on the romantic possibilities. Plus, he was twenty-four years old. He'd been through his share of relationships, and the next time around he wanted something more substantial.

An eighteen-year-old? That was just asking for trouble.

Sure, physically speaking, she was grown up, but she probably still lived at home and had never paid so much as an electric bill in her life.

She was feisty, though, and he liked that. He'd always wanted a wife who had a mind of her own, not just some doormat for his own ambitions.

Easy there, big guy, he told himself. *Give it another two or three years.*

"You know where my dad is?" Catherine said.

"He left awhile ago to meet the investigator at the burn site."

"Okay. Guess I'll check back later."

"Okay, then. Well, uh, good meeting you, Catherine."

"You, too, Caleb."

With that, Catherine Campbell pivoted toward the waning sun, leaving the rookie with her silhouette burned into his mind.

PART TWO

SMOKE

APRIL 2008

CHAPTER 3

Along the bay wall of the Albany Fire Department, Station One, grimy gear and smudged boots stood beneath yellow helmets that hung from hooks. Caleb Holt had just added his own to the collection, the word *Captain* stenciled upon it.

Ten years he had served this city. Now, at age thirty-four, he had earned the second trumpet on his white officer's shirt—one of the youngest ever to do so. He'd dreamed of this since age eight, and even though he dreaded some of the grisly scenarios he came upon in the line of duty, he loved his job, this city, and the group of guys he worked with.

Lieutenant Michael Simmons: a tall, rangy black man with an angled chin.

Driver Wayne Floyd: a loose-limbed jokester, with gelled hair above expressive blue eyes.

Firefighter Terrell Sanders: a stocky, bald black man, always ready for a debate.

Rookie Eric Harmon: a young, sturdy fellow, still trying to find his place.

15

In the manner of firefighters everywhere, they were a dependable bunch, fun-loving, and ready to go to any lengths to protect the citizens in their care.

Why, then, did Caleb have this gnawing unease in his gut?

Still smelling of soot and smoke from this morning's warehouse blaze, the young captain panned the bay area, where a red ladder truck sparkled and its bugle gleamed, ready to sound the alarm. A wide orange stripe, bordered with blue, ran along the cinder-block walls, broken only by the city's Fire and Rescue emblem, which boasted outlines of an ax, a helmet, a ladder, and a pike pole.

Everything looked good.

And still, that sense that something was wrong.

He brushed it aside and stared off at the water tower across the street. That tower had been here for years, ready to serve this historic firefighting community. On the firehouse lawn, a flagpole waved the American and state flags in the clear day's breeze.

"Wisdom, Justice, Moderation . . . In God We Trust."

So read the words beneath Georgia's thirteen stars on a field of blue. The Peach State, one of the original colonies, was a great place to live.

Good job. Good location. Good crew.

But none of that solved the problems at home.

Caleb wandered outside, while Terrell Sanders used hand motions to guide Engine One back between the fire poles into the middle bay. The backup signal sounded, then Wayne hit the brakes as Terrell banged on the side of the truck.

Eric, the rookie, jumped down from the cab and rounded the front end. Beneath suspenders, his blue shirt was tucked into firefighting pants with reflective strips down the sides. He approached Terrell, his head hung low.

16

"Terrell, man," he said. "My bad."

"This ain't no game." The black man poked a finger into his chest. "What you did was wrong. You playin' with people's lives."

"C'mon, man."

Terrell shirked any further discussion and stomped off in his boots, with Wayne at his heels.

Caleb went to the dumbfounded rookie. "Eric?"

"Yes, sir?"

"He's got a right to be upset with you. You left him in a dangerous spot and tried to be a hero."

"But, Captain . . ." Eric took a breath and lifted his arms. "I thought I heard someone calling for help."

"It was coming from *out*side the building."

"But it . . . It was so dark. I couldn't see anything."

"That's why you have to stay with your partner. He had no choice but to assume something had happened to you, and that you needed his help. You *never* leave your partner. Especially in a fire."

Eric nodded and looked down.

"My rookie year," Caleb said, "we almost lost one of our captains."

"Captain Campbell?"

"That's right. His partner was running low on air and left him on his own in a burning store. The reason I'm even standing here today, as a captain, is because of the things that man taught me, but he could've been gone just like that. On your own, your chances of survival drop in a hurry."

"Sir, weren't you the one who—?"

"I got lucky, Eric. I found him with seconds to spare. Now, listen. Terrell's worked with me the past three years and he's a pretty good guy. Give him time to cool down, and then you give him a proper apology."

"Captain, I know that I was wrong, but did you hear the way he—"

"And make it sincere."

"Yes, sir."

Caleb slapped his station's newest member on the shoulder and left him on his own. To his credit, Eric kept his mouth shut and faced the lonely duty of washing down the truck and equipment.

IN THE FIREHOUSE dining area, Capt. Caleb Holt and his crew were gathered for lunch. They worked twenty-four-hour shifts, with forty-eight in between, clocking in at eight a.m. Alarms had kicked off this morning for them, and he knew they were all famished after skipping breakfast.

"Round two, gentlemen." Lieutenant Simmons appeared with a second plate of hot wings and set it on the table along with a bottle of hot sauce.

"Wrath of God," the label read. "Hotter Than the Lake of Fire."

"Bring it on," Wayne said. "How come you only make this once a month, Lieutenant? This stuff's good."

"'Cause man can't live on chicken wings alone, Wayne."

Wayne rubbed his belly. "This man can."

"Nah, you need the four food groups."

Caleb grabbed a few wings and passed the plate down the table. "He eats the four food groups—steak, fish, chicken, and pork."

"Hey, that's all I need," Wayne said.

Simmons made a face. "What you need is a bath. I can smell you from over here."

Despite the banter, Caleb noticed Terrell shooting Eric a hard look. The rookie dropped his gaze to his plate and kept eating.

"What I smell like," Wayne explained, "is a hardworkin' man.

18

You should never be ashamed to smell like a man. That's why I don't wear deodorant."

Eric looked up. "You don't wear deodorant?"

"Only if absolutely necessary. Now, if this Wrath of God sauce came in a roll-on, I'd be wearing it every day." Wayne tapped a few drops onto his wings.

"I don't see how you eat that. That's insane hot."

The alarm sounded and all five men froze, ready to burst into action. After four beeps, the dispatcher clarified that the call was going to Caleb's previous station: "Engine Six, Battalion One, respond to 1516 Brookfield Drive. Vehicle fire in back parking lot. Time out, 12:41."

Caleb relaxed and went back to eating as the voice droned on through the speakers. He knew matters would be safe in the hands of his Station Six counterpart, Captain Loudenbarger.

"Thank You, God," Wayne exclaimed. "I never mind putting out fires, but not while I'm eatin' chicken wings."

"Don't say that unless you mean it." Simmons pointed at him with a pair of barbecue tongs.

"What're you talkin' about?"

"Don't be thanking God if you don't mean it."

Terrell rolled his eyes. "Aww, c'mon, man. How could anybody really mean that?"

"Excuse me?" Simmons was all business.

Caleb said, "Better watch out, Terrell. You're about to get a sermon."

"All that God stuff? Man, you might as well believe in Spider-Man."

"Hey, I went to school with a kid named Peter Parker," Wayne cut in.

"You don't think God is real?" Simmons pressed.

"Oh, absolutely . . . ," Terrell said. "*Not.*"

"That was his real name, too," Wayne prattled on to no one in particular. "We used to call him Spidey."

Simmons kept his focus on Terrell. "Why do you think there is no God?"

"Why do you think there *is* a God?"

"Don't go there, Terrell." Caleb had been through this discussion before.

"He wasn't no Spider-Man," Wayne continued. "Kinda walked like a chicken."

Simmons refused to be derailed by the driver's nonsense. "Okay, Terrell," he said, gesturing with a half-eaten wing. "So outta all the knowledge there is to know out there, how much do you think you know?"

"Outta *all* the knowledge?"

"All of it. How much do you think you know?"

Wayne's monologue continued unimpeded. "We used to say, 'Hey, Peter—climb that wall for us, dude.' He hated that."

"Aww, I don't know. I'd say I know two to three percent. And nobody could know more than five."

Simmons turned his gaze toward Terrell. "So, Terrell, outta the ninety-five percent you don't know, you're positive there is no way God exists?"

"How do *you* know He exists?"

"I talked to Him this morning."

"See, you can't even say that, man."

"I'm pretty sure," Wayne mumbled between bites of chicken, "that Peter wore Spider-Man underpants to school. Just to make himself feel special."

This was too much. The others turned toward him in unified disbelief.

"What?" Wayne said.

"What're you talking about?" Caleb demanded.

"I'm saying that Peter Parker is *real*."

"And so is God," Simmons added.

"No," Terrell said. "He ain't."

"I'm telling you, He is."

"Man, you done lost your mind."

"All right, all right." Caleb wiped his hands with a napkin. "Eric, you've got cleanup duty. Wayne, I need you to finish the fire report."

"I'm all over it."

Caleb stood to leave, with Wayne and Simmons right behind him. He noticed his rookie lingering at the table while Terrell finished a last chicken wing. He knew it was best to let Eric and Terrell work out their differences, but he felt the need to listen in—just in case a referee became necessary.

"Hey, man." Eric's tone was almost bashful. "I, uh . . . I blew it today."

"Mm-hmm."

"I shouldn't have left you like that, Terrell. It won't happen again."

"Better not, rookie."

"It won't."

"I know it won't." Terrell pushed away from the table. "'Cause I might not come back for you next time."

Caleb turned away, letting the dining room door close behind him. Those words had triggered anew his sense of discontentment.

His wife of seven years, Catherine, his dream girl—she'd been giving every indication that their relationship was over. Which meant he was failing as a husband. It was a feeling that didn't set well with him, and he'd tried to shove it down beneath his officer duties. Last night, though, they'd argued and Catherine had issued

21

a warning similar to Terrell's: *"You spend all your time rescuing other people, but when are you here for me? Never, Caleb. We hardly even talk. Well, don't expect me to come running after you. I can't do it anymore."*

With that memory rumbling through his head, Caleb headed up to his office. Seven years was a good run. They'd given it a shot. At this point, he just wasn't sure he had the energy to keep trying.

Or the heart.

He sat at his desk and pulled out the station logbook. Enough of that. He had work to get done, always more work.

CHAPTER 4

The crew at Station One went without another call for the afternoon. Caleb was following his friend Lieutenant Simmons into the living area to catch the latest election results on TV, when a hand grabbed hold of his arm.

"Hey, Captain?" Wayne said. "When're you gettin' your boat?"

Caleb shrugged free. "I'm still saving for the one I want."

"Well, you just let me know. I'm right here and waiting."

"And why's that?"

"Isn't it obvious? It's about time I showed you my skills on the water. Maybe you haven't heard yet, but this boy can ski barefooted on one leg."

"Well, uh . . . That gives me something to look forward to."

"Oh yeah."

Caleb blinked in amazement. Did Wayne have no limit of self-confidence? He turned away and joined Simmons in front of the muted TV, where images flashed of the day's news.

"Hey, look," Simmons said. "Isn't that your wife?"

Caleb nodded.

Simmons picked up the remote and ratcheted the volume.

Catherine's voice purred through the speakers as she responded to a Channel 10 reporter: "Yes, we're grateful for the cancer center housed in our new medical tower, and we believe it will greatly impact the lives of our patients."

Shots of hospital equipment rolled as the reporter spoke. "Catherine Holt, public relations manager of Phoebe Putney Memorial Hospital, went on to say that they will continue to provide world-class medicine for southwest Georgia. For WALB News, I'm Rebecca Mills."

Simmons nodded. "Your wife, she's a good woman."

"Pretty, too," Wayne said. "You're a lucky man."

Yeah? Well, you don't live with her, Caleb thought.

"How long've you two been together?"

"It's been what, Caleb? Seven years?" Simmons said.

"Something like that."

"Betcha still remember the first day you met." Wayne toggled an eyebrow. "A man doesn't forget that kinda thing."

"That was a long time ago," Caleb said. "C'mon, guys, we got stuff to do."

"Like what?" Wayne tapped his watch. "Man, it's already dinnertime."

"Then stop jabbering and go throw in some pizzas for us."

"It's not my—"

"You want kitchen cleanup?"

"Pizzas," Wayne said. "Coming right up, sir."

AT PHOEBE PUTNEY, Catherine Holt was feeling proud of her accomplishments. Dressed in a professional skirt that flattered her slim figure, her clicking heels echoed along the tiles as she strode

24

down the hall. She was at the top of her game, overseeing public relations at a thriving medical center and gaining the notice of her peers.

She passed a tall, clean-cut doctor in the corridor. Dr. Keller, was it? He was the facility's newest man of mystery, unassuming, yet boyishly handsome.

She approached the nurses' station with a padded day planner in hand, purse dangling from the crook of her elbow. Her identity badge—with her new position in red print—clung to the lapel of her buttoned suit jacket.

"Hey, Tasha," Catherine said.

Tasha looked up from her desk. She had a stethoscope around her neck and wore a brightly colored smock. "Hey, Cat. Just saw you on TV. Lookin' good."

"Oh, I missed it. I was giving a tour of the new cancer wing." She set purse and planner on the counter, then glanced at her watch. "Hey, has Robin left yet?"

"No, she's here." Tasha called to the back room. "Robin? Cat's here."

Robin Cates, a young nurse with a long, blonde ponytail, walked out in a blue tunic. She removed her glasses. "Hey." She gave Catherine a hug.

"How are you?"

"I'm good. How're you?"

"Good." Catherine shook out her hair and leaned an arm on the counter. "Are we still on for tomorrow?"

"Four o'clock. You still want those scented candles?"

"Absolutely, bring 'em on. I wanna try them all."

"Good."

"And I'm gonna see my parents later. I thought they might like some, too."

25

"Ohhh." Robin lowered her voice. "Tell me, how are they?"

"You know, it's been a year since Mom's stroke. I've been trying to get her a new hospital bed and wheelchair, but their insurance doesn't cover it, and . . . I don't know. It's just so frustrating for my dad. He wants to help her, but he can't afford it. His own health issues have already cut into their retirement."

"I'm so sorry."

"It's all right." Catherine closed her planner and gathered up her keys. "Anyway, I need to run. But I'll see you tomorrow, right?"

"Right. I'll see you."

"Okay, bye."

Catherine turned to leave and bumped into Dr. Gavin Keller, whose eyes were fixed on the clipboard in his hand.

"Whoa. Hey, Catherine."

She felt flustered. "I'm so sorry, Dr. Keller."

"Call me Gavin, please."

"Gavin." Catherine liked the sound of that. He was one of the staff's newest additions, and she'd heard that he sought the slower pace and better opportunities that had eluded him in Orlando. "I'm sorry for almost running you over."

"Anytime," he said. "It's good to see you."

Anytime? What was that supposed to mean?

"You too," she said. "Take care."

As she headed down the hall, she was keenly aware of Gavin's appreciative gaze, and even from the nurses' desk his smooth baritone reached her.

"Sweet girl," he was saying. Then: "Tasha, would you file this for me?"

"Sure, Doctor."

Catherine paused and glanced back over her shoulder.

Tasha's face marked Gavin's departure with skepticism, followed by a none-too-subtle whisper to her coworker: "If I didn't know better, Deidra, I'd say the doctor has a thing for Cat."

Short and wide Diedra pursed her lips in agreement.

The two nurses exchanged a look and said in unison: "Mmm-hmmm."

Catherine hurried on, her cheeks flushed and her heart racing.

CATHERINE EASED HER Toyota Camry into her parents' driveway. Though they'd scaled down, by necessity, this lower-income house was nice enough—a single-level dwelling, guarded by shade trees and a row of bushes.

She knocked, but her dad's hearing had suffered of late, and she suspected he couldn't hear her. The door was unlocked, so she let herself in. Poking her head into the sitting room, she found Mr. Campbell helping his wife from the couch into a stock wheelchair.

She tried not to well up with tears. Even now, in his midsixties, her father had the strong yet caring arms of a fireman. She was reminded of being a young girl, pretending to sleep so that he would carry her from the sofa to her bed.

"Hello?" She gave a soft knock.

"Ohh. Hi, sweetheart."

"Hey, Daddy. How are you?"

"Great." The retired Captain Campbell gave her a hug. "Good to see you."

"You, too."

"How's my favorite son-in-law doing? We haven't talked in a while."

Catherine acted like she hadn't heard that and bent to embrace her mother, letting their cheeks gently touch. "Hey, Mama. How are you, huh?"

Joy Campbell nodded. Although her gray hair was brushed, her eyes wide and alert, there was something sorrowful behind those pupils. The stroke that had put her in this chair had also stolen her ability to communicate by any means other than the small chalkboard in her lap.

"She's doing great today," Mr. Campbell said. "She had a good lunch, she took a nap, and we were thinking about watchin' a little TV before heading off to bed tonight. She still loves to catch those game shows."

"*Wheel of Fortune.* I bet she still guesses 'em quick as ever."

"She certainly does."

Catherine slid fingers through her mother's hair, over her ears. "Any word yet on getting her that custom bed and wheel-chair?" She took her mom's hand.

"No," Mr. Campbell said. "They think as long as her current chair is working that she doesn't need anything else. But she can't sit in this one very long without it hurting her back. I have to wash her sores twice a day."

"We'll get you one, Mama." Catherine squeezed her hand gently. "And a better bed, too."

Mrs. Campbell gave a brave, close-lipped smile.

Mr. Campbell walked to the doorway. "Can I get you something to drink, dear?"

"Sure, Dad. Do you have any sweet tea?"

"With lemon?"

"You know me," she said, thinking how nice it was to be known and understood. These days, there wasn't much of that in her own home. Twice as big, with only two occupants, the Holt residence still felt claustrophobic.

She turned longingly to her mother. "Mama, I wish we could talk."

28

Mrs. Campbell's eyes reflected the same desire.

"It's been *so* long since I've heard your voice. I miss you."

Mrs. Campbell bent to her chalkboard and wrote: I   M_SS YO_ T_ _.

Catherine filled in the empty spaces and squeezed her mom's hand. They sat together, eyes locked, sharing love much louder than words.

CHAPTER 5

Caleb Holt was off duty, ready to get some sleep and time away from the guys. He knew Catherine would be heading to work in a few minutes. Through the tinted windows of his truck, he saw her car in the garage between his mountain bike and a stack of supplies that included a blue Igloo.

How many times had they used that ice chest? Once? At that lake party last summer?

And the bike?

Catherine had bought it for his birthday last year, but he preferred jogging. It burned more calories and gave him some physical outlet after his twenty-four-hour shifts.

He parked his burnt-red GMC Sierra in the driveway. Purchased from Jay Austin Motors, the truck was his pride and joy. He left just enough room for his wife to back out, and headed into the kitchen through the garage.

She emerged from the hallway, hair brushed and shiny over her pin-striped suit. The flared pant legs gave a fluid look to her movements. She'd always had a presence about her, a catlike grace befitting her nickname.

Not that it did much of anything for him anymore.

She cut around the bar into the kitchen. Remained silent.

So that's how it would be, huh? All these amenities—stone flooring, marble countertops, frosted-glass chandeliers—and they had nothing to say to each other.

Caleb set his duffel bag on the dining table and removed his captain's jacket. He tugged at his shirt, loosening up for a day off, and turned to the refrigerator—so new and shiny, he could almost shave in front of the monstrosity. One day, Catherine had reasoned, they would need the refrigerated storage space when they had children. Well, their professional existences had kept that reality at arm's length. At this rate, he wouldn't be a father till age forty.

Across the kitchen, Catherine was fiddling with that coffee grinder she adored. The woman and her caffeine. What was wrong with Maxwell House from a tin?

"You have breakfast already?" he asked.

"Yes."

He grabbed the milk from the refrigerator, shook it, and set it on the bar. "What'd you eat?"

"I had the last bagel and a yogurt."

He passed her on his way to the cupboard, where he pulled out a nearly empty box of Coney Bombs cereal.

Great. When was she going to get around to buying another box? He turned to chastise her, even as she returned the half gallon of milk to the fridge. The one he'd just pulled out.

"I was going to use that," he said.

"Then get it back out when you're ready."

"I am ready. Would you just let me do things in the order I want?"

31

"How am I supposed to know?" Catherine said. "You leave stuff out, and it usually sits there till I come cleaning up after you. Like I have nothing better to do."

"What about the shopping? You planning to make a grocery trip soon?"

She poured creamer into her travel mug. "Caleb, with the way your schedule works, you've got more time to go than I do."

"Hey, I just asked you a simple question. You don't need to get smart with me. You could've at least saved me some breakfast."

"Well, I never know when you're eating at home or going out. You don't tell me these things."

"Catherine, what is your problem?" Caleb's scavenging turned up a granola bar. Better than nothing. He slammed the cupboard door and turned. "Did I offend you by walking in the door this morning?"

"No. You just can't expect me to work every day and still get the groceries, while you sit at home looking at trash on the Internet and dreaming about getting your boat." She dipped a spoon into a bowl of sweetener and stirred her coffee.

Couldn't she even extend the courtesy of looking at him?

He stabbed a finger at the air. "Hey, you chose to take this job, and no one said you had to work full-time."

"We need the income, Caleb—especially since you tuck away a third of your salary saving for a boat we don't need. You've got twenty-four thousand dollars in savings when we have things in our house that need fixing."

"Like what?"

"The back door needs to be painted, the yard needs better landscaping, and I keep telling you I want to put more shelves in the closet."

32

"Those are called preferences, Catherine. Those are not needs. There's a difference. If you wanna spend your money on that stuff, go ahead. Fine. But I've been saving up for my boat for years." He turned his back, disgusted by this whole conversation. "You're not taking that from me."

"This is so pointless. I don't have time for this."

"Yeah, go on." He watched her scoop up her belongings as he tore into the granola bar. "And shut the door on your way out."

She did. Forcefully.

In the hallway something clattered onto the carpet, and when Caleb went to investigate, he found one of their wedding photos dislodged from the wall. He jammed it back onto its hook, not even waiting to see if it settled evenly.

LATER IN THE afternoon, Catherine hosted Robin Cates and her passel of scented candles. Robin was on the couch, the Holt wedding album in her lap. Catherine took a seat next to her, with a bag of cookies and two drinks. She was dressed casually, done with the headaches of her workday. From the unlit candles on the table, she selected a lavender one and drew in its floral sweetness.

"Oh," Robin said. "Just look how happy you are. Catherine, these pictures are gorgeous."

"Thanks."

"Someday . . . ," her friend said wistfully.

"Robin, you're a hopeless romantic. That's not real life, you know?"

"But it's every little girl's dream, right?"

"Yeah. And then we grow up."

Sounds of a car in the drive were followed by a visitor's knock on the door.

"Caleb," Catherine called down the hall.

He emerged from the master bedroom, outfitted in a gray T-shirt and navy sweatpants. Catherine saw Robin give him a quick approving look, then drop her gaze back to the album.

Another knock.

"I got it," Caleb said. He passed through the dining room.

Catherine didn't need to see their visitor to know it was Lieutenant Simmons. Simmons had arrived in Albany five years ago, after serving in Iraq, and quickly become one of her husband's best friends.

"Hey, Michael," Caleb was saying.

"You ready?"

"Yeah, let me get the drinks."

Catherine saw him duck into the kitchen and heard the fridge open. "Caleb, are you leaving?"

"Told you already, I'm going out with Michael."

"You didn't tell me."

"I did too." He appeared in the archway, bottles of Gatorade in hand. "It was this morning. Or maybe last night."

"Well, when will you be back?"

"Later." He turned to leave.

"You think, on your way, you could go by the store and—"

The door slammed on her sentence and she clenched her jaw.

Beside her, Robin was still looking through the album as though nothing had happened. "Oh, I love this one. You were such a beautiful bride."

Catherine dared not open her mouth. She nodded in feeble agreement, thinking how much easier it was for some people to

34

hold on to the fairy tale. The reality was that this castle was no longer big enough for a fair maiden and her handsome prince.

SIMMONS LEANED OVER the Sierra's truck bed, his dark eyes taking in the blanket of greenery that stretched toward the woods. "That your property all the way out there?"

"Last time I checked," Caleb said.

"And is that a pond I see back through those trees?"

"I've never taken you out there?"

"No. But, uh, I'm not into romantic walks with my guy friends, thank you. You ready to bounce?"

"Ready."

"You tell Catherine we're going to the gym?" Simmons asked.

"Nah, she's good." Caleb opened the driver's door. "Oh, hold on. I left my wallet inside, and I need to put some gas in this beast. Man, if I go back in there, she's gonna think up some errand to send me on."

"I can go in."

"Then she'll just ask you, and we'll both be in the doghouse. Hold tight. I'll be right back."

Caleb bounded back through the garage, turned the door handle slowly, and eased himself through the opening. He could hear Robin and Catherine still talking, could hear the flap of the wedding album's pages and the crinkling of candle wrapping.

"Mmm, that smells so good," Catherine said.

"Aren't those incredible?" *Flapp.* "Oh," Robin said, "I love this church. Does it still look like that?"

"That was many years ago. I have no idea."

Caleb glided into the kitchen on the soles of his tennis shoes.

35

Flapp.

"And your cake—oh my goodness, Cat."

Seven years ago, Caleb had been so enraptured with his new bride and thoughts of the honeymoon suite that he couldn't even remember what flavor that cake had been. Vanilla? Carrot? A Christmas fruitcake, for all he knew.

Flapp.

"Your dress was so pretty, I can hardly stand it," Robin gushed to Catherine. "Okay, so if you could go back to your wedding day and talk to yourself, what would you say?"

No reply.

Caleb palmed his wallet from the counter, then started to sneak back out, but his wife had still given no response and he found his curiosity getting the better of him. What did women talk about when the men weren't around? Would she exaggerate his attributes, as guys were known to do? Brag about his earning power and the silky nightwear he'd bought for her last Valentine's Day?

"Don't do it," Catherine answered at last.

Caleb froze.

"What?" Robin said. "Don't do it, as in . . . you wouldn't marry him again?"

"I mean, if you want me to be honest."

Caleb felt his head spin, knocked off balance by his wife's confession. She didn't mean that. Did she? Every couple had their ups and downs. It would pass. She was just being a woman, living in the emotions of the moment.

"But I thought you guys were doing pretty good, Cat. I mean, you've been married for seven years."

"Seven *bland* years," Catherine responded. "I don't know. We started off great. It was so romantic, but we just went downhill from there."

36

Caleb stood at the counter, trying to stay still. He heard Simmons come back inside, and even the lieutenant seemed to recognize the need to be quiet.

"I don't even feel like I know who he is anymore," Catherine said. "We fight more than we do anything else. Lately, I just catch myself thinking that . . . that this is not the man I wanna grow old with."

Turning, Caleb saw Simmons give a jerk of the head. It was time to leave. Yeah, that was the best plan right now—to leave before it got worse. But how much worse could it get?

"Catherine, I am so sorry. I had no idea it was that bad."

"It's all right," she said to Robin. "I . . . I'm just tired of playing this game, you know? We've been heading in different directions for a while."

"So, what're you gonna do?"

Caleb held his breath, straining to hear his wife's answer.

Silence.

Simmons was gesturing, trying to curtain Caleb's eavesdropping.

Still not a word.

Well, Caleb figured, that was about right. Catherine had been giving him nothing for weeks now—no affection, no understanding, and certainly nothing close to a civil conversation. Was it wrong of him to expect those things in his own home?

He eased outside with his wallet and carefully closed the door. He climbed behind the Sierra's steering wheel, turned the key, and cranked up the stereo. Simmons, to his credit, nodded his chin with the music and made no comment.

CHAPTER 6

I n the station weight room, Simmons completed his final bench
  press and sat up for a breather. Sweat was glistening on his
forehead and dripping down his jaw. His stereo was plugged in
beside him, blaring music and keeping the adrenaline flowing.

On a nearby universal machine, Caleb churned out the rest of
his reps, letting the weights smash against each other—up, down,
clang . . . up, down, *clanggg*—as he worked out his frustration.

At last he sat up, panting. "My triceps are burning."

"You're complaining?" Simmons said. "Man, I think those
weights are ready to apologize for whatever they did wrong to you."

Caleb smirked, then reached for his Gatorade. Simmons turned
down the music and wiped at his neck with a towel.

"It ain't working, Michael," Caleb said. "How is it that I get
respect everywhere I go except in my own house?"

"I've been there. That's a hard place to be."

"What'd you do about it?"

"I realized that it wasn't my marriage that was broken. I just
didn't know how to make it work."

38

"What does that mean?"

Simmons thought about it a moment, then pointed to a treadmill. "That treadmill's not broken, but if you don't know how to run it, it ain't gonna work for you."

"What? Are you saying I need counseling?"

"Well, I think everybody needs counseling."

"Hey." Caleb raised a finger. "Look, man. I am not about to go talk to somebody I don't even know, about something that's none of their business."

"All right. Well, Catherine does need to respect you. But just remember that a woman's like a rose. If you treat her right, she'll bloom. If you don't, she'll wilt."

"Where'd you get that?"

Simmons took a sip of his juice and grinned. "Counseling."

Caleb threw his empty bottle at Simmons, who only smiled as Caleb smirked and looked away.

CATHERINE WAS STRAIGHTENING up the house. She and Robin had shared Papa John's pizza after a relaxing, soul-sharing afternoon. On top of that, Catherine had bought some beautiful candles. She lit one now, trying to set a mood, to establish some atmosphere in this cold, immaculate dungeon. The house was like one of those model homes—presentable, even impressive on the surface, yet empty and lifeless within.

She heard Caleb's truck pull into the driveway. She held on to a slim hope that he would have something nice to say about the scent she had picked out, maybe show some interest in her day.

Something other than: *"How much money did you give Robin for those things? What? You bought some for your mother, too? Like that's gonna do any good, when what she needs is a good wheelchair. I mean, a candle? C'mon."*

That would be so predictable. So Caleb.

She slipped back to the bathroom and ran a brush through her hair, touched up her mascara. She waited as the door opened and closed, as his feet scuffed through the kitchen—no doubt streaking the floor she had polished this morning. Not that he would notice.

She heard the refrigerator open. Telling herself to give him the benefit of the doubt, she flicked her hair back, squared her shoulders, and walked into the kitchen.

Her first observation: He had snuffed out the candle, and only a thin wisp remained in the air above the counter.

One more of her hopes . . . up in smoke.

"What're you doing?" she said, despising the sound of her own voice, but unable to halt the flow of disappointment.

"I see you left me no pizza," Caleb shot back. He was in his workout clothes, a ring of sweat around the collar of his T-shirt. He closed the refrigerator, then moved toward the cupboard.

"Caleb, I just lit that candle. I like the way it smells."

"Well, I don't. Did you leave me any dinner at all?"

She brushed her hair over her ear and looked down. "I assumed you were eating with Michael."

"Does it not occur to you that there are two people living in this house and both of them need to eat?"

"You know what, Caleb—if you would communicate with me, maybe I could have something for you."

He slammed the cupboard door, still empty-handed. He approached the bar, setting both hands on the marble and facing her. "Why do you have to make everything so difficult?"

Catherine braced herself across from him. Well, at least they were looking each other in the eyes. That was a first this week.

"Oh," she said, "*I'm* making everything difficult? It seems to me like I'm the one carrying the weight around here, while you're off doing your own thing."

"Excuse me? I'm the one out there working to pay this mortgage, and I pay for both of the cars."

"Yeah, and that's all you do. I pay all of our bills with *my* salary—"

"Which you agreed to do." He jabbed a finger at her. "That's fair. Do you not like this house? Do you not like your car?"

"Ohhh." She felt things coming apart inside but couldn't hold herself back—not now that he had dragged this into the open. "Caleb, who takes care of this house? *Me.* Who washes all the clothes? *Me.*" He turned away—typical—and fumbled with a basket of packaged goodies for something to munch on. She continued, refusing to be muffled by his lack of attention. "Who gets all the groceries? *Me.* Not to mention I'm helping my parents every weekend. You know, I've got all this pressure on me, and the only thing you ever do for anybody is for yourself."

IT WAS BAD enough to have his wife throwing out accusations and waving her hand at him, as though he were a defendant on the stand, but what really got under Caleb's skin, what really stuck in his craw, what turned up the heat so fast he thought he would explode, was her blatant disrespect for him as a husband and as a man.

She was staring at him now, her voice raised.

Would she be the one to deride his every maneuver while he crawled through a building in search of victims? Or as he applied pressure to a severed artery and watched the life go out of a college kid's eyes? He had a crew of men that backed him up without question, and here in his own home he couldn't butter bread without her questioning his technique.

Eye to eye. Nose to nose.

Okay, was that how she wanted to do this? Oh yeah—he knew how to fight on these terms.

"Let me tell *you* something," he said. "You don't know the first thing about pressure." He whipped around the counter, getting right up in her face, punctuating his words with his hand in the air. "You think I . . . I put out house fires for myself? Or rush to car wrecks at two a.m. for myself? Or pull a child's body out of a lake for myself? You have no idea what I go through!"

"Oh yeah," she said. "Well, what do you do around here other than watch TV and waste time on the Internet? You know what, if looking at that trash is how you get fulfilled, that's fine, but I will not compete with it." She turned to leave.

"Well, I sure don't get it from you."

"And you *won't*." She snapped around, speaking to his back now as he looked in yet another cupboard for food.

All Caleb had wanted was a bite to eat, a shower, and some peace of mind. Now he tried to avoid meeting her eyes for fear of letting the animal within roar to life for the kill.

Her words were right there, though, buzzing through his head.

"You know why?" she ranted on. "Because you care more about saving for your stupid boat, and pleasing yourself, than you ever did for me!"

Caleb slammed the doors shut so hard he could feel the floor shake.

"Stop! I'm *sick* of you!" He turned and came at her, veins bulging in his neck and in the hand that jutted toward her. He edged her back, cornering her against the wall. Something in his

42

male psyche had snapped, further provoked by the terror in her eyes. "You *dis*respectful, *un*grateful, *self*ish woman!"

Catherine teared up and shook her head. "I'm not selfish—"

"How dare you say that to me!" He was out of control, his voice gravelly and cracking in rage. "You constantly nag me, and you drain the life outta me. I'm tired of it!"

Catherine was sobbing now, her chest heaving. She closed her eyes and turned her head down and away, flinching at his every word.

But he wasn't done.

"If you can't give me the respect I deserve—*look at me!*—then what's the point of this marriage?"

She shook her head back and forth, her chin quivering, her lips sealed shut. He paced, turned, looked back at her. He felt like a tiger measuring its prey, and he hated himself for it, hated the fury that seemed so volatile just beneath the surface of everything ordered and tidy about their lives, yet he meant everything he'd said.

He was done. Finished.

Catherine covered her mouth as she bleated: "I want out. I just want out."

"If you want out . . ." Caleb got back into her face and threw his whole body into his closing statement. "That's *fine* with me!"

Catherine collapsed over the counter, sobbing.

Caleb knew he should feel something for this woman he had sworn to honor and cherish—he'd been convinced he would die for her—but now all he felt was relief to be done with it. The torture could end for both of them.

He stormed out the back door, arms shaking with rage. His hands turned into iron fists, in need of a physical outlet. He stomped to the edge of the driveway, turned, stomped back again, searching for an object on which to take out the brunt of his anger.

43

The large green trash can caught his attention.

He walked up to the inanimate container and kicked it. Hard. It toppled onto its side, sending garbage bags tumbling onto the dirt. That only spurred him on. He hefted it with both arms and sent it crashing into the wall of the brick house, spilling refuse like entrails from a wounded beast.

He'd drawn first blood, so to speak. He had won.

Easing off now, he turned.

And realized he had an audience.

Mr. Rudolph, the elderly next-door neighbor, was standing ten yards away in a threadbare bathrobe and cinched pajama bottoms. His eyes were hooded and hard to read. Vulturelike, he stood hunched at the shoulders with one hand holding the lid of his own trash receptacle, the other dangling a kitchen garbage bag over the opening.

Oh, great. This was just wonderful.

Caleb dropped his hands to his sides, thought of shoving them into his pockets in a show of nonchalance, then simply offered a half wave. "Uh . . . Mr. Rudolph."

The man replied in a low monotone. "Caleb."

Caleb nodded, then went to work setting things back where they belonged and cleaning up his mess. Mr. Rudolph dumped his own trash. Caleb shot him one more look, hoping to have won back approval.

With a blank stare, Mr. Rudolph pulled tight the folds of his robe and trudged back to the safety of his own home.

IN THE MASTER bedroom, Catherine cried until there were no tears left. Her cheeks burned with the salty trails of her grief and anger. She didn't deserve to be treated this way. After an hour

44

curled alone on the bed—*their* bed—she felt herself begin to turn numb.

It started from somewhere deep within, a place that had held out a thin hope until tonight. Well, that hope had been snuffed out, and she closed the door on it now, once and for all.

She stood and shuffled toward the dresser. The numbness spread with icy resolve from her chest, through her arms and legs, and up into her face. She stared at herself in the mirror, noticing that her lips had turned bloodless and pale, pressed into a thin, hard line.

A candle burned on the dresser, beside a framed photo taken four years earlier while Caleb and Catherine spent a weekend at a bed-and-breakfast in Charleston.

Had that vacation ever happened?

Were those people in the picture just photo doubles, paid to smile and look good?

No, that was them. It was real.

They'd loved each other in a previous lifetime, but things had changed.

Catherine Holt removed her wedding ring and stuffed it behind the garments in her top dresser drawer. Down the hall, the spare bedroom door closed loudly behind the harried movements of her husband. Smart man. He had no place in *her* bed, not tonight. Not ever again, for all she cared.

She slammed the drawer shut. Turned off the lamp. Blew out the candle.

This flame had gone out for good.

CHAPTER 7

At Station One, Caleb watched his guys going through routine daily procedures. He was seated on the front fender of a fire truck, thumbing through a boat catalog while enjoying a splash of sunshine coming through the open bay doors. Nearby, Wayne and Terrell were following Eric, observing the rookie's every move as they went over a checklist for the truck.

"Airpacks?"

"Check."

"Pikes and axes?"

"Check."

Caleb loved the history of this place. This was the city's central station, built in 1970 with two levels, and it took a lot of work to keep it in tip-top condition.

"Think I got it all," Eric said.

"You sure about that?" Terrell said.

Holding the clipboard, Wayne wore a blue ball cap over his cropped blond hair. "Have you tested the torque on the lug nuts?"

"You serious?" Eric said.

"Every little thing, man. Tires, fluid levels, wiper blades, brake lights—every component has to function correctly. The chrome and silver's gotta shine. Just imagine us showin' up at a fire with a coupla hoses left behind, huh?"

The inspection continued. All around, the brass fire poles gleamed and the bay floors were spotless. Caleb knew his guys were whipping the kid into shape.

"That's it," Eric said finally, closing a compartment door and looking toward Terrell for assurance.

The squat black man gave a thumbs-up.

"We got it," Wayne said. "We're good to go."

Eric put his hands on his hips and flashed a smile of confidence. "I think I got the hang of this."

"You think you know the truck?"

"Yeah."

"Good," Wayne said. "All right, I'll tell you what. Terrell and I are gonna go inside and get something to drink. I want you to bring us a hose stretcher."

Eric's expression went blank.

Wayne clapped him on the arm and exchanged a subtle look with Terrell.

"Uh . . . all right." Eric mouthed the words *hose stretcher* and turned to begin his search.

Caleb watched Wayne amble over to Terrell, who was propped against the front fender of the truck. Wayne wore a smirk.

Terrell said to him, "Man, that's mean."

"Now you're defending the rookie?"

"He's still learning."

"That's the whole point. It's good for him."

Caleb smiled. All newbies had to go through some practical

47

joking as part of their six-month probation period, testing if they had what it took for this job.

Years ago, he'd also had to earn the respect of his peers, though rescuing Captain Campbell from the grocery store fire had done that quicker than usual. Some of his original crew had held that against him, angered by the favor he curried.

Nothing came easy to young firefighters in a town that took its pedigree as seriously as Albany, Georgia. You earned each trumpet on your lapel. This city's first heroes had operated in 1836, forming bucket brigades to put out fires. They'd graduated to horse-drawn engines and large cisterns, and only decades later had they enjoyed the luxury of fire hydrants and pressurized hoses.

Chief James, the original, had died serving his fellow citizens.

Chief Billy Brosnan, a legendary innovator, had later served the area for forty years, and his name was still bandied about in larger cites as a standard for excellence. Recognized nationally and internationally, he'd even headed the International Association of Fire Chiefs for a short time.

Caleb was snapped out of his thoughts by conversation from the other side of the truck.

"Uh, really?" Simmons was saying. "You planned her party for Saturday?"

"I told you about it, Michael," said a female voice. "I already went by the store and picked out your mother's gifts."

Caleb knew that was Tina, Simmons's wife. Sure enough, she came into view wearing a tan brushed-leather skirt, black knee-high boots, and a jean jacket over a white turtleneck. She was holding Simmons's hand, seemingly still enamored with her husband of eight years.

"Oh." Simmons snapped his fingers and turned to Tina. "I forgot to tell you. I got Friday off, so I'll be there for the game."

"Good."

Still holding her hand, he said, "You know, I ain't gonna let my son down."

"I know you won't."

"Hey, we still got that hot date tomorrow, right?"

"Oh, so now it's a *hot* date?"

"Mmm," Simmons said. "Life's too short to have any other kind."

"You're right about that," Tina cooed.

Looking through his boat catalog, dreaming of open water and sports fishing, Caleb heard the couple kissing and felt almost guilty listening in on them. Obviously, though, they weren't too worried about privacy here between the trucks in the bay. Caleb threw another glance around the corner.

"I love you, baby," Simmons told Tina.

"Aww. I love you, too." Her free hand cupped her husband's face, her eyes looking into his. Slowly, she pulled her hand away. "I will see you in the morning."

"All right."

"You stay safe, Michael."

Simmons put both hands on his waist, his mouth spreading into a sappy grin as he watched her go.

It was all so gushy, so nauseating. It was hard for Caleb to believe he and Catherine had been that way at one time. This morning, as he'd passed his wife in the kitchen, he'd noticed she was no longer wearing her wedding ring. That had cut deeper than any words she'd spoken.

What had gone wrong? Long ago, hadn't they been lovesick, too, like Simmons and Tina?

Now Caleb was just sick of it all.

Fumbling sounds broke up the quaint farewell between

49

Lieutenant Simmons and his wife. Circling the other truck, Eric was still searching for the mysterious hose stretcher. Caleb was about to stand and intervene, when Simmons broke out of his reverie and spotted the bewildered rookie.

"Eric, what're you doing?"

"Umm . . . Well, I'm . . . Wayne told me to grab a hose stretcher."

"A *hose* stretcher?"

"Yes, sir."

"Eric." Simmons wrapped an arm around the kid's broad neck and leaned close. "You *are* the hose stretcher."

To his credit, Eric took the lieutenant's hard slap to the back without complaint. Simmons walked away and Eric dropped his head in embarrassment. "Aww, man." He turned, pulled down an open compartment door with a clang, and headed toward the lunchroom.

On the engine's front bumper, Caleb chuckled. With no one to share the moment, however, his laughter turned hollow in the empty bay.

CHAPTER 8

Later that evening, Catherine found herself in the caring hands of her friends—Robin, Tasha, Deidra, and Ashley. They'd seen her puttering around the hospital all day, and asked how the public relations manager could be the one looking so dour. Once the word *relationship* was tossed up as part of the trouble, it was all over.

Time for some girl talk.

A table for five, alfresco, at a trendy restaurant.

"Men and women?" Tasha folded her arms and rested them on the white tablecloth. "They don't think alike, that's a proven fact."

"Doesn't take no sociologist to tell me that." Diedra took another bite of her dinner roll. "Any wife, mother, sister, any girl who's ever lived with a man, they can tell you—there is a whole world of difference. Men, they don't work right."

"Aww, that's not fair," Robin said.

"It's true."

"Some of the time, sure," Tasha said. "But I know a coupla sistas who ain't got it all straight neither."

Robin nodded. "We're all human. All of us need help every now and then."

"Which is why we're here," Deidra said. "Right, Cat? You need us."

Catherine gave a weak yet genuine smile. She wore a scooped blouse with a silver padlock resting against her collarbone on a chain. She remembered how she had opened that lock, figuratively, nearly a decade ago in the fire bay. She'd met Caleb Holt's eyes, seen a man who was strong, cute, and heroic, and she'd let down her guard. Let him in. Let him play king of the castle.

And now she only wanted to run away.

Or go back to sleep.

Here at this outdoor dining area, with lights strung along the latticework and the amber moon low and large overhead, she wondered: Was there any way to go back to being Sleeping Beauty? What if the kiss that had awakened her was a bad joke and she wanted to reverse its effects?

"Thanks," she said to her cluster of friends, "for getting me away. This is nice. I don't know, maybe I'm just overreacting to everything. I mean, Caleb and I used to have something there. Maybe I should just talk to him and—"

"Oh no you don't," Tasha cut in, waving her fork. "Honey, I agree with you. You got to get out. He don't deserve you."

"You can say that again." Deidra looked Catherine directly in the eyes, wagging her finger. "A real man's gotta be a hero to his wife before he can be a hero to anybody else—or he ain't a real man."

Ashley said, "Catherine, do you need a place to stay? I can't imagine living in that house with him."

"No," she answered. "I decided last night that I'm not the one who's leaving. *He's* the problem, not me."

Tasha waved her fork again. "That's right, girl. Stand your ground, and make him respect you. If there's one thing a man understands, it's . . ."

"IT'S RESPECT," CALEB said. Here in the bay, between polished floors and parked vehicles, his words sounded hollow. He was seated on the step of Engine One, checking the threads of a hose coupling. The station was quiet, the bays locked down till the next emergency, amber moonlight peeking through the windows.

He jabbed his arm toward Lieutenant Simmons, who was leaned against the wall. "Respect," he reiterated. "That's the issue. That's the reason our marriage is failing. She shows me no respect at all. And the saddest part about it is . . ."

"HE DOESN'T EVEN have a clue." Catherine leaned both arms on the table, mindlessly tearing her dinner roll into pieces. She could feel the emotion rising up in her all over again, angered by her husband's thoughtlessness.

"You got that right," Deidra said. "Men never do."

"I mean, he thinks our marriage has been fine for the most part. You know, he probably thinks . . ."

"OUR MARRIAGE HAS been fine until this year." Caleb held out his hands, as though open to suggestions for a problem he knew did not exist. "Now, all of a sudden, she goes off the deep end."

"Do you really think this happened all of a sudden?" Simmons said.

"I don't know what to think. I don't understand her. She's

emotional about everything. She's easily offended and way too sensitive . . ."

"HE'S SO INSENSITIVE." Catherine felt her voice crack and looked to her friends for understanding. "You know?"

"Oh, we know," Tasha said.

Ashley rested a hand on her arm.

"I shouldn't even be . . ." Catherine paused.

"Say it, honey. Just say it."

"I . . ." Catherine felt safe with these ladies. Yes, she had to say this, had to get it off her chest. She swiped a finger at the corner of her eye, where frustration was beginning to bubble over in hot tears. "I don't think he truly cares how I feel. And he doesn't listen to me, even if I say it over and over and over again . . ."

"AND THEN SHE starts nagging me." Caleb was up on his feet now beside the fire engine. He waved off the very thought of his wife's pestering, like a man batting away a bee. "Saying that I don't listen to her, or . . . or something like that. It drives me crazy. I feel like I'm going . . ."

"INSANE."

Catherine was admitting the worst now. She worked at a hospital, for heaven's sake. She was supposed to have it all together. She made good money, had the attention of half the men in the cafeteria, and portrayed the very image of a woman with all her stuff together. If she let them know what went through her mind, would they have her committed to the mental ward?

That would be sure to hit the news in a city the size of Albany. But at this point, it no longer mattered to her.

"You know," she said to her girlfriends, "he just doesn't understand my needs. I feel like we are completely and totally . . ."

"INCOMPATIBLE!" CALEB STABBED a finger at his friend Lieutenant Simmons. "There's no other word for it. She's probably off whining to her friends, making me sound like a criminal. I can see them all right now, crying, having some sorta group hug . . ."

THE WOMEN WHISPERED words of consolation, their arms around Catherine's shoulders, their hands touching hers. Deidra got up from her seat to come hug her from behind and rest her cheek on Catherine's hair.

"It's gonna be okay, sweetie," Tasha said. "It's gonna be all right."

"Oh, girl. Oh, girl," Deidra said.

Catherine was covering her eyes with her left hand. She could feel her chin quivering with emotion. The tears flowed freely now, spilling onto the white tablecloth and splattering on chunks of torn bread.

This wasn't her. This wasn't the professional, put-together woman she wanted to be.

She couldn't help it, though. She was coming apart.

"You'll get through this," Ashley said.

"We're here for you," Robin said. "You'll be happy again. Don't worry."

"He's not good enough for you."

Deidra massaged her shoulders. "We got your back. Whatever you need, whatever you need . . ."

HE DIDN'T NEED this anymore. Caleb Holt knew that beyond a shadow of doubt. He folded his arms, his eyes hard and unblinking.

"So," Simmons said, "you think it's past the point of no return?"

No return?

That sounded like surrender, like giving up. But who was Caleb fooling? Marriage wasn't a game, some contest in which all the spoils went to the victor. This was supposed to be a joint venture, right? A partnership. And his partner wanted nothing to do with him.

"Michael." He looked up and gave Simmons a flinty stare. "I don't have a reason to return."

CHAPTER 9

Sixteen-year-old Bethany Dawson braked her silver Kia at a stoplight in downtown Albany, turned up the volume on a Third Day song, then fidgeted with her hair in the rearview mirror. She liked her new highlights and hoped they made her look older. With her thin, high voice, she was tired of being mistaken for someone years younger. Not to mention, her squeaky tones gave people the impression she was ditzy.

Like, how ridiculous. She wasn't even blonde, okay?

But Kelsey was. Slouched in the passenger seat, Kelsey was scrolling through names on her cell phone.

A maroon sports car pulled alongside, and Bethany glanced through her open window to see two guys she knew from high school. Both good-looking. Both seniors. Their flirtatious smiles made her feel awkward and confident, all at the same time.

"Bethany," Kyle called over.

"Hey, Kyle. Hey, Ross."

"What's goin' on?" Ross said, his arm draped over the steering wheel.

"What're y'all doing?" Bethany said.

"We're heading down to the Pizza Barn to meet some friends." Kyle gave her a confident smile. "You wanna come?"

She turned to Kelsey for a reaction, hoping the sparkle in her eyes wasn't too obvious.

Kelsey's eyes were sparkling, too. "Sure," she said.

"Hey," Kyle said, "we'll race you there. And if you win, we'll buy."

The girls were all over that.

Kyle leaned back in his seat, staring straight ahead. The road was clear for blocks, and sunshine was just beginning to break through the clouds over the central water tower. "Ready. Set—"

Punching the gas, Bethany caught the boys off guard.

Behind her, she heard Kyle's frantic yells: "Go, go, go!"

Free pizza? The attention of two upperclassmen? Even in her Kia, Bethany told herself this was one race she just had to win.

CALEB MADE SURE the crew was attentive to every detail as they washed the truck on the pad outside the bay. The radio was playing that new tune from Third Day—a band he especially liked, considering their Georgia roots. He loved the South, the traditions that had made it resilient, and the focus on family. Not to mention the good weather. You couldn't pay him to trade Albany's sticky-hot days of August for the bone-brittle chill of upstate New York or Wisconsin.

No, sir. No thank you, ma'am. And y'all enjoy that ice storm, you hear?

On the other hand, the embarrassment of watching a white man try to dance in the presence of cool perfection . . . Well, that was cause for concern.

Wayne, however, showed no concern at all.

"Oh yeah. Better look out, Terrell." Wayne shook his hips while washing the engine, then slid his head back and forth as though it were resting on a swivel stick. "'Cause I'm about to give you a li'l bit o' this, and a li'l bit o' that."

Hokey didn't even begin to describe it.

"You're about to *what*?" Terrell coughed a sharp laugh into his hand. "You got to be kiddin' me. Whatever you think you look like, that ain't what everyone else is seeing."

"Do I sense some jealousy?"

"Jealousy? Wayne, you're an embarrassment to every color-challenged person who already can't dance."

Wayne was not to be dissuaded—a li'l more of this, and a li'l more of that.

Caleb could see that Eric wasn't sure whether to laugh out loud or hide behind the truck. It took some getting used to these guys, but it was all in fun, and he had a feeling the rookie would fit in soon enough.

"Eric, you still got a dull spot on that driver's door," Caleb said.

"Yes, sir."

Caleb left the dance scene and headed into his office, where the lights were down low and a screen saver of his dream boat bobbed on virtual waves. What he wouldn't give to be out on the Gulf right now, away from the drudgery of the station and the embarrassment of a marriage that was going up in smoke.

BETHANY MEASURED THE distance to the railroad tracks ahead and figured she would make it before Ross and Kyle caught up in their low speedster. She'd got the jump on them, and anyway she was a girl. They'd back off after giving her a scare. She was sure of it.

She was wrong.

"Bethany, slow down," Kelsey begged from the passenger seat.

The road was narrowing to one lane in each direction, and Ross seemed intent on overtaking the girls before they reached the crossing. He showed no signs of backing down. The nose of his car pulled even with the Kia.

Bethany set her jaw and narrowed her eyes. A split-second glance showed the boys laughing, whooping, and having a good time. They were used to this sort of game, to the stare-down, the whole macho deal.

Who did they think they were? She'd show them.

She crushed the pedal to the floor.

"Bethany!"

The train tracks were rushing at them, silver and shiny, growing larger, larger. The car would sail over the embankment, probably get some air, and come down hard. What if they slid into the tree on the other side? What if—?

With Kelsey's scream in her ears, Bethany Dawson panicked.

And slammed on her brakes.

The sudden deceleration pulled the wheel in her hands, causing the driver's side front panel to veer into Ross's sports car. There was a crunch of metal, followed by an angry yell that turned into screams—from the boys, from Kelsey buckled in beside her, and from the grinding of the vehicles.

Then, overcorrecting, she spun her car the other way, and the world went haywire in a flash . . .

Tires squealing; brakes and rubber lacing the air with burnt odors; the entire steering column coming at her, pinning both legs as the Kia pinballed off the cross-arm warning pole; air bags deploying; then, finally, in slow motion, sliding sideways up the pavement and slamming down into the groove between the tracks.

CALEB'S CELL PHONE rang. Caller ID told him it was his father. "Hey, Dad."

"Son, you busy?"

"No, not really."

"I heard your message. What's going on?"

"Well." Caleb kept his voice even. "I think Catherine and I are done."

"Oh, I doubt that. Everyone goes through rough times."

"No, it's . . . it's over. She said she wants out."

"Well, we've all felt that way before, son. She's a good woman and she's worked hard to get where she is in her career. Giving up just doesn't seem like her style."

"She's probably right, though," Caleb said. "It's just not working."

"Listen, why don't I come down so I can talk things over with you."

"Uh . . ." Caleb knew his parents had gone through a recent spiritual revival of sorts, and he had a sudden vision of his father pushing religion on him. All that God-talk was fine for them, but it wasn't really Caleb's thing. Nevertheless, he caught himself saying, "Sure, you can come over. I'll be home."

"Okay. Well then, I'll—"

The fire alarm sounded throughout the station, setting bells ringing.

"Dad, I gotta go."

Caleb stood and snapped his cell phone closed. The clock was ticking in his head now, counting each second the crew took to get moving through those bay doors. Every moment mattered.

Overhead, the female dispatcher's call came through the fire-house speakers: "Public Safety to Engine One, Battalion One. Respond to the intersection of Roosevelt and Kelley. Ten-fifty-I Rescue. Time out, 12:21."

Car accidents were often the worst.

Caleb rocketed from his office into the bay, dreading what he and his crew might find. He saw Simmons coming toward him as Terrell slid down the fire pole. "Hey, this one's close by. Lieutenant, you and Terrell get the other truck and go with us."

"Ten-four," Simmons said.

Already standing in their boots, Wayne and Eric were suiting up, pulling heavy fire-retardant gear over their station uniforms. Caleb yanked suspenders onto his shoulders, gearing up in stride as he'd learned to do over the years. He climbed aboard the engine, with Wayne in position as driver and Eric in the cab's backseat pulling on his scuffed yellow helmet.

"Okay," Caleb said. "Let's roll."

The driver gave the affirmative and flicked overhead switches, kicking in the lights and sirens. He blasted the deep horn as he pulled onto North Jackson Street, with the aerial following close behind. They threaded tree-lined avenues on their way through town. The emerging sun was pleasant and cheery, giving no indication of the life-threatening scenario they might soon encounter.

Caleb spoke into the radio. "Engine One is en route to Roosevelt and Kelley, Ten-fifty rescue."

Dispatcher: "Ten-four, Engine One."

Terrell's voice: "Aerial One is responding with Engine One."

"Lieutenant," Caleb radioed to Simmons, "you and Terrell have the Hurst tools ready if we need them." He then turned to Eric behind him. "You stay with me when we pull up."

Eric, his forehead already pricked with sweat, gripped the handhold by his door. "Yes, sir."

The engine turned, running parallel to the train tracks now. Trees and houses were set back from the area, but the scene was rapidly becoming congested with well-meaning citizens.

"We've already got a crowd," Wayne said.

Caleb craned his neck for a view of the accident. "Can you see it?"

"We've got one car on the tracks."

"You're kiddin' me."

Rarely serious off duty, Wayne was all business while on a call. "No, it doesn't look good, sir." He blew the horn to clear people out of the way.

Caleb got on the radio again. "Engine One is Ten-twenty-three. We are Roosevelt Command. We have a two-vehicle accident with possible entrapment. One of the vehicles is on the train tracks. Please notify the train dispatcher to stop all trains in progress."

"Ten-four, Command. Be advised that EMS is en route."

Eric was squirming in the back.

"Rookie," Caleb ordered, "you come with me."

"Let's go, guys," Wayne said.

Caleb hopped down, moving past horrified pedestrians with cell phones glued to their ears. The other truck halted. Caleb pointed out the maroon vehicle in the ditch where a pair of passengers sat motionless. "Terrell, you two go check out that car and let me know what you got. Wayne, pull me an inch-and-three-quarter line from the truck."

"Got it, sir."

Caleb and the rookie hurried past glittering glass and strewn car parts, toward the silver Kia, where a group had gathered in hopes of being of some help. Steam was escaping from beneath the sedan's hood. The roof was caved in and the front windshield obliterated—clear evidence of a rollover. The vehicle was smashed beyond repair, its rear passenger-side wheel twisted at an odd angle where the axle or U-joints had given way.

"Eric, you check out the passenger."

"Yes, sir."

"All right," Caleb addressed the crowd for their own safety. "I want you all to stay clear of the tracks and the vehicle." Only with a firm voice would he be able to establish control and restore some calm to all concerned. He knelt beside the driver's door. "Ma'am, I'm Captain Holt of the Albany Fire Department. We're here to help you."

"Help me, please," the girl said in a thin voice. "I can't get out."

"What's your name?"

"Bethany. Please, help—"

"Bethany, I'm gonna do everything I can to get you outta there. Okay?"

She nodded.

Caleb saw that Eric was attending to the unconscious female passenger, checking vital signs, assessing the damage. The rookie was doing good.

Back to the trapped driver.

"Please," Bethany whimpered.

Caleb couldn't help but notice she was a teenager. Just a kid. Her forehead was furrowed, left nostril dripping blood, chest heaving. He had to keep cool or risk spreading panic and fear, thus hindering his own decision-making.

"Can you tell me where you're hurting, ma'am?"

"My legs are hurting. Please help me."

"All right," he said. "We're gonna help you."

Bethany's eyes were pleading, pleading. They seemed to say: *I'm dying and you're the one person who can save me.* Except, he couldn't always do that. He had lost a few over the years, and he'd gone to bed more than a few times with that very look burned into his nightmares.

"I . . . I can't . . . move my legs," she told him. "I'm stuck."

"I'm here to help, you understand? We'll get you outta here."

Caleb leaned in through the window and pushed aside the spent air bag to study the situation. What he saw stole his breath away.

CHAPTER 10

Bethany was losing blood quickly, her left leg nearly severed by jagged metal that had rammed through the car's firewall. From her pinned position, she was unable to see her predicament, and Capt. Caleb Holt knew it was best to keep her attention diverted. He didn't need her going into shock.

"Okay," he said. "Where else are you hurting?"

"My neck is hurting. Please." She was sobbing. "Please help me."

"Listen, we're gonna get you out of here. You're gonna be just fine, all right? Just hang on."

"Please don't leave me, please don't leave. Don't let me *die*."

Caleb met her eyes, knowing those very pupils might stare holes through his soul for years to come. He couldn't let that stop him, though. She needed his strength. He reached a hand toward her and gave an assuring nod. "I promise you I am not going to leave you. Bethany, you're gonna be all right."

Eric spoke from across the crumpled roof, reporting the passenger's situation. "Captain, she's alive but not responding."

"Get the spreaders."

"Yes, sir."

As Eric turned to fetch the necessary tools, Simmons and Terrell hurried up the rail embankment.

"Captain." Simmons tossed a thumb back over his shoulder toward the boys in the sports car. "Those two are gonna be okay. They've got minor injuries."

"All right, we've gotta cut these girls out. Terrell, help Eric with the Hurst equipment. Lieutenant, I need you to check for gas leaks."

"Yes, sir." Simmons pulled off his helmet and crouched down beside the mangled chassis.

Close by, a few men were watching the events and murmuring among themselves. Farther back, a police vehicle had pulled up to start crowd control.

Caleb returned his attention to the trapped girl, who was shaking now, becoming more desperate with each breath. Glass fragments glittered like a busted necklace around her throat. He set a hand on her arm. "Bethany, we've got an ambulance coming. I'm gonna stay right here with you."

A gasp. "Okay."

"In a moment, you're gonna hear a loud noise. That just means we're getting you out faster."

She was still with him. "Okay."

"You're gonna be all right."

A train whistle sounded in the distance. Caleb turned toward it and stood to full height, eyes widening as they followed the glistening rails around the bend. The train was not yet in sight, but the rumble of its weight could be felt through the very earth beneath him.

"Captain?" Simmons rose to his feet. "Did I just hear a train?"

Caleb grabbed his radio and barked into the transmitter. "Dispatcher, this is Roosevelt Command. We have a car on the train tracks. Notify the train dispatcher to stop all trains in progress!"

"Roosevelt Command. Be advised, we are currently unable to make contact with the train dispatcher. We will continue trying."

Caleb's face contorted in frustration and sudden determination.

"There's a train coming," an onlooker called out.

Others were realizing the predicament now. "Hey! A train's coming. A train's coming!"

Terrell and Eric approached with the Hurst tool. A hydraulic implement created for tearing into metal and peeling it apart, it was a powerful item, though not particularly fast.

"No, no, *no*. We don't have time! C'mon," Caleb said, gesturing at his crew. "We're gonna have to push it out of the way."

Bethany was crying harder now, terrified by the train's approach and the panic rippling through the crowd.

"C'mon!" Caleb yelled again. "Let's *go*, let's *go*!"

No time left for being calm, for bedside manners or pep talks.

The ticking clock in his head had wound down to the final minute, and this, in his experience, was when things slowed to a crawl—the mind's mechanism for dealing with an emergency in a rational and efficient manner.

Caleb leaned in and tried to get the Kia in neutral so that they could push it unhindered. He noticed, from the corner of his eye, a person pointing at something along the vehicle's rear end.

The twisted rear tire. Was it caught on the tracks?

The train whistle blew again.

"C'mon," Caleb urged.

Simmons repositioned his helmet and jumped to the back, Eric hooked his hands beneath the front wheel well, and they started pushing in the same direction. Terrell grabbed hold of the passenger-side door. Caleb again wrestled with the gearshift, finding staunch resistance. As the firefighters pushed, they realized there was indeed something causing the car to hang up on the trestles.

Another whistle. Louder now.

Caleb took quick stock of the resources at his disposal. From among these onlookers, he might need a hand. Lots of hands. And quickly.

He saw a Marine in fatigues, two strong young black men, a tall fellow with a slight paunch, pairs of concerned women, and a businessman a few yards back. They each jumped out at him in Technicolor, options to choose from and put to use. The only problem: he was prohibited from commanding civilians to put themselves in harm's way. He could, however, accept any aid that was offered.

Bethany was yelling, "Please *help* me. Don't let me *die*. Please!"

"Captain, it's not rolling," Simmons huffed. "We gotta drag it off."

"Okay, get the chain. Get the chain!"

Terrell turned in his yellow helmet and shouted, "Wayne, hook up the chain. Hook up the *chain*."

Wayne was already running from the ladder truck with the box of chain in hand, instructing people to move their parked cars out of the way. Some heard, while others were focused only on the train now rolling around the bend.

Loud, short bursts from the horn.

Triple headlights blazing.

Caleb looked down the tracks and gauged the distance to be about six hundred yards, still over a quarter mile. But depending on how many cargo cars were behind that engine, it might require a full half mile to come to a screeching halt.

Bethany was in full panic now. "Helpmehelpmepleasedo-something..."

"The *train*." Pedestrians were pointing their fingers and yelling. "The *train*!"

Simmons said from the back, "Captain, we don't have time. We gotta *pick* this car up."

"All right, Eric—you grab the front. Grab the front."

The rookie shifted around and bent his stocky legs.

"Lift on three, all right?" Caleb said. "One, two, *three*."

The four firemen grunted, putting every effort into lifting the Kia free, yet it moved only an inch before settling back down. Wayne realized the chain was out of the question, dropped the box, and dashed forward to lend a fifth hand. The entire crew was now positioned around the car, while on either side of the tracks, police officers on foot tried to corral people away from the intersection.

Simmons called out: "*Again*."

"Okay." Caleb counted: "One, two, *three* ... *Arggghh*."

This time the vehicle felt ready to comply, then snagged and dropped back, having shifted only a few inches from its previous position.

"We gotta get this car off the tracks! One, two, *three*."

Still nothing.

The crowd was alive with screams now as the locomotive had cut the distance in half. Brakes were shrieking, but it was apparent to all that the engine would come hurtling through this intersection before stopping.

"*Again*, Captain!"

Caleb was about to count it off once more, when he spotted a cluster of men dashing up the embankment from both sides. The dire situation had finally snapped them out of fear and into activity. A Marine. A young black man. A guy in a dress shirt and tie. And a policeman.

"One, two . . . *three!*"

With the hands of nine capable bodies, with straining legs and backs and shoulders, the car broke free and began to move laterally over the rails. Each sound of the horn reenergized the load bearers.

Another blast. A half foot.

Blast! Half foot. *Blast!*

The screams were horrendous now, the entire crowd lost in a moment of sheer panic and terror.

"Lord, *help us!*" Simmons cried out.

"Ahhhaahhhaahhhaahhh . . ."

They were so close, so very close.

Situated on the corner of the car nearest the oncoming train, Lieutenant Simmons threw his head back, clamped his eyes shut, and hefted with both arms while using his thighs to nudge the car that last few inches from doom. A wave of hot, oily wind struck him as the engine careened past and then—

The nick of metal against metal.

Kaa-bammm!

Simmons screamed as his helmet was torn clear from his skull, the chin strap snapping like a rubber band. The massive metal beast had caught the back flap and knocked it twenty feet from where he stood. Frozen in shock, head still back and eyes still closed, he let out a terrified howl that competed in volume with the thunder of the passing train.

Now that the car was cleared, Caleb and the other men dropped it beside the tracks. The Marine beside Simmons pulled him down away from danger and rested a strong hand of comfort upon his back.

The locomotive was slowing to a stop, at last.

In the Kia's front seat, Bethany was still bawling between gulps of air.

CHAPTER 11

"G et the spreaders," Caleb reminded the rookie, now that the car was off the tracks. Time was still a factor here, despite the disaster they had averted.

The sound of approaching ambulance sirens soothed him. On the rails, the train's brakes had fallen silent, and the conductor was now stumbling back along the embankment in a daze.

"Medic," Wayne called from the car. "Medic!"

A pair of EMS personnel rushed to his assistance. One slipped through the back window to better reach the unconscious passenger from inside, while the other, an older gentleman, tore away the expended air bag for visibility.

"You're gonna be all right," Caleb told Bethany in the driver's seat. "You're okay, you hear me? You're gonna be okay."

He looked up and saw Simmons inching down the slope, still dazed. The Marine had his hands folded over his camouflage cap, taking deep breaths. Terrell and Eric had the generator running and tools connected, ready to cut through the car's window supports and roll back the dented roof. In the vehicle itself, the EMS guys had draped both girls in shrouds to protect them from any bits of glass or metal that might pop loose during the procedure.

Terrell angled the Hurst tool's Jaws of Life into place and started cutting.

The medical team stepped back, and Caleb said to the nearest one, "We got two males over there with minor injuries. These girls are pretty bad. Driver's suffered severe trauma to both legs. Her name's Bethany."

"We got it. Thank you, Captain."

Caleb sighed, taking it all in. He saw witnesses staring off in silence, their faces grim masks of shock. Others wiped away tears of joy and relief. A few of the volunteer rescuers were still nearby, and he pulled off his gloves as he approached the Marine and the young black man who had jumped into the fray.

"Gentlemen." Caleb shook their hands. "Thank you for your help."

"You're welcome."

"I don't know about you, but that had me scared."

"You ain't kiddin'," the black kid said.

Caleb turned to the Marine. "There's no way we could have moved that car without you. Thank you."

"You're welcome, sir."

"You guys are heroes now. You know, the news is gonna want to interview both of you."

"Nah," the first man said.

The Marine agreed. "We're good, sir. We don't need that."

They both patted Caleb on the shoulder and walked away.

The captain collected his lieutenant's ill-fated helmet and turned back toward the truck. On the grass, Simmons sat with arms draped over his knees and eyes closed.

"Thank You," he was whispering. "Thank You, Lord."

"Hey, are you okay?"

Simmons looked up, brows knitted together over relieved eyes. "Captain, I just needed a minute."

Caleb handed him the cracked helmet.

The man took it in both hands and stared at it as though expecting to find his head contained within. "Well," he sighed. "I broke my record for how close I could come to death and still live."

"Yeah? Well, don't break it next time."

"I wasn't trying to break it this time."

Caleb gave him a contemplative look, then rose to leave.

"Hey . . . ," Simmons said. "Don't tell my wife."

When it came to life and death and near misses, there were some things better kept between the guys. Among firefighters, it was the bond of the brotherhood. Caleb nodded, clapped a hand around his friend's arm, and left him to his thoughts.

BACK AT STATION One, the firemen climbed down from the trucks, shucking suspenders and heavy firefighting gear. Caleb battened down a loose hatch on the truck. Around the corner, Eric and Simmons were stepping out of their brush pants and boots. Despite the air of relief, there was palpable concern in the ranks. They could've lost a teenage girl. Or even lost one of their very own.

"Hey, Lieutenant?" Eric said.

Simmons looked up. "Yeah?"

"This kinda thing doesn't happen all the time, does it?"

"Risking our lives? Yes. Playing chicken with a train? First time."

"Aren't you afraid of dying?"

Terrell was peeling off his jacket and he caught Caleb's eye. They both turned toward their comrade to hear his response.

"No," Simmons said, "'cause I know where I'm going. I just don't want to get there 'cause I got hit by a train." He grabbed his commemorative helmet and headed toward the doors at the back of the garage. "Eric, why don't you come help me work on some dinner."

"Long as you don't make me eat that hot sauce of yours."

"The Wrath of God?"

"Stuff's hot as—"

"Hey, now."

The two men brushed by the fire pole on their way out, and Caleb grinned at their repartee. He moved to follow them out of the bay, intending to write up a fire report before grabbing some food.

"Hey, Cap'n." Terrell stopped him. "Hold up for a second."

Caleb paused.

"You, uh . . . you know where you're going?"

"I'm going to my office," Caleb said.

"No, I mean . . ." Terrell fidgeted. "You believe in heaven and hell?"

"I . . . I don't know."

Wayne climbed down from the truck beside them.

"Well, when I die," Terrell said, "I'm going in the ground, and that's where I'm stayin'."

Caleb shrugged. "You know, you and Michael both seem so sure. But one of you is wrong."

Terrell sloughed that off. "It ain't me."

"How do you know? Hey, listen, you might not agree with Michael, but you and I both know . . . he's the real deal." Caleb turned toward the back of the bay as Terrell folded his arms across his wide belly.

"What about you, Wayne?" Terrell said.

76

"Don't drag me into this."

"Man, you believe in heaven and hell?"

"Maybe," Wayne confessed. "I'm open to the possibility."

"I'm not."

"Yeah, we know."

"Well, what if y'all are wrong and it's all a big joke?"

"Then," Wayne said, loud enough for Caleb to catch it, "I guess I'll be stuck lying in the ground next to your sorry bones. And who says the dead can't dance?"

"You kiddin'? You're *alive*, Wayne, and you still can't dance."

THREE DAYS LATER, following a weekend that included softball games and birthday parties, Lieutenant Simmons walked back into the fire station. He was early, by twenty minutes. This gave him time to enjoy relaxing on a kitchen stool with the morning's *Albany Herald* spread out on the counter.

To his left, a CPR poster hung from the wall. To his right, a list of janitorial duties was taped to a cupboard. Everywhere he was faced with the job's requirements, and he took them seriously.

During his two-year tour north of Baghdad, as an Army tank mechanic, he'd witnessed the daily struggle between life and death, between freedom and captivity. It was hard coming back to a complacent culture after seeing the things he'd seen. He felt, sometimes, as though he owed his buddies back in Iraq more than he could give them here on friendly soil.

What he could give, though, was his best—to his wife, his son, and his fellow firefighters.

"Whatever your hand finds to do, do it with all your might . . ."

He lived by those words from Ecclesiastes. Or tried to, anyway. He'd been given a second chance and he meant to use it wisely.

77

PART THREE

ASHES

MAY 2008

CHAPTER 12

Caleb parted the dining room blinds and saw his parents' car cut into his driveway. John and Cheryl Holt had made the trip over from Savannah, and he figured he should be thankful for their concern. On the other hand, as a healthy American male— a self-made man, right?—he believed he should be able to tackle the problems in his marriage on his own. Surely there was a logical solution. Something obvious.

Of course, he wasn't dealing with a logical creature, was he?

See, there was part of the problem.

He ushered his parents inside. Offered sweet tea to his mother. Set out a bowl of snacks that went untouched. Apparently they had no more appetite for this conversation than he.

"Son, can you tell us what's been going on?" John said solemnly.

Feeling defensive and helpless all at the same time, Caleb situated himself on the living room love seat, alone—how fitting— and faced his parents on the matching sofa.

John wore a ring of white hair around his head and a pair of wire-rimmed glasses that gave him a sage, scholarly appearance.

Cheryl had short, graying hair, glasses, and looked her usual presentable self in a peach top and pearl necklace.

"Caleb," she said with a heavy Southern accent, "I just can't help worryin' about you two. Is Catherine doin' all right?"

"Catherine? Whose side are you on, Mom?"

"Oh, it's not about sides. She's a daughter to us, by her marriage to you."

There was no arguing that point. Caleb had experienced similar acceptance from Catherine's family. Of course, with his recent struggles, he'd made no real effort to communicate with them. He and retired Captain Campbell hadn't even gone fishing together this year, and that was a first.

"So," he said. "I might as well just get it all out . . ."

John nodded. "That's why we're here, son."

With no further preamble, Caleb wheeled out his frustrations. It felt good to share them with someone, even if John and Cheryl weren't exactly shining examples of marital bliss—at least they hadn't been in the past.

Caleb's childhood had been full of slammed doors, clanging pots and pans, and shouts loud enough for an occasional visit from the local patrolman. Even worse were his parents' long bouts of silence, during which they wouldn't speak. They'd circle around each other, warily, like they'd come upon a dead animal in the road.

That had been worse than the yelling—walking on eggshells and never knowing when the next eruption would occur.

Still, they were his mother and father. He would weigh any advice they could give, especially in light of the love they seemed to have rediscovered in the last few years. They not only loved each other, they seemed to *like* each other.

Good for them. At least someone was happy.

"Caleb," John said, peering through his glasses, "how long has this been going on?"

"I don't know, Dad. Uh . . . we've had our arguments now and then, but it seems like now she is constantly frustrated with me. I mean, I walk in the *door* and she's mad about something."

His mother leaned forward, hands folded and eyes full of care. "Have you given her a reason to be upset? I've never known Catherine to be unreasonable."

"Listen," Caleb said, "I could've saved the lives of two people at work, but if I'm not here helping wash the dishes, I'm a horrible husband."

"She needs your help here as well, son. Doesn't she help her parents out every week? She can't do *every*thing around the house."

"Mom, what is this? You sound like you're taking her side again."

"Well, if she's working every day and she's trying—"

"I do not need you to tell me I'm doing everything wrong. I've got Catherine for that. I am not the problem. *She* is."

On the table, a multilevel candle arrangement stood as a reminder of Catherine's most recent obsession. Here she was, smelling up the house with all these fancy things—just beeswax, after all—and it seemed to Caleb like a subconscious dig at him.

He was a fireman. And what did she do?

She went around lighting fires, while he tried to put them out.

"If she would give me one ounce of respect," Caleb said, "then maybe we'd have something to build on here."

"All I'm saying," Cheryl responded, "is that if she's working—"

"Sure, she's working, and I'm happy for her. That doesn't mean she can rob me of my dreams, okay? I know things have been tight for her parents, but we've done stuff to help them out. For crying out loud, I rescued her dad from that building."

John Holt tilted his head. "You're still resting on those laurels?"

"I'm not resting on anything, Dad. I'm just stating the facts. I can't go around saving lives, putting out fires, and then paying everyone's bills on top of that. We all have our burdens to carry, right? And if I'm smart enough to save a little, then what's wrong with me enjoying that?"

"Nothing."

"That's right. Nothing."

"You just have to put yourself in Catherine's shoes," Cheryl said. "She's—"

"What about her putting herself in *my* shoes, huh?"

"Cheryl." John rested a hand on his wife's wrist. "Please, let's hear Caleb out. I wanna know what's going on with him."

"Dad, can I please have a few minutes to talk with you? Alone?"

Cheryl looked hurt. "Caleb, I just want to help you and Catherine."

"Dad?"

John turned. "Honey, why don't you let us take a walk? It's all right."

Cheryl sighed and looked off out the window. "Okay."

John put on a light jacket over his shirt and followed Caleb out the back door. They funneled down the steps onto a path that eased beneath Spanish oaks and draping moss. A pond rippled in the slight wind, lapping at the old wooden posts of a dilapidated dock used years ago by a summer camp. Puss willows stood in patches at the water's edge.

Caleb kicked at leaves on the trail. "Why did you have to bring her?"

John acted insulted. "Caleb, 'cause she's my *wife*. And your mother. No one loves you more than she does."

"She's just . . . she's always fixing me. She's *still* trying to fix me." Caleb shoved his hands into the pockets of his corduroys. "I'm not broken."

"Son, if you're looking for a perfect mother, I'm afraid there's not one out there. But she's a good woman. And I love her more now than I ever have."

"I'm not saying I don't love her, Dad. It's just that . . ." He made a fist with both hands and grimaced. "She—she . . . she grates on me."

"Have you not seen a change in her in the last few years?"

"Yes. She treats you better. But you've also put up with a lot."

John chuckled at that. "And so has she."

"Dad, I'm glad you didn't split up, but I would've understood if you had."

"Do you know why we didn't?"

Caleb mulled it over. "Not really. She realized she couldn't do any better?"

"Not quite. Caleb, the Lord did a work in us—in both of us."

"The *Lord*?" Caleb shot his dad a look and came to a stop in the shadows of a hovering live oak. "You're giving credit to God?"

"Why does that bother you? You've always believed in God."

"If there's a God out there somewhere, He's not interested in me and my problems."

"I disagree. I'd say He's *very* interested."

"Then where's He been in my life?"

"I'd say He's been at work all around you, and you just haven't realized it. You haven't exactly given Him an open invitation." John turned, hands in his pockets, and strode into the sunlight of a nearby clearing. He seemed impervious to his son's aggravation. "What is this place?"

Caleb came alongside. Around a dormant campfire pit, stumps that served as seats faced an old wooden cross. "Uh, there used to be a summer camp across the lake. I think this must be a part of it."

John studied the cross. "Son, I used to be where you are right now."

"Sick of it all?"

"Oh, definitely."

"Ready to throw in the towel?"

"The towel?" His father grinned. "More like the entire laundry basket."

Caleb wondered where this was leading. His parents had never said much about their marital difficulties, and, true to form, the recent turnaround had gone mostly unexplained. This might provide some interesting insight.

"I know you and Mom had some rough years," he said.

"We sure did, didn't we? Back then, God didn't matter to me. But I can't say that anymore." John lifted his chin, letting the sun splash over his face and smooth his wrinkles into a look of contemplation. "I never understood why Jesus had to die on the cross for my sins. I always thought I was a good person, and I—"

"Dad, Dad, Dad, *please*. We had this conversation last month. I'm glad this new faith is working for you and Mom. I really am. It's just . . . it's not for me."

John turned sad eyes to the ground, seeming to ponder an appropriate response to his son's condescension.

Caleb turned away. He'd already said more than he intended.

"Tell me this, Caleb." John's tone stopped him in his tracks. "Is there anything in you that wants to save your marriage?"

He stared at his dad and weighed the question. Did he want to save this marriage? Was he really willing to put any more effort into this failing relationship? "Maybe," he conceded. "If Catherine wanted to. But she doesn't. She wants a divorce."

"Is that what you want?"

"I want *peace*. And what difference does it make, anyway? If she signs the papers, Dad, it's all over."

"Have you agreed to start the process with her?"

86

"No, but I think we both understand where this is all headed. I've got plans to meet with my lawyer tomorrow."

John remained quiet a moment. "Caleb, I want you to do something for me."

"What?"

"I want you to hold off on the divorce for forty days."

"Why?"

"I'm gonna send you something in the mail. Something that'll take that long to do."

Caleb folded his arms. "What is it?"

"It's what saved our marriage."

"Dad." Caleb took a deep breath. "If this is a *religious* thing, then I'd rather you didn't—"

"Look at it as a gift from your father. Take one day at a time, then see what happens."

Caleb wrestled with the idea. He rubbed the back of his neck and thought it over. It was worthless, of course, and all it would do is put him through needless torture for the next five or six weeks. On the other hand, it might prove just as annoying to Catherine. As a couple, they'd already put each other through enough grief— why not put up with a little more?

"Please, son." John rested a hand on Caleb's shoulder. "If for no other reason, do it for me. I'm asking as your father."

"Forty days?"

"Forty days."

Caleb eyed his dad, then stared out over the sun-dappled pond. On the other side, the dock that had stood strong long ago was now rotted, leaning and broken into pieces that seemed to have no purpose at all.

CHAPTER 13

Catherine set down her lunch tray in the hospital cafeteria and took a seat, her posture upright in her dark jacket, silky hair draped over her shoulders. She'd picked out broccoli and chicken for her meal, and it smelled good. She peeled the wrapper from her straw, propped it in her cup of sweet tea, and prepared to dig in.

"Eating alone?"

She looked up to see Dr. Keller standing next to her table. He wore a white physician's coat over slacks, with a stethoscope hanging down his striped oxford-cloth shirt. She gave him a friendly smile. "Oh, hello, Dr. Keller."

"Gavin."

"Gavin." She tucked her hair back behind her ear. "Sorry. How are you?"

"I'm doing well. I just, uh, need a place to put my plate down. Is this spot reserved?"

"Um . . . Deidra was supposed to meet me, but you're welcome to join us."

88

"Well, if you're gonna twist my arm, but I don't wanna be any trouble."

Trouble?

The doctor seemed friendly enough, but she wasn't going to let him get too close to her or anything. She was still married, after all. For a few more days, anyway. Weeks, tops. She didn't mind the company of a well-mannered man, an intelligent individual who looked her in the eye and showed interest in her. It's what every woman wanted, wasn't it—if that desire hadn't been plucked from her by lies and abuse?

Guys had always given Catherine attention, but in all the wrong ways. Caleb hadn't been like that. Yes, he'd noticed her, but he'd spent the next three years wooing her, waiting for her to get a little older, giving her time to become a woman.

Once he'd gotten his prize, though, he'd let all that fall by the wayside.

Catherine Holt was an independent person, and she prided herself on that. Inside, however, she knew there was still a little girl who wanted to be appreciated and understood. That need hadn't disappeared at the altar.

And here was Gavin . . .

The way he looked—it was intriguing. It didn't stir physical desire so much as an emotional longing. A sense of connection.

Catherine touched her hair again, giving the doctor a coy look as he took his position next to her. "Are you gonna eat wearing your clean white coat?"

"Well, I do need to keep up with the latest fashions." Gavin wrapped up his stethoscope and set it on the table. "It seems all the doctors are wearing one these days, but it's probably not too smart during lunch."

Catherine watched as he removed and set his jacket to the

side. He looked nice in his dress shirt and tie. She noticed he wore no wedding ring.

Stop, Cat. Don't even think like that.

She said, "I didn't know doctors cared about staying in style."

"Well, we have to keep up with the attractive fashions the public relations employees wear." His fingers brushed her elbow. "Wouldn't want to look bad."

"I see." She felt blood rushing to her cheeks. "Since there's only one person in that category, I'm sure she'd feel honored."

"She should."

Catherine glanced up and met his eyes, feeling her insides flutter.

"She's pretty amazing," Gavin added in a low voice.

With a demure chuckle, she returned her attention to her meal. She couldn't remember the last time she'd felt this sort of emotion, this mix between clouded confusion and clear-eyed delight. His flirting seemed inappropriate, if not downright unprofessional. Yet it felt nice. Very nice.

IN THE FIREHOUSE locker room, Wayne sauntered up to the mirror with his toiletry bag. He had his stereo propped on the adjoining sink, and the rhythm coming through those speakers was one he could not deny.

"Oh yeah."

Booming bass notes filled the space, grabbing him by the hips and shaking them from side to side. Why fight the obvious talent he possessed?

"You're lookin' good," he told his reflection.

With his Fire/Rescue shirt hanging loose over his navy blue shorts, he began applying dabs of gel to his spiked hair. It took work, took time, but it was this attention to detail that kept him in favor with the ladies. Sure, he carried some extra weight around his middle. And yes, his hairline was receding, but none of that could overcome the mesmerizing effect of his big baby blues.

He gave himself a wink.

Yep. Just like that, he'd been known to turn a woman to mush.

Or at least that's how he imagined it. Hadn't actually happened yet, but there was still time. He was only twenty-nine, just reaching his prime.

Alone in the locker room, he wiped the steam from the mirror and leaned in till he could see nothing but larger-than-life Wayne. He envisioned a girl on the other side of that glass, eyeing him, wanting him, but intimidated by his devastating good looks.

"Hey," he said to his pretend partner. "You look *good.*"

He applied double dabs of gel and answered back. "Thanks. I try to take care of myself."

He let the music move his hips.

He raised his elbows, looked left, looked right, bobbed up and down.

"You like this song?"

He toggled his eyebrows in response. "Oh yeah."

He looked left, right, again. "You feel that?" Left, right, dip down, and back up. "It's called chemistry. And we got it."

The music hit a sudden pause. With an exaggerated look at his reflection, Wayne dropped out of sight, all the way down to a crouch, then rose back up as the beat resumed. His legs were dancing, his hips shaking, and his eyes gazing deep into the mirror again. He nodded and gave what he hoped was a seductive smile, even though it looked a little, well . . . goofy.

"That's right," he assured his imaginary girl. "Wayne won't leave you."

He put all his energy into the music now, swiveling his head, bobbing, weaving, showing himself and his girl and the entire world that this white boy had some rhythm.

"Yeah, *boy*."

The click of the door behind him brought the dancing to an abrupt halt. Back to normal. He could see through the glass Terrell entering the locker room, and already the short black man was shooting him a look of suspicion.

"Hey, man," Terrell said. "You seen my bag in here?"

"No." Wayne shook his head. "I ain't seen it."

"All right. It's probably in my locker."

Wayne applied toothpaste to his brush and waited for Terrell to turn the corner and head for the showers so that he could start dancing again. But why should he be embarrassed? No, Wayne wasn't embarrassed. It was just that the dance of love, the interplay between a man and a woman—that was private. Plus, he didn't want to give away any of his secrets. He'd rather save those for the real deal.

He winked at the mirror.

See, don'tcha worry. Wayne is back.

He double-checked that Terrell was out of sight, then cocked an eyebrow at the mirror. "Where were we?"

He picked back up where he'd left off, dancing, shooting eyes at himself, losing himself again in the dream of a relationship with an attractive woman.

"Ha-ha-*haaaa!*"

Wayne spun his head and saw Terrell peeking at him from around the shower-area wall, his face contorted by rowdy glee.

"Aww, c'mon, Terrell!"

"Woooo." Terrell mocked his moves, gyrating arms and hips.

"That ain't funny! This ain't no show."

Terrell doubled over, barely able to control his whoops and hollers.

"This is *me* time." Wayne's voice cracked. "*Terrell*, where's my privacy?"

Still chortling, the other man stumbled out of sight. "Wayne, you too funny."

Wayne saw nothing funny about it.

CAPTAIN CALEB HOLT and Lt. Michael Simmons were at a table in the kitchen area, with the lighting limited to one bulb over the stove. They'd eaten Chinese takeout earlier, and the rest of the crew was off watching TV in the living area. The station duties were complete, night was settling over the city of Albany, and they could only hope that nothing disastrous would happen on their watch.

"Forty days?" Simmons said. "Does Catherine know?"

"I'm not gonna tell her." Caleb stirred his coffee with a pair of chopsticks. "If she wants to go ahead and file, that's up to her."

Simmons hesitated. "Divorce is a hard thing, man."

"Well, if it brings peace . . ."

"Caleb, you want the right kind of peace."

"What do you mean by that?"

"You know what that ring on your finger means?"

"It means I'm married." Caleb took a sip of the coffee.

"Yeah. But it also means you made a lifelong covenant—you were putting on *that* ring, while saying your vows."

"Try telling that to my wife. She's not even wearing hers these days."

"Really?"

"Not for the past coupla weeks." Caleb shrugged. "Not that I care."

"Yeah, it's hard to care when you're afraid of getting hurt. You know, the sad part is that when most people promise 'for better or for worse,' they really only mean for the better."

Caleb shifted in his seat. "Listen, Catherine and I were in love when we got married, but today . . . We're two very different people, all right? It's just not working out anymore."

Simmons took a breath and looked around the table. He took hold of the salt and pepper shakers, hefting them for the captain to see. "Caleb, salt and pepper are completely different. Their makeup is different, their taste, and their color. But you always see 'em together."

"Yeah?"

"So when you . . . Hold on just a second."

Caleb pressed a fist to his lips and waited.

Simmons set the shakers down and scooted back in his chair to fetch something from a drawer. He came back with a tube of superglue.

"What're you doing?"

Simmons said nothing, simply ran a line of liquid down the side of the pepper container and attached the saltshaker to it.

"Michael." Caleb stretched out his hand. "Hey, what'd you do that for?"

His friend pressed the two shakers together, letting the glue set, then held the joined pair up for observation. "Caleb, when two people get married, it's for better or for worse, for richer or for poorer, in sickness and in health."

"I know that. But marriages aren't fireproof. Sometimes you get burned."

Simmons set his glue project on the table. He fixed his captain with a stern eye. "Fireproof doesn't mean that a fire will never come, but that when it comes you'll be able to withstand it."

Caleb cleared his throat, shot a stern glare back, then snatched up the shakers. "You didn't have to glue them together." He started to tear them apart.

"Don't do it, Caleb."

"What?"

"If you pull 'em apart now, you'll break either one or both of 'em."

This was ridiculous. Caleb saw what Simmons was up to now, and he didn't like it. He set the shakers back down—hard. He said, "I am not a perfect person, but better than most. And if my marriage is failing, it is not all my fault."

"But, Caleb, I have seen you run into a burning building to save people you don't even know. Now you're gonna just let your own marriage burn to the ground." Simmons punctuated this last remark with a swipe of the hand, as though taking out an entire building.

This confrontational attitude not only stunned Caleb, it angered him. What right did this man have butting into his personal business? They were coworkers, yes. Friends for the past five years.

But that gave Simmons no right to act like he had all the answers.

Caleb leaned across the table. "Michael, you are my friend, and I've allowed you to speak freely with me on this job. Don't abuse it."

Simmons stared down, his eyes dark and unreadable.

Caleb stood and marched out of the room. He had a headache, and he still had a full night ahead. He hoped things would stay quiet so he could get a little sleep—assuming he'd be able to sleep at all.

HE WENT JOGGING the next morning after work, clearing his head by sweating out his frustration. As he rounded the bend on the return leg of a three-miler, he saw the postal truck pulling away from his house.

He stopped at the box. Collected the mail. And there it was, in a padded tan envelope, as promised by his father.

Well, let's see what good this'll do.

CHAPTER 14

Caleb waited till he was in the house to rip open the envelope. Standing in the living room, he pulled out a small, brown-leather journal. Despite its small size, it had weight to it. Significance. It looked old enough to have been pulled off a shelf in King Arthur's court—an ancient relic, fit for old people. Just because it'd worked for his mother and father did not mean it would work for him and Catherine.

He flipped to the first page and read the title:

The Love Dare.

With a quick perusal, he saw the entire book had been written in his father's hand. How touching. He propped himself on the arm of the couch and scanned the introductory section.

As he read, he imagined his father's voice.

My son,

This forty-day journey cannot be taken lightly. It is a challenging and often difficult process, but an incredibly fulfilling one.

If you will commit to a day at a time for forty days, the results could change your life and your marriage. Consider it a dare from others who have done it before you.

I love you,
Dad

Caleb was intrigued now. Figured it couldn't hurt to read on.

Day 1

The first part of this dare is fairly simple. Although love is communicated in a number of ways, our words often reflect the condition of our heart.

For the next day, resolve to say nothing negative to your spouse at all. If the temptation arises, choose not to say anything. It's better to hold your tongue than to say something you'll regret.

"Be quick to listen, slow to speak and slow to become angry" (James 1:19).

Caleb was still perspiring, his pulse still up from his run, and he decided it was time for a shower. This book, this love thing, seemed like a well-intentioned gesture from his dad, but he couldn't imagine something so simplistic having any lasting effect.

"Say nothing negative . . ."

That was like asking him to stop breathing for a day. And even if he succeeded at holding his tongue, Catherine would be sure to take advantage and give him all the berating he could handle. It'd be like walking into a boxing ring with his hands tied behind his back.

Ding, ding, dinggg!

"And in one corner, we have Capt. Caleb Holt, a hero at his job but a big whopping failure within the walls of his own home.

"And in the other corner, Catherine Holt, public relations director, beautiful, tenacious, and never one to back down from a fight . . ."

Until now.

She wanted out. Those were her very own words.

AT 7:42 A.M. Caleb was heading out for another shift at the fire station. From the hallway, he heard Catherine pour herself a mug of coffee over the sink, then turn away as he entered. She was in a bathrobe, hair already done and makeup on. She'd be going to the hospital soon, and maybe she could do him a favor on the way.

He dropped his gym bag and a dirty uniform shirt on the bar. He pulled on his captain's jacket, hurrying, trying not to give her time to think before he presented his request—just two people, nothing more than roommates, taking care of business.

"Do you have time to take this to the dry cleaner's today?" he said.

Catherine's reply was sharp and immediate. "You'd think, after two days off, you would've already taken care of that." She didn't even turn to look at him.

Caleb propped both hands on the counter, ready to go at it. Ready to tell her exactly what he thought of her attitude.

"Say nothing negative . . ."

In bed this morning, he'd decided this would be Day One, yet here he was, wanting to take that back already. Maybe he could start tomorrow, *after* giving her a piece of his mind.

"Say nothing . . ."

Okay, he could do this.

Caleb gripped the counter, rolled his neck, and held back the torrent of words that flooded his mind. At last, he shot an exasperated look at his wife's back, stuffed his shirt back into his bag, and stormed out the front door as she stirred sweetener into her drink.

Off to a great start.

CHAPTER 15

In the station, Caleb found five guys gathered at the meeting room table. They had open books, sheets of paper, and sharpened pencils. It was like elementary school all over again, except this was life-and-death knowledge at their fingertips.

Eric was saying, "If nobody's in the house, you pull cover lines to protect the houses on either side, then attack the fire through the front door."

"Not bad." Caleb moved to a covered cake dish on the counter. He took off the lid and started cutting himself a slice. "Just be sure to remember that when you're at a fire."

"Hey, Cap'n," Terrell said. "What's the story on that cake?"

"If you're not an officer, it's a dollar a slice."

"For real?" Eric said.

Wayne rolled his eyes. "C'mon, rookie. You can't fall for everything."

Caleb held up a coin. "Terrell, you tell me which hand the coin is in, and you can have as much cake as you want."

101

Terrell stood and studied his captain. Caleb feigned to move the object from his left hand to the right, while both remained closed. He shrugged, waiting for a decision.

"It's in the other hand," Terrell said.

"Which one is that? Left or right?"

"Left, okay. You never pick the obvious choice."

Caleb opened his left hand and showed that it was empty.

"It was in the right hand?" Terrell whined. "Aww, man, I *knew* that."

Caleb revealed that his other hand was empty as well.

"He gotcha." Wayne pointed a finger. "Terrell, you think you're so slick."

The others joined in the laughter.

Caleb walked over to Terrell, dropped the coin in his lap, and said, "Well, you can't figure out everything. But the cake's on me."

Terrell's frown didn't keep him from going to collect his consolation prize. "You know," he said, "everything can be explained. Gimme time, and I'll figure out how you did it."

Wayne reached into his own pocket for a coin. "I got a magic trick."

"Man," Terrell said, "any trick *you* do can be figured out in five seconds."

"You don't think I can stump you?"

"Ain't nothing you can do, Wayne, that would impress me."

"Nothing?"

The black man put the lid back over the cake. "Here. You make this cake disappear, then I'll be impressed."

Simmons got up from the table, motioning as though shoveling food into his mouth. "Give him three minutes and we know he could make it disappear."

102

"You got that right, Lieutenant," said Terrell.

"All right," Wayne said. "Give me the cake dish."

"No, no, no. Stand over there and do it. I ain't lettin' you touch it."

"You can't do that, man. I gotta have room to work."

"If you can't work from there, you ain't the real deal." Terrell's left hand remained on the cake dish, while his right lifted a slice to his own mouth.

"Terrell," Caleb urged, "I say let him try."

"Sure, Cap'n, but I ain't giving him the cake. He's always braggin' about what he can do, and how well he can do it. I been trying for years to be impressed with Wayne, and I'm just sayin' . . . It's been a long wait."

As Terrell spoke, Lieutenant Simmons slipped behind him unseen, from the other entry into the kitchen, and motioned to Caleb.

Caleb took his cue. "Wayne," he said, punching the driver in the arm, "Terrell's right. The only thing you can do better than him is dance."

Terrell almost choked on his bite of cake. "Excuse me?"

Caleb turned on the stereo.

The light came on in Wayne's eyes as he noticed Simmons still in hiding. Realizing his opportunity, he jumped in with both feet—quite literally. "That's right," he taunted. "That's what I been talkin' about. Everyone here knows I can lay it down better than you, Terrell."

"Give us all a sample," Caleb said.

Wayne started dancing to the music as Terrell stared in disgusted disbelief. The rookie was laughing, and Caleb couldn't conceal his own wide grin.

"Are you kiddin' me?" Terrell waved a hand, shooing away this disgrace to people of rhythm everywhere. "There's no way you could be serious. He moves like a drunk hippopotamus."

The hippopotamus continued, unfettered.

Eric and Caleb egged him on.

Terrell let go of the cake lid, still unaware of Simmons just behind him. He stepped toward the center of the room, ready to throw it down. "Look, man. You gotta *flow* with the music, like this." He started dancing. "It's gotta be smooth, Wayne, and *soulful*. You can't just lumber around like that."

Wayne's gyrations came to a slow halt as he turned his attention to the suave movements of his fellow fireman.

Caleb gave Simmons a slight nod. The lieutenant gently lifted the cake lid and removed the entire dessert. He retreated back the way he'd come, disappearing from view.

"Wayne, I hate to break it to you," Caleb said. "But it looks like Terrell's got you beat. The man can dance."

"*Thank* you." Terrell's face made clear his disdain of the competition.

"But Terrell, I still think Wayne can make that cake disappear."

"I know I can," Wayne said. "Stand back and watch some *real* talent."

Caleb joined his driver in the center of the room. "Do it, Wayne. Do it. C'mon, just like I taught you."

"Are you serious?" Terrell was confused. He took a step back, blocking the counter with his wide body, and returning his hand to the lid to guard the object in question. "Show me whatchu got, big guy."

"I've been holdin' back on you, man. But it's time," Wayne said with a flourish of his hands and a wild-eyed look, "for the master to work. Hold the music, please."

Eric turned off the stereo. Wayne stared toward the counter, putting his face through a variety of facial contortions that were more slapstick than mysterious. Terrell watched him as if he had gone certifiably crazy.

"That's it," Caleb said. "Pull it all out, Wayne. You got it. Make it happen."

Wayne pointed, waved his hand once more in a final dramatic gesture, then dropped both arms as if worn out by this exhibition.

"Good job, man! You did it." Caleb gave his driver a high five.

"Very nice," Eric agreed, clapping. "I'm impressed."

Terrell sneered and gave the three of them a vacant stare. "Do y'all think I'm stupid? If I check to see if it's gone, you'll just laugh at me for even lookin'."

"No," Caleb said. "That cake is gone."

"Very funny."

"Think what you want, Terrell. If you don't believe, you can't see it. C'mon, guys," Caleb said to the others. "Let's get back to work." He strolled out with Wayne and Eric on his heels. He slapped Wayne on the back. "Way to go, man."

Terrell was still shaking his head.

Just through the door, Caleb paused. He glanced back and saw Terrell venturing a peek beneath the cake lid.

"No," Terrell gasped. "No way." He checked along the counter, in the cupboard, searching everywhere for the missing baked goods.

Caleb and the others tried to control their snickers from the shadows in the other room, but Terrell caught them as he stomped by.

"Wayne?" he said. "Where is it?"

"I can't tell you, man. You're not a believer."

"Tell me, Wayne. I mean it. Where'd it go?"

While the two faced off, Caleb gestured to Simmons, who was hidden around the corner. The lieutenant snuck back through the other doorway and returned the cake to its position beneath the lid.

"It ain't funny, Wayne. Where is it?"

"You want me to bring it back?"

"Yes, I do."

"Okay." Wayne rolled his hand and bowed. "After you."

Terrell led the march back into the other room. As he reached for the lid, Wayne gave it a hard stare and snapped his fingers once.

"Done."

"You," Terrell said, "are a fool." He lifted the lid and was stunned to find the cake staring up at him. "What? How'd you do that?"

"A magician never reveals his tricks."

"That's right. You just have to believe." Caleb led his driver away again, leaving Terrell alone with the cake and a head full of questions.

"Wayne!" Terrell yelled.

Wayne kept walking.

CHAPTER 16

Caleb sat at his bedside, his back against the wall, reading the next entry in *The Love Dare*. His shift was over, and he was back at the house. The clock read 8:20 a.m., and he could hear the shower running in the master bedroom. Catherine had always cared about looking good for work, but this morning she was really pushing her schedule to its limit.

The best thing to do? Ignore her mood and just get through this.

Day 2

It is difficult to demonstrate love when you feel little to no motivation. But love in its truest sense is not based on feelings, but a determination to show thoughtful actions, even when there seems to be no reward.

In addition to saying nothing negative to your spouse today, do at least one unexpected gesture as an act of kindness.

Caleb looked up into the early morning daylight and sighed. An act of kindness? What good would that do? As part of his job, he already protected lives and led men into life-threatening situations. What could one little gesture on the home front accomplish?

Well, best to get this over with.

He padded into the kitchen and filled the carafe. He was at least capable of making her morning brew. He poured water into the coffeemaker. Added a filter. Ground the beans and scooped them in. Pressed the button.

Easy enough.

A few minutes later, he heard Catherine rumbling around in the bedroom. He spread a cloth place mat on the counter, set out the sugar bowl and spoon. He poured rich, dark liquid into her favorite red mug and positioned it in the mat's center. Turned it slightly, to make the handle more accessible.

Hey, this might even earn him a smile. That'd be a change.

Catherine came tripping into the dining room, adjusting the strap on a high-heeled shoe. Since when had she worn that pair? They were the tallest ones she owned, normally reserved for special occasions. She'd even told him they made her feet hurt if she had to wear them all day.

He opened a cupboard and tried to downplay his kind gesture. "Oh," he said, pointing, "I, uh, poured your coffee."

She snatched up her purse and keys. "I don't have time for coffee."

And off she went.

Caleb put his hands on his hips. What? He'd done all that to brighten her day, maybe earn a little goodwill—and she didn't have *time* for coffee? She *always* had time for coffee. It was her morning ritual.

He heard her car start up and pull out of the garage.

He thought of drinking the sludge himself.

No, he needed to get some rest after his long shift. Instead, he grabbed the cup and dumped it into the sink. He yanked the plug on the coffeemaker. Still irritated, he took the carafe in hand and poured the entire steaming contents down the drain.

THAT NIGHT, CALEB brushed his teeth in preparation for bed. He had his father's book in hand as he faced the sink, his way of making plans for tomorrow. He'd enjoyed the day off. Surfed the Internet. Checked his savings account, and calculated his chances of getting a boat before next summer.

A boat? A personal toy?

The words in *The Love Dare* didn't come as a ringing endorsement of that plan. Quite the opposite. He could almost hear John's voice of reprimand.

Day 3

Whatever you put your time, energy, and money into will become more important to you. It's hard to care for something you are not investing in.

Along with refraining from any negative comments, buy your wife something that says you were thinking of her today.

Do *what?*

Caleb stopped brushing. He felt the toothpaste dribbling from the corner of his mouth, yet he was frozen by the audacity of tomorrow's assignment. He could hardly even read the rest of the entry. He was supposed to invest in her? That made her sound like some kind of project.

Really, this was starting to get sappy. And didn't women always complain that men objectified them?

Of course, they were usually referring to men's obsession with their physical attributes and the way that they—

Well, anyway, that wasn't the point. Caleb knew how to invest money, and he was more than capable of maintaining the equipment at the station. This sounded like a similar concept, putting his energy and resources into those things he truly cared about.

Or those people. Whatever.

He spit out his toothpaste and slammed the book shut.

MR. CAMPBELL WAS surprised to see an incoming call from Caleb Holt's cell phone. Months had passed since he'd last heard from his daughter's husband, not that he let that worry him. Young people these days had a lot on their plates, and Mr. Campbell had no intention of becoming one of those nosy, puttering retirees.

"Hello, Caleb," he said into the phone.

"Good evening, Captain Campbell."

"How's my favorite son-in-law?"

"Your only son-in-law."

He chuckled. "Keeps things simple that way. So, are you ready for another fishing trip up the North Flint River? My rod and reel are getting rusty."

"Uh, that'd be a lotta fun, I'm sure." Caleb cleared his throat. "I just, uh . . . Well, I'd have to schedule some leave days, and then coordinate it with Catherine's schedule. I'm not sure how that would work right now."

"Say the word and we'll figure a way."

"Yeah. Okay."

"Is everything all right, Caleb? Is there something I can help you with?"

"Everything's fine. Fine."

"You sure?"

"Yeah, uh, I just wanted to get some advice."

"Now, how long are you gonna milk this?" Mr. Campbell gibed. "You pull me from a fire one time, and now you think you can pick my brain any ol' time you like?"

Caleb's voice warmed at their worn joke. "I warned you, sir— you've gotta teach me everything you know."

"Sorry about that. I'm retired now."

"Oh, and I'm the one milking it?"

Mr. Campbell smiled through the phone. He didn't mind retirement, but he missed his days in the line of duty. Some people thought his early departure had been a result of that close call in the late-night grocery store bonfire, but that wasn't it at all. Even now, at sixty-five, he still had the courage to face choking smoke, skin-puckering heat, or the carnage of a road accident.

It was his body that wasn't cooperating, particularly a weak hip that'd started threatening his capabilities on the job. More important, however, was his relationship with Joy. She had suffered through many sleepless nights, and the emotional wear and tear of his work had started to affect her physical well-being.

Since leaving his position in 1999, Mr. Campbell had grown closer than ever before to his wife. Though some men became unbearable when stuck at home, he found peacefulness in Joy's presence. He'd even taken up watercolor painting—and wasn't there some poetic justice in that, after decades of working with water as his medium?

Of course, Joy's recent stroke had complicated things.

Mr. Campbell helped her as best he could—from the chair to the toilet, from the chair to the bed—and harbored some nagging guilt that his former high-stress job had precipitated her body's shutdown. Each time he cared for her bedsores, he reminded himself it was the least he could do for this precious wife of his.

"So tell me, Caleb," he said, "what do you need to know this time?"

"It's about Catherine."

"Oh? How so?"

"I'm, uh . . . I'm wondering if you think she'd rather get a pair of shoes or a bouquet of flowers."

"Thinking ahead for her birthday, are you?"

"Sure," Caleb said. "Something like that."

"Flowers or shoes, huh? I guess I'd have to go with the shoes. Even as a little girl, she used to put on her mama's heels and go strutting around the house." Mr. Campbell rested a hand on his belly and reminisced. "Come to think of it, though—there is one problem with that idea."

"What's that?"

"Well, you probably know, Caleb, but she's got real specific tastes when it comes to clothes and that sorta thing."

Caleb remained silent.

During the lull, Mr. Campbell heard his wife's wheelchair coming down the hall to his study and that gave him an idea. "You know, you oughta ask Catherine's mother about this. Joy'll be better in that department. In fact, you're more than welcome to come on over and—"

"Uh, thank you, Captain. Actually, it's no big deal."

"You sure? 'Cause we can—"

"I'm sure. Hey, I gotta run, but thanks for the input."

"Anytime, Caleb. Anytime."

The line went dead, and Mr. Campbell looked up to see his

wife in the doorway. She was holding aloft her chalkboard with three words scrawled on it:

TELL HIM ROSES.

CALEB REGRETTED EVEN making last night's call to his father-in-law. All he was looking to do was hurry through one of *The Love Dare*'s requirements, not go on some complicated shopping expedition. The very thought made him shiver.

He glanced around to assure himself his crew was on task. With trucks in constant need of attention, Wayne and Eric had been sent to check tire pressure on all vehicles. Simmons was speaking with dispatch about road construction updates that could affect their routes if sent on a run. Terrell was in the kitchen, straightening the place up, and—Caleb suspected—still trying to figure out the trick behind the cake disappearance.

Caleb slipped into the first bay with his phone and made his move.

"Blooms 'N More," a woman's voice answered. "May I help you?"

"Yeah," he said. "I, uh, need to order some flowers for my wife."

"Well," said the woman on the other end, "that's awfully sweet of you."

"I can do this over the phone, right? I just give you my credit card info or something?"

"Sure. Did you have anything particular in mind, sir?"

"No, no. It doesn't matter."

"Okay. We could go with a dozen roses."

"Sure. I mean—hold on, how much does that cost?"

"Uh, it's forty-five dollars for a dozen."

"Forty-*five*? No. That's too much. Do you have something cheaper?"

"Well, we have a small bouquet of wildflowers for twenty-five."

"Yeah." He breathed a sigh of relief. "That's more like it. Let's go with the twenty-five. You don't happen to have any coupons or sales running, do you?"

"Umm. Not at the moment, sir."

"Okay, how about a box of chocolates or something?"

"We have a red heart-shaped box that's very popular."

"And how much are those?" He leaned against the bay wall, between the rows of soot-stained coats and fire helmets.

"Six dollars."

"For a box of . . . Aww, you're killing me."

"Or there's a smaller, gold-foil box for two-fifty."

"That's better."

"Will there be anything else, sir?"

"Okay," Caleb said, "how about a little stuffed bear?"

"The small bears go for eight, and the large—"

"All right, forget the bear."

"No bear. Got it."

"How long is it gonna take to throw something like that together?"

"We can have it ready for you in half an hour. Would you like a small card to go with the flowers?"

He braced himself. "Should I even ask how much those run?"

"Is free okay?"

"You've sold me. I'll take one."

"We can write a message on it for you, if you'd like. Also free."

Caleb considered the option, but could think of no appropriate message, nothing he meant from the heart. This florist woman—

she was the expert, right? He'd get her advice. "What do guys usually put on things like that?"

"Well, you do hope she likes this stuff, right?"

"Yeah." Caleb pushed away from the wall. "That sounds pretty good."

The lady cleared her throat. "'I hope you like this stuff'?"

"Perfect. Okay, here's my credit card info." Before hanging up, he remembered to throw in a quick "Thank you."

The florist responded in a droll voice, "You're welcome, Romeo."

CHAPTER 17

Catherine entered the house through the garage. She'd had a decent day, and even brushed past Dr. Keller a few times, yet the moment she turned the car into their subdivision, she found her mood plummeting and a headache coming on.

Not right now, honey. I have a headache.

Wasn't that the old excuse? Well, she didn't need any excuses of late.

Life in this house, with Caleb, was no longer something she enjoyed. She'd made it clear that she had little interest in physical companionship, and Caleb reciprocated by turning his interests elsewhere—like the Internet. She didn't know whether she should be upset that he sometimes forgot to delete all the history from his online meanderings, or if she should be glad he no longer tried so hard to hide it from her.

Maybe he hoped it would spark some jealousy on her part. Or that it would get her stimulated in the way it did him.

Instead, it just turned her stomach.

She'd been an object before, in a short-lived high school

relationship that left her feeling dirty and used. She certainly had never expected her husband would be of the same ilk, but of late, things had been going downhill for both of them. Truthfully, not much would surprise her anymore.

She *was* surprised, however, by the flowers on the table.

Arranged in a simple glass vase that looked almost like a Mason jar, the wildflowers were thin and pitiful, and could've been plucked from any neighbor's front yard. Although a small box of chocolates was supposed to sweeten the deal, the ridiculous card betrayed Caleb's inadequacy in the romance department.

"You hope I'll like these?" she murmured, reading his short note. "Way to splurge, lover boy."

Her lips curled in disgust; then she dropped the card to the dining table and marched off to the bedroom where she could get out of these clothes and high heels. At the rate things were going, she might as well start packing.

CALEB WAS IN the firehouse kitchen, grabbing some A-1 steak sauce to go with his plate of sirloin and home-style potato wedges. At the counter, Lieutenant Simmons was thumbing through the *Albany Herald*.

"You want some of these potatoes, Michael?"

Simmons shook his head and turned back to the newspaper.

Caleb thought back to their conversation the other evening, after Simmons had glued the shakers together. Caleb had used his position unfairly, taking a cheap shot at their friendship under the guise of his superior rank.

"I've allowed you to speak freely . . . don't abuse it."

Who was the one being abusive there? It was just the sort of thing he had sworn not to do when becoming a captain late last year. True, there were levels of respect between officers, but Simmons had spoken as a friend, whereas Caleb had lashed back as a superior.

"Look, man," Caleb said. "I got an extra steak. All yours, if you want it."

Simmons raised an eyebrow. "Steak?"

"If you want it."

"Sure. How 'bout we split it?"

"How 'bout you take the whole thing and stop being ridiculous."

"Yes, sir."

They exchanged a smile, and Caleb knew things were back to normal.

At the table by the window, in the slatted light through the blinds, Eric, Wayne, and Terrell were once again preparing for the testing that was to come. Though they'd spread books, pencils, and highlighters across the table, they were more engaged in verbal saber-rattling than actual study.

"Man, you done lost your mind," Terrell said to Wayne.

"Terrell, I can bench three hundred right now."

"For real?" Eric asked.

"Why can't we all come to the same obvious conclusion?" With hair gelled and spiked, Wayne looked around to make sure he had the attention of all present. "That I . . . am the man."

Caleb strolled forward and sat at the head of the table. "All I know is that the *man* left a thermal-imaging device on the bumper of the truck last night."

"Mm-hmm." Terrell shot the driver a censoring look.

"That's an eight-thousand-dollar piece of equipment, Wayne."

"All right. My bad, Captain. But that still doesn't change the fact that when it comes to difficult situations, I can take it."

"Man, I can't take this much ego. Wayne, you been braggin' on yourself for ten minutes," Terrell complained.

"It ain't braggin' if it's true." Wayne gestured with his pencil. "Last week at the apartment fire, I pulled off two attack lines, laid my own supply line, and caught a hydrant in under two minutes."

Caleb snagged Simmons's eye and made a drinking motion. Simmons nodded and angled toward the fridge.

"So what?" Terrell said. "There's other folks that could do that, man."

"Not from *this* station."

"Tom McBride could," Caleb said.

"At Station Four?" Wayne sneered. "Are you kidding? He might could do it in two and a half, but he can't do it under two."

"Mmm, I don't know."

"Captain, he's strong, but he's not as fast. I could take him any day of the week."

Caleb shrugged. "You know, Wayne, you seem pretty high on yourself. I think confidence is a good thing, but you . . . you're over the top."

"Man, he way over the top," Terrell agreed.

Wayne lifted both hands. "I can back it up. That's all I'm sayin'."

Simmons walked into view with two bottles of hot sauce, the slogan printed along the bottom: *Hotter Than the Lake of Fire*. He set them in front of Caleb, then drummed the table with his hands. "Wrath of God, baby."

Caleb grabbed the nearest bottle, eyeing the list of ingredients.

"What's that for?" Eric asked.

"We're about to have a little contest," the captain told his crew. "We're gonna see if Wayne really is the man—that is, if he's up to the challenge."

"Oh," Wayne said, "I'm all about this."

Caleb slid the second bottle across the table, then unscrewed the cap from his own. "All right, I'll go first."

"What're . . . What're you gonna do?"

Caleb fixed his attention on the bottle with the flaming yellow-and-red label. He shifted in his seat, readying himself. "Michael, time me."

Wayne shot a worried glance around the gathering.

"You got it," Simmons said. "Ready? Go."

To wide-eyed stares, Caleb tilted the bottle to his lips and started guzzling. The best thing was to make this quick and show little reaction. He might let his eyes water, but that was the most he would let his driver see from him.

"No, way," Eric said.

Caleb backed off, pressing his fist to his lips and feeling the furrows in his forehead deepen. He forced the mouthful down, then tilted his head back for another go.

"Man, you crazy," Terrell said. "Look, he gonna drink that whole thing."

Caleb winced, scrunched his eyes shut, gulped, took a deep breath, then forced the last of the bottle's contents down his gullet in a series of short swallows. He slammed the Wrath of God down, held his forehead, and reveled in Wayne's expression of intense worry.

"Twenty-three seconds," Simmons declared.

"Ooooh." Terrell was chuckling.

Caleb blinked a few times, wiped the red juice from his chin, and shot his gaze to the other end of the table. "All right, man. You're up."

The guys turned their heads toward Wayne.

"All right," he conceded, "that was impressive. Until I do it in under twenty."

"Two-zero?" Eric said.

Wayne stared Caleb in the eyes and twisted off the bottle cap.

He tossed it back over his shoulder in a show of fearlessness that was about to be put to the test.

"We're all watching, Wayne. Let's see it."

"Time me."

"Oh, I'll time you," Simmons said. "Ready?"

"Ladies . . ." Wayne lifted the bottle.

"Go!"

Wayne started with valiant resolve, draining a third of the contents in throat-clenching, Adam's-apple-wobbling gulps. His face reddened and he fell forward, trying not to spurt the juice back out.

"C'mon, Wayne," Caleb said.

"Go, Wayne," Eric said.

"It's *hot*."

"I thought you could take it," Terrell ribbed him.

With watering eyes, the driver tucked back in for another long draught from the bottle. He came up for air, whipped his head to the side, and screamed.

"Uh-huh," Terrell said. "You gotta drink that, bro."

"Fourteen seconds," Simmons called out the time.

Wayne's next attempt was shorter than the first two, and he spewed droplets across the table and his own arm. "Ahhhh, it *burns!*" He pounded the table and gasped for air. The bottle was still half full.

Eric was laughing.

Terrell said, "Where the man at now, huh? I thought he said he could take it."

Wayne guzzled some more, then pounded the table with his palm and yelled through lips doused in dripping red sauce: "*Aahhh. My mouth's on fire!*" He dashed toward the bathroom. "*Aahhh!*"

Caleb watched his exit with serene calm.

"Cap'n," Terrell said, "how'd you do that, man? You don't even feel sick?"

"You could do it, too, Terrell"—Caleb held up his empty bottle and grinned—"if you replaced yours with tomato juice."

The black man guffawed and clasped hands with Eric in victory. Lieutenant Simmons broke into a wide smile and clapped.

"That's classic," Eric said. "That was awesome."

"I doubt we'll hear any more of his bragging for a while."

"Code of silence," Simmons said. "Nobody tells him for two weeks."

"Code of silence," the others agreed.

CHAPTER 18

Catherine strode through the Staff Only doors of the cancer wing, wearing her glasses and low black pumps beneath a fitted skirt and jacket. If she was going to catch the attention of Dr. Keller, she was no longer going to do it in spikes, thank you. Already her lower back was feeling better than it had in days.

"Dr. Anderson," she called after a gray-haired man in the hall.

He turned from a wall chart. Nurses passed by.

"Hi." She touched his arm. "I just wanted to remind you about your interview in ten minutes." She knew how helpful a gesture could be, and she wasn't above using her female allure to imprint important matters in the minds of the male staff.

"Catherine, thank you," Dr. Anderson said. "I'll certainly be there."

"Sure. And congratulations on your cancer research award. You deserve it."

"I appreciate that."

Her cell phone rang and she let her hand drop from the doctor's arm. He moved toward the nurses' desk while she answered the call. "This is Catherine."

"Hey. It's Caleb."

"Caleb?"

"You know, your husband?"

She wondered why he would be calling her at work. This was abnormal.

"I wanted to call and check on you," he said.

Catherine's pulse sped up. She thought about an encounter earlier in the day with the doctor—the other, younger doctor. Had she been too obvious in her exchanges with Gavin, too flirtatious? Had word got back to Caleb somehow?

But she'd done nothing wrong.

So as not to raise his suspicions, she tried to mask her rising annoyance. "You wanted to check on me? What for?"

CALEB WAS SEATED by his storage locker in the station, *The Love Dare* open on his lap and the phone pressed to his ear. He detected a tone of irritation in his wife's voice, but that was no surprise. They never called each other at work, so she had to be wondering what was up.

"Uh, you know," he said. "Just to see if you needed anything."

CATHERINE SPUN ON her feet and put all her weight on one hip. This was strange. Something wasn't right, but she couldn't place her finger on it. Caleb sounded almost . . . *nice*. Still, there was a quality to his voice that seemed forced.

"You called to see if I needed anything?"

"Right," he said. "Yeah, uh, you want me to bring something

home for you? Or, uh, or get something from the store in the morning?"

Warm fingers brushed Catherine's elbow and she turned to see Gavin walking by. He was in scrubs, with a blue surgical cap over his head. For some reason, he looked even more handsome at this moment. They made eye contact and she smiled at him.

"Catherine?"

"Listen, Caleb—you've never asked me this before. What's going on?"

"I just wanted to see if you needed anything, that's it."

"I'm fine."

"Okay. All right. Well . . . Good-bye."

Catherine snapped her phone shut. The sensation of Gavin's touch still burned along her elbow as she shook her head and stalked off down the hall.

CALEB SHRUGGED. HE'D had only the slightest of hopes that his wife would soften and ask for his assistance, but he'd harbored a greater fear that she would request something beyond his means or his willingness to comply. Thankfully, she'd let him off the hook.

He gazed down at the notebook in his hands. So be it.

"Day Four," he said. "Done."

He closed the notebook, tossed it into his locker, and slammed the door shut. He could now get on with the rest of his afternoon.

CATHERINE SLID HER padded planner onto the counter of the nurses' station, where Tasha and Deidra were busy with paperwork and phones. She leaned forward on her elbows and closed her eyes, drawing in a deep breath.

125

"Hey, Cat," Tasha said. "How ya doin', girl?"

"Confused." She slipped off her glasses. "I don't know. My husband's acting weird."

"What's he doing?"

"Well, in the last few days he has fixed me coffee, bought me these pitiful little flowers, and a few minutes ago called just to"— she lowered her voice in imitation of a man's—"to see if I'm doing okay."

"Really?" Tasha tucked her chin and gave a skeptical look.

Deidra stepped in, one hand on her hip. "I'll tell you what he's doing. He's trying to butter you up for a divorce."

"And why would he do that?"

"Oooh," Deidra said, wagging her pen in the air. "Before my cousin Lawanna got a divorce, her husband started doing the same thing. Started acting all nice and sweet and everything. The next thing we know, he walks away with the house and most of their money. He hasn't even talked to her since."

An emptiness gnawed at Catherine's stomach. Was she being made a fool of? Was that Caleb's angle here?

Deidra seemed to have no doubt. "Don't you let him deceive you, girl."

Tasha was in agreement. "Mm-hmm."

Catherine started to seethe.

SEATED AT THE computer in jeans and a loose pullover, Caleb heard Catherine's Camry pull into the driveway earlier than usual, and his heart jumped into his throat.

Mid-afternoon? She wasn't supposed to be home yet.

He had the shades closed, the room darkened against the sun and any curious neighbors. He double-clicked items in his recent

126

history and hit the Delete key, worried that she might be angered by them, while almost longing to be discovered. He'd rather get this all out in the open, rather deal with the real issue, than act like it didn't exist and that their lack of marital intimacy was of no concern to him.

He was a man, after all. What did she expect?

They hadn't slept in the same bed—let alone the same bedroom—for weeks now. Didn't the Bible even tell husbands and wives not to refrain from their physical union for long periods of time?

Okay, so maybe God wouldn't consider that valid grounds for indulging in Internet sleaze, but Caleb hardly cared at this point.

His wife was in the house now. Coming down the hall.

Tap, tap, tappp . . . Delete.

The lighting changed as she flicked on a switch; then her keys and purse dropped to the table. He could hear her picking through the day's mail. With his back to her in the desk chair, he cleared his throat and tried to act relaxed.

"You're home early," he said.

"Did you clear your history?"

"What?"

"Did you wipe the Web sites off so nobody would see where you've been?"

His eyes felt bleary. He kept his mouth shut and his back turned.

"You know, Caleb, you're not fooling anybody." Catherine's voice was on that edge between steady and about-to-unwind. "I know exactly what you're trying to do, buying me flowers and calling me at work."

"And what is that?"

"I'm meeting with a lawyer next week, and don't you think for one second I'm buying into this nice-guy routine."

"What're you talking about?"

"You're not getting one *dime* more than you deserve. When this divorce is final, I'm taking my share."

He bolted from the chair to confront her. "Is that what you think I'm doing?"

"No." Catherine slapped down the pile of mail and strode right up to him, eyes blazing. "I *know* that's what you're doing."

"Yeah? Well, you're wrong. You know, you never assume I would do anything worthy of respect, anything honorable!"

"Honorable? *Honorable?* What were you just looking at, Caleb? What was on that computer screen? Was that *honorable?*"

He brimmed with anger. He wanted to throw hurtful barbs back at her, words that would tear her down and make himself feel bigger than her.

He kept his lips clamped shut.

"Who do you think you're fooling?" she pressed on. "Do you know why your sweet little gestures mean nothing to me? It's because *that's* the kind of man you've become." She jabbed a finger at the computer. "When you're alone, that's what you default to, and there is *nothing* honorable about it."

Caleb watched her march away. He chose the opposite direction and stalked out the back door to the porch, both arms wrapped over his head. He was ready to explode. With clenched fists, he turned and saw his aluminum baseball bat leaned up against the house.

He took hold of the bat, flexed his fingers around the handle, then swung with all his might.

The green trash can tumbled onto its side with a dull thump.

He hit it again.

And again.

The blows rained down until it was obvious he could inflict

no more damage, at which point he heaved the worthless bat into the backyard with a loud grunt. She had no idea of the torture she was putting him through. Still simmering with fury, guilt, and self-righteous despair, he searched for something else to destroy.

Then he realized, once more, he was being watched.

Perfect. Just perfect.

Standing at his grill on the neighboring back patio, Mr. Rudolph stared unblinkingly at Caleb. His spindly form was decked out in a flower-print Hawaiian shirt, and he clutched a wire brush in his hand.

Caleb collected his breath. "Mr. Rudolph."

The elderly man's dry voice bridged the distance. "Caleb."

Embarrassed, Caleb pried the phone from his pocket and headed for the cab of his Sierra pickup, chased there by the sounds of the bristles of Mr. Rudolph's brush grating against iron.

JOHN HOLT WAS in his easy chair, reading the newspaper, when the phone rang. He'd just returned from a men's prayer luncheon and was still dressed in slacks and a long-sleeved shirt. He reached for the phone on the end table.

"Hello?"

There was no preamble, just a harried voice. "It's not working, Dad."

"What's not working?"

"This whole 'love dare' thing. It is not working."

John folded the paper and set it aside. "Tell me what's going on."

"I have been doing everything that it says to do, and she has completely rejected all of it."

"Caleb, this process takes forty days, not four."

"What is the point of driving down a dead-end road, when you know it's not going anywhere?"

"You don't know that yet. Caleb, you're not a quitter, and something tells me you're doing just enough to get by."

Silence from the other end.

"Am I right, son?"

There was a long exhalation of air. Caleb said, "I *feel* nothing."

"I understand, but this is not based on feelings. It's a decision. You can't give up yet. Keep taking it a day at a time."

Another sigh. "Yes, sir."

"I love you, son."

"You too, Dad."

John heard the line disconnect. He wished he could be there with his only child, but there were other ways to fight such battles. He sat forward, arms crossed over his knees, wondering why he hadn't lifted up his son's marriage for consideration at the earlier prayer luncheon. There was no need for gossip or hearsay, but there was a definite call for unified petition before God's throne.

Cheryl entered from the kitchen and sat facing John from the other chair. "How is he?" she asked.

"We've gotta start praying for him more."

"That's all I've been doing for the past few days."

John reached for his wife's hands. "Then let's do it together."

130

CHAPTER 19

Catherine was seated across from her mother, looking into those soft eyes and that speechless mouth that was filled with so much wisdom. Framed photos on the end table showed Catherine as a little girl, and she thought back to the dreams she'd had at that age.

Dreams of a prince. And a fairy-tale romance.

Of course, that was not reality.

What had happened, though, to the love she and Caleb once shared? Once he had won her hand, he acted like he'd been let off the hook. Didn't he realize that marrying her just meant he was the one who'd gotten the job? Why would he think there was no more work involved?

"I don't know what to do, Mama."

Joy Campbell nodded for her daughter to go on.

"I know you always told me to hang on during the hard times," Catherine said, "but it's just . . ." Her lower lip began to tremble and her voice caught. She pushed a strand of hair back from her face and tried to find the strength to continue.

131

There were some things too shameful to divulge, even to her mother.

The Internet, as great a tool as it was, had also brought temptation into her home, only a few keystrokes away from her husband's itchy fingers. Times had changed. In her mother's era, such things were hidden in boxes in the attic or garage. Now lurid images could be loaded onto the computer screen whenever he desired.

How could Catherine possibly compete with that?

"I don't know what to do," she mumbled.

She wasn't an airbrushed image. She required actual care and devotion—things Caleb seemed to have forgotten.

Her mother reached out and touched her knee.

Catherine tried again. "You don't know what I've been competing with. I mean, when he looks . . ." Her voice failed her completely this time. Her lips quivered with the feelings of betrayal that had lurked beneath the surface for months. She buried her face in her hands, felt the prick of tears at her eyes. She pulled her hair back, shaking her head. "He makes me feel so humiliated, and he doesn't even know it."

Mrs. Campbell gripped her hand, holding on tight.

"When, Mama?" With tears rolling down her cheeks, Catherine met her mother's eyes. "When did I stop being good enough for him?"

THE NEXT TWO weeks passed with no discernible improvement. Caleb followed each day's suggestions from his dad's notebook, but they seemed like small pebbles stacked against a flood of old patterns and emotions.

How did that saying go? *Insanity is doing the same thing over and over, while expecting different results.*

132

That described this futile exercise to a T.

Of course, his dad would probably tell him that sometimes you did the same thing over and over because it was the right thing to do, regardless.

With these thoughts rumbling through his head, Caleb found himself once again at the computer on his day off. He reached for the Power button, then hesitated. He'd wasted hours yesterday, thinking of boats and fishing and time alone and other things he knew were off-limits to a married man—which only made them more enticing, of course.

He raised his head, took a deep breath.

On the wall, a large rectangular panel of dark wood hung as a keepsake from his grandfather. Crafted by the old man's hands, the panel had once graced the lobby of a church on the outskirts of town.

In 1982, the building had crumbled in a fire. Caleb, only eight years old, had been there with his family among the onlookers. Aghast, they'd watched the firefighters battle the blaze, and to this day Caleb could feel the heat on his face and taste the ash that had curled through the night. The steeple burned like a torch lifted high into the sky, smoking as a heavy rain began to fall.

That evening, Caleb knew what he wanted to do when he grew up.

This panel, salvaged from wreckage and returned to its original splendor, was a tangible reminder of his purpose, his heritage, and the suddenness with which life could take a disastrous turn. The words "Live—Laugh—Love" lined the tan middle portion. Furthermore, the panel hung as a symbol of his grandfather's godly demeanor and of the words that now graced the man's tombstone:

"In life, a friend of all . . . In death, a friend of God's."

Caleb snatched his hand back from the computer.

What was he doing?

Taking hold of Catherine's college graduation photo next to the monitor, he thought about the woman who had stolen his heart there in the firehouse bay ten years earlier.

And he made his decision.

There came a time to start putting out fires, and that time was now. He shoved back in his chair and walked away from the computer desk.

CATHERINE SPENT THE next two weeks going through the motions of work and public relations. She tuned out Caleb's meager advances and gestures, determined that she would no longer play the fool in this relationship.

Yesterday she'd put on a brave face for the cameras, standing before Phoebe Putney's hedged garden area, answering questions from a female reporter. She'd cradled her hands in front of her, a picture of professionalism.

When it came to her husband, though . . .

The answer, Catherine had decided, was to stop trying, stop caring, and stop feeling. Like a local anesthetic, this tactic actually seemed to work.

She was no longer dying inside.

Or, if she was, she couldn't feel it. And that was all that mattered.

"Catherine," Gavin said, catching her in the corridor on the fifth floor. "Have you taken a break yet this morning?"

"Uh, no. I was—"

"It's a beautiful day. Would you like to join me out by the fountain?"

"Sure, Gavin," she said. "I've got a few things to put in my office, but I'll meet you out there in five minutes, okay?"

"Make it ten. I'll stop at the café and grab us some drinks."

"Mmm. Sounds good."

"A skinny vanilla latte for you, is that right?"

"How'd you know?"

"I pay attention." Although the doctor's tone was polite, the passion in his gaze was undeniable.

"I'm impressed, Gavin."

"Well, good. That's what I was hoping for."

She joined him there ten minutes later, on schedule. As the fountain bubbled, she did too, reacting to his dry humor and brightening at his flattery. She was a married woman, true. But he didn't know that, not since she had removed her ring and left it in the dresser drawer. Of course, Gavin might've heard it through the hospital grapevine—there was no stopping the rumor mill around this place—but he might assume that she was currently separated.

His intentions are completely noble, she told herself.

Hers, on the other hand, were not quite so honorable. She'd pointed the finger at Caleb, but was this really any different?

She pushed that thought aside and laughed at Gavin's next joke.

By increments, she was giving herself away.

A FEW MONTHS ago, Catherine would've seen it as a black-and-white matter. She should not be opening her heart to another man—not to mention that workplace romances were almost always ill-advised. At twenty-eight years of age, she knew better.

These days, however, the matter didn't seem so clear-cut.

She felt her heart skip a beat as she entered her office and saw something waiting for her beside her business-card holder.

It was a Hallmark greeting card, accompanied by a single long-stemmed rose. Already, the deep red petals were sending their sweet aroma through the room.

For a moment, she wondered if it could be from Caleb. He never visited her here at work, but he had been acting strangely the past few weeks. Maybe this was another one of his attempts to soften her up for the kill.

She settled into her chair and lifted the rose, holding off on opening the card. She drew in the bloom's soft scent with eyes closed.

Caleb?

Or Gavin?

She pulled out the card and, at the sight of the doctor's scribbled signature, felt a heady delirium rush through her. It reminded her of falling in love all over again, and she dashed from her office.

She found the good doctor in the corridor. "Thanks, Gavin."

"You're welcome," he said. "My pleasure."

"That was very thoughtful of you."

"So, my bedside manner is improving?" Behind placid eyes, his question was loaded with innuendo.

Catherine leaned back against a door frame, clutching her planner, lifting one foot up on her toes. She knew Tasha was just over there, within earshot, at a desk. In her peripheral vision, she also spotted her friend Anna eyeing her from across the nurses' station.

None of that seemed to matter.

"Oh," she said, "we've had a few complaints, Doctor, but one particular woman says you've been as nice as can be."

"You mean the great-great-grandmother on the second floor?"

"Don't give me that." Catherine leaned forward, laughing, and squeezed his hand in a playful gesture. "You know exactly who I mean."

Gavin smiled. "I'm beginning to think that I do."

From the left, Catherine felt Anna's stare drilling into her with unspoken accusations, but she refused to pay it any heed. Let the older nurse think what she wanted. Catherine was a grown woman and she could make her own decisions. This was her life.

And no one else's, thank you.

CHAPTER 20

Lieutenant Simmons was manning the barbecue on the station's side patio. Grease sizzled, coals spat, and the scent of grilled meat wafted through the air. Close by, Caleb was reading this day's entry in *The Love Dare*. Recently, he'd been sharing portions of it with his friend.

Simmons flipped medium-well-done patties onto a plate, then looked up from beneath his fireman's ball cap. "So what day are you on, Caleb?"

"Eighteen."

"And?"

Caleb glanced back at the men circling the ladder truck. Although they were doing their job, probably paying no attention to his conversation, he didn't feel like sharing the details of his little dare. Simmons was his friend, and that's as far as this would go.

Simmons flipped another burger.

"And," Caleb answered, "it's still difficult. Every day has me adding a new concept to the way I treat Catherine."

"For example?"

"Well, here . . . Day Sixteen was about praying for her." He looked up. "I kinda skipped that one." He flipped the pages and continued. "Day Seventeen was about listening to her, and Eighteen's about studying her again."

"Studying her?"

"Yeah. Here . . ." Caleb read aloud: "'When a man is trying to win the heart of a woman, he studies her. He learns her likes, dislikes, habits, and hobbies. But after he wins her heart and marries her, he often stops learning about her.'"

Simmons scraped at the grill, all ears.

"'If the amount he studied her before marriage was equal to a high school degree,'" Caleb continued, "'he should continue to learn about her until he gains a college degree, a master's degree, and ultimately a doctorate degree. It is a lifelong journey that draws his heart ever closer to hers.'"

"That's a pretty good concept. I never thought about it like that."

"So do you study Tina?"

Simmons tilted his head. "Yeah, but I don't think I've got my college degree on her yet."

Caleb smirked and looked down at the notebook.

"You think maybe I could borrow that book?"

Caleb's head snapped back up. "You?"

"Just to brush up, you know? Maybe work on my master's."

"You don't need it. You and Tina, you seem pretty happy together."

"That's exactly why we need it."

"You lost me."

"Well," Simmons said, "you know how we're always trying to teach fire prevention around here, going into the schools, doing community work and all?"

"Yeah?"

139

"You and Catherine, me and Tina—we're in the hot seats. Just 'cause we wear the rings doesn't mean we're safe. We have to do all we can to keep our relationships fireproof."

Caleb let that sink in, while choosing not to dwell on his wife's absent ring.

"So," Simmons said. "Tell me a little bit more about, uh, studying her."

"Well, I'm supposed to make her a candlelight dinner and then ask her a whole list of questions."

"Hmm. My advice is, go all out."

Caleb wore a confused expression. "Meaning?"

"Don't go cheap. If you don't cook, get it from a good restaurant. Take it home, use your best dishes, glasses, music . . . everything." Simmons aimed the grill spatula at Caleb. "You make sure it's a memorable date."

KP: KITCHEN PATROL. Terrell chose to sweep while Wayne was left to do the dishes. The driver seemed okay with that, smiling, boasting as usual, as he cleared the table and shoveled garbage into the trash can.

"I just tell 'em I'm a fireman," Wayne said, "and the women can't stay away."

Terrell came to a halt. "What women?"

"The ones kissin' up to me every Friday night."

"Man, whatchu talkin' about? You ain't had a date in a year."

"Hey, I'm like a fine wine. I need about thirty-five years to reach perfection." Wayne tossed down a napkin, sucked in his gut, and gestured at himself. "But the lady that gets Wayne Floyd, she'll get a complete package."

"You mean, a complete wreckage."

"Nah. I'm two hundred and fifty-five pounds of pure love. All you need to make marriage work is a li'l bit of romance, and that comes from right here." With two fingers, Wayne inscribed a heart on the front of his blue Fire/Rescue shirt.

"What?" Terrell could hardly believe his ears. "That's easy to say when you ain't never been married. I been with my wife almost five years, and it's a lot harder than you think, man."

Terrell continued to pepper the driver with jibes and sarcasm, yet none of it was mean-spirited. Wayne was Terrell's opposite—tall, Caucasian as they came, blue-eyed, and blond. Their camaraderie as firemen was only strengthened by the playful banter. Sometimes Terrell even lay in bed just thinking of new ways to get under Wayne's skin.

Some nights that's all Terrell Sanders had to think upon.

Truth was, the past few months his wife had made a habit of sleeping on the couch or going to her sister's place downtown by the river.

Yeah, marriage was hard. No doubt about that.

Wayne was not to be discouraged, though. Not tonight.

He put glasses away in a cupboard and said, "You watch, Terrell. One day I'm gonna walk in here with a tanned beauty on my arm, and I'll show you how easy it can be."

Captain Caleb Holt walked in, trailing barbecue smoke and a pair of bees as he brought plates and condiments from the outside patio area.

"I'm tellin' you, Wayne . . ." Terrell propped both hands on his broom handle and jeered. "The only thing you'll ever come in here with, hanging from your arm, is a bucket o' chicken."

Wayne grinned. "Yeah, you wish."

Caleb slipped up beside Wayne and clapped a hand on his shoulder.

The driver stopped. "What?"

"It was tomato juice," Caleb stated, before leaving the room.

A befuddled look crossed Wayne's face. He shrugged, glanced toward Terrell, and shook his head as if to say: *What was that all about?*

FOUR HOURS LATER, with a calm, humid night settling over Albany, Terrell shifted in his bed on the station's upper sleeping level. Although sometimes they got awakened by the sound of the alarm, he hoped this evening would allow him a long rest. He needed it. On his days off, he'd found little peace sleeping alone in that king-size marriage bed.

Sudden movement cut through his drowsiness, followed by a yell.

"To*mato* juice? Man, that's wrong!" Wayne shot up from his bed, the one between Eric's and Terrell's, his face a mask of indignation. He punched at his covers. "That's *wrong!*"

"What's wrong?" Eric sounded groggy.

In shorts and a T-shirt, Wayne jumped up on his bare feet. He stabbed the air with his finger. "I drank the *real* stuff while *he* drank tomato juice."

"You just got that?" Terrell asked.

"You know what that stuff *did* to me?"

"Go to bed, Wayne," Simmons barked from around the corner.

"There were some *serious* repercussions."

The crew chuckled in the darkness, while Eric begged for silence.

"It's on now! That's just *wrong*, man." Wayne grumbled as he adjusted his blankets and flopped back on his mattress. "You done lit a fuse. Somebody's gonna get a karate-chop sandwich."

CHAPTER 21

The tip of Caleb Holt's lighter touched the first tapered candle, then the second. Shadows edged the dining room, and the fire's golden glow danced on polished silverware.

Taking his lieutenant's advice, Caleb had pulled out all the stops. He'd ironed and spread out a white linen tablecloth, then set the table with the finest dishes and crystal stemware. After picking up a steak dinner for two from an upscale restaurant, he'd raced home so he could serve it hot the moment Catherine arrived.

She had no idea, of course. She'd always liked surprises, though, and he hoped his efforts would soften something in her.

The Camry's headlights cut across the lawn. She was here.

Caleb hit the stereo remote, starting the romantic music he'd selected. He placed the steaks on their individual plates, beside bowls of garden-fresh salad and Parmesan breadsticks.

In dress shirt and slacks, he waited.

The side door opened, ushering Catherine into the candlelit atmosphere. She had her purse over her arm, one hand on the strap as though protecting herself from getting robbed. She wore a fitted, striped shirt that was fashionable yet casual. The highlights in her hair caught the soft lighting, and her eyes . . .

Her eyes were deep and brooding—beautiful, yet distant.

Caleb's heart seemed to stop.

She was stunning.

Catherine stood in the dining room doorway, taking in all he had done. He lifted his chin in her direction and eased her chair from the table. All he wanted was one flicker, one blink. Anything to show a softening on her part.

Please, Catherine.

She said not one word. She strode off down the hall to the master bedroom. He watched her go, yet refused to give up hope. She'd be back. She was just needing to change her clothes after a long day at work. Or to collect herself emotionally.

No, she hadn't just rejected him. Had she?

CATHERINE TOSSED HER purse and keys onto the dresser and braced herself against the furniture, caught off guard by her husband's gesture. Soft music floated down the hall, a man's voice crooning something about being on top of the world.

What had gotten into Caleb?

Sure, Deidra had cautioned her about these sorts of male tactics, but it was hard not to believe those green eyes of his, sincere and unblinking. Those eyes that had peered into her soul, when she was not much more than a girl, and invited her into his life.

She knew those eyes, didn't she?

And just now, she'd seen no deceit.

Of course, that could be his intent—to put on a good act and appear as innocent as possible, before dropping the hammer.

She looked at herself in the dresser mirror and saw a woman who desired affection, security, and independence. She had given a good portion of her life to this relationship, and somewhere along the line, somewhere between her graduation from college and her promotion at the hospital, the bonds between Caleb and her had gone slack. They'd both been pulling, keeping that strand tight, but now it was loose and dangling—like a downed power line.

Useless. Nothing but arcing sparks.

Other women she knew had played the fool. Her own grandmother had let a husband squander his weekly earnings on a gambling addiction.

"He's got a good heart," Grandma used to say. *"He'll change."*

Yeah, right. If Caleb wanted me, he wouldn't need those images on the computer. He wouldn't treat me like a second-rate servant. He wouldn't . . .

Catherine pivoted from the mirror and marched back to the dining room.

SHE WAS COMING back. Caleb wanted to believe that was a good thing, but the hurried steps implied something other than loving surrender.

"What're you doing?" Catherine demanded.

Caleb had both hands on the back of the chair. "Maybe I'd like to have dinner with my wife."

She looked down, swung hair from her face, then met his gaze. "Let me be real clear with you about something . . ."

He waited.

She advanced two steps. "I do *not* love you."

Caleb's chest felt like it had been crushed beneath a falling beam. He could barely breathe. He didn't trust himself to speak. He watched her turn, heard her clicking shoes carry her away, and then he blinked back tears that turned quickly from despair to rage.

The Love Dare?

What a joke.

He plunged his hand into his water glass, then used wet fingers to snuff out both candles—*hissss, hissss.*

With a coat snatched from the hall closet, he rushed outside and paced beneath the starry Georgia night. What he wouldn't give to have one of those stars fall right now, wiping out his existence in a fiery flash.

He dragged a patio chair across the concrete pad, dropped into it, and pulled out his phone, ready to give his father a piece of his mind.

JOHN HOLT WAS at his desk, going through bills by lamplight. The cordless phone rang beside him, and caller ID provided a clue as to the purpose of the call.

"Oh, son," John mumbled. "This is when it gets hard."

He answered the phone. "Hello, Caleb."

"We're done, Dad! I am not gonna keep doing this. I have tried and there's nothing there. It's not *worth* it."

The rush of words came as no surprise. John remembered— oh, how he remembered—the struggles he and Cheryl had gone through. "I understand, son, but you're halfway there. That was the most difficult for us, too."

"But at least you had some hope. Catherine has given me nothing."

"There was a point when we had no hope either. Our marriage

should have ended, Caleb. You can't listen to the way you feel at the moment. There's no doubt that she's seen you trying, right?"

"No. She doesn't care. None of this means anything to her. Dad, I tried."

John contemplated what to do. He thought of his own father, a craftsman with wood, a godly example, and one who had been there as a calming influence for John and Cheryl. "Caleb, are you off tomorrow?"

"Yeah. Why?"

"I'm coming to see you. We can talk then."

"Dad, you don't have to do that."

"I want to, son. I'd like to come."

Caleb paused on the other end, then sighed. "All right."

CATHERINE FELT SO weak. She wanted to be strong, to hold it all together and show her self-reliance. Here, though, in the face of her collapsing marriage, she could muster only the strength to curl beneath the covers, work clothes still on, and cry.

She held the pillow to her face and felt hot tears spread through the material. She tried to mute her own whimpers. Had she made a mistake? Were Caleb's efforts genuine?

No, he had slammed the back door on his way out to the patio. He was mad—and why? Because she'd called his bluff.

Why, then, did it feel like she was the one with the losing hand?

Catherine cried herself to sleep, feeling helpless, wishing she could go back and tell the truth to that dreamy-eyed girl she had once been: Lasting romance was for storybooks, and that was it. There was no *happily ever after.*

Or, in her three-year-old words, *happily after ever.*

CHAPTER 22

"Dad, I feel bad that you drove four hours just to come see me."

"It was good," John said. "Gave me time to think and pray. So, uh, what are you on? Day Twenty?"

"Yeah. Yeah, something like that."

With his dad at his side, Caleb circled around a fallen log, past thick foliage that served as a carpet to towering pines, oaks, and pecans. Sunbeams spilled through the greenery, like glowing drops of water, and filtered through strands of moss. This trail behind Caleb and Catherine's house was guiding them back to the old camp spot with the wooden cross.

"Twenty," John said. "Yeah, I'd say the halfway point was the hardest."

Caleb hooked a thumb into his pocket. "Why?"

"Well, it's when you determine whether your heart's in it or not. It makes you check your real motives when things get difficult."

"Did Mom give *you* a hard time?"

"Oh," John chuckled. "I thought your mother had a pretty good attitude about it."

"Well, Catherine's not buying any of it."

"And why do you think that is?"

"Because she doesn't love me. She doesn't even like me. Dad, she's just about ignored everything I've done."

"Are you reading everything on each page?"

"Of *The Love Dare*? What, you mean the Bible verses at the bottom?" Caleb groaned. "No, no, I'm not, Dad. I told you, that is not what I need."

"And what do you need?"

"I need Catherine to wake up to the fact that we're about to get an ugly divorce. I'm trying to prevent that, but I cannot do it by myself."

"That may be true, but I think you need more than that."

"Dad, if you're gonna tell me I need Jesus—please don't. I don't need a crutch to get through life." Caleb scraped his leather hiking boots over the ground, snapping twigs beneath his feet.

"Oh, son, Jesus is much more than a crutch. He's become the most significant part of our lives."

"Why do you keep saying stuff like that? 'He's the most significant part . . .'? How is that?"

John lumbered along the trail, unhurried. "When I realized who *I* was and who *He* was, I realized my need for Him. I *needed* His forgiveness and salvation."

"See, I don't understand that. Why do I need His salvation? What, am I gonna be thrown into hell? For what? Because I got divorced?"

They had reached the clearing, where scattered stumps still waited for campers who had been gone for years. There was something serene about this place, away from the rough-and-tumble of life.

"No," John said, turning in his ribbed tan sweater and dark corduroys. "It's because you've violated His standards."

"What? Thou shalt not kill? Dad, I help people. I am a good person."

"According to you. But God doesn't judge by your standards. He uses His."

Caleb's mind was racing. See, this was too much for anyone to live up to. This was why all that religious talk turned people away. No wonder fundamentalists of all sorts ranted at a world gone astray. That gave them all the justification they needed to point their fingers and rain down condemnation.

"Okay, Dad. And what're God's standards?"

"Well . . . truth."

"Okay."

"Love."

"I'm honest."

"Faithfulness."

"I care about people. I am those things."

"Sometimes. But have you loved God, the One who gave you life? His standards are so high," John said, gesturing, "that He considers hatred to be murder. And lust to be adultery."

The words pierced to Caleb's core. He thought of all the times he'd harbored hatred toward others—even toward his wife. And the hours he'd wasted in front of the computer, committing adultery in the hidden places of his mind.

"But, Dad, what about . . . what about all the good I've done?"

"Son, saving someone from a fire does not make you right with God. You've broken His commandments, and one day you'll answer to Him for that. Your only hope is God changing you, and your pride is keeping you from getting there."

Caleb planted himself on one of the stumps, his back turned toward the sunrays that radiated around wooden crossbeams. In his father's voice, he detected no arrogance or scorn, only untamed truth and desperate love. Caleb leaned forward, knotting his hands over his head. The weight of the world was here on his back—his failure as a husband, the lack of respect from his wife.

And now he had to carry the burden of being some awful sinner?

It was too much.

It seemed easier to look away than face the truth.

"Caleb, if I were to ask you why you're so frustrated with Catherine, what would you say?"

That brought his head back up. Caleb could almost imagine the list scrolling from his mouth. "She's stubborn. She makes everything difficult for me. She's ungrateful. She's constantly griping about something."

"Has she thanked you for anything you've done the last twenty days?"

"No. And you'd think after I've washed her car, changed the oil, done the dishes, and cleaned the house, that she would *try* to show me a little bit of gratitude. But she doesn't."

John pursed his lips, pushed both hands into his pockets, and began shuffling along the campsite's perimeter.

"In fact," Caleb snarled, "when I come home, she makes me feel like . . . like I'm an enemy. I'm not even welcome in my own home, Dad. That is what really ticks me off!"

His father's eyes were down, loafers still sliding through the leaves.

Caleb shifted his weight on the stump, making sure every word was heard. He could feel the veins popping on his neck and forehead as he vented the feelings he'd bottled inside. "For the last three weeks, I have bent over *back*wards for her. I've tried to demonstrate that I still care about this relationship. I've bought her flowers—which she threw away."

John's rolled shoulders and downcast eyes showed no reaction.

"I have taken her insults and her sarcasm, but last night . . . That was it," Caleb growled. "I made dinner for her. I did everything I could to demonstrate that I care about her, to show value for her. And she *spat* in my face. She does not deserve this, Dad. I am not doing it anymore! How am I supposed to show love to somebody *over* and *over* and *over* who constantly rejects me?"

His dad came to a halt at the solitary cross. He looked up, then leaned against the vertical beam as he studied his son through wire-rimmed glasses.

Caleb blinked against the sunlight.

"That's a good question," John said.

Caleb lifted his gaze to the cross, this ancient symbol of love and sacrifice, then let it come back to rest on his father. With the meeting of eyes, something flashed through Caleb's thoughts. "No." He hardened his jaw. "No, that is *not* what I'm doing."

"Isn't it?"

He shook his head. "Dad, that is not what this is about."

"Son, you just asked me—how can someone show love over and over again when they are constantly rejected? Caleb, the answer is, you can't love her because you can't give her what you don't have."

Caleb rubbed his forehead, shielding his face from his father. If God was real . . .

If it was true that Jesus had died for him . . .

No, this was too much, too fast.

"I couldn't truly love your mother," John said, approaching Caleb with slow steps, "until I understood what love really was. It's not because I get some reward out of it. I've now made a decision to love her, whether she deserves it or not. Son, God loves you, even though you don't deserve it. Even though you've rejected Him. Spat in *His* face."

152

Caleb lifted his eyes to the wooden beams. Is that what he'd done?

He felt pierced by his own hardened heart and arrogance. Who was he to complain? By comparison, his own suffering to show love was pitiful.

John's voice turned tender. "God sent Jesus to die on the cross and take the punishment for your sin because He loves you, Caleb." John knelt, resting a hand on his son's shoulder. "The cross was offensive to me until I came to it. But when I did, Jesus Christ changed my life. That's when I *truly* began to love your mom."

Caleb gave his father a sideward glance.

"Son, I can't settle this for you. This is between you and the Lord. But I love you too much not to tell you the truth. Can't you see that you need Him?"

Caleb held his chin in his fist. The warmth of his father's hand, the depth of his concern, worked like oil flowing through the cogs and wheels of Caleb's heart and mind. The friction that had been tearing at him, burning through him, began to ease, and now his position became clear.

His father was right. He had broken God's laws. He had hated, lusted, even lied. He had judged his wife for the very things he had done himself. He had scorned the God who had given him life, and he knew if he stood in judgment before the Almighty, he would be found guilty.

Tears pooled in his eyes. He nodded and lowered his chin.

"Caleb, can't you see that you need His forgiveness?"

"Yes," he whispered.

"Will you trust Him with your life?"

Caleb peered at his dad, witnessing in those aging eyes unwavering acceptance, grace, and love. The change in John Holt was real.

I want that, too. Whatever it takes. I can't do this without You. Save me, Jesus.

Nodding, Caleb felt his father's arms enfold him—and he sensed the hint of a greater, larger embrace that would never let him go.

CHAPTER 23

There was no magic involved. Captain Caleb Holt's life didn't turn overnight into a landscape of wondrous bliss. In fact, the next day Catherine's tone was more spiteful than ever.

"So, what'd you and your dad talk about?"

"You and me," Caleb replied.

"Oh, great," she snapped. "Now you're dragging others into our problems, huh? You made him drive all the way from Savannah just so you could poison him against me? What stories did you feed him this time?"

"Catherine, I—"

"Forget it. I don't even wanna know."

"Actually, I—"

"You're gonna be late. I don't want to cause you any trouble at work." She swiveled from the kitchen back toward the master bedroom—or *her* bedroom, as Caleb had come to think of it.

"I'll call you," he said.

"My phone'll probably be turned off. If it is, don't worry about me."

Caleb's thoughts raced back to Day One in the notebook, the one that had implored him to say nothing if he had nothing kind to say. At least this time it was easier, and he clung to that small victory.

IN THE MEETING room at the Albany Fire Department, Station One, Capt. Caleb Holt joined the rest of his crew as they waited for the previous shift to head home. Five men stood with duffel bags in hand, weary from last night's multiple false alarms at a warehouse on the edge of town.

"I think someone was messing with us," Captain Harris told Caleb.

"At two in the morning? That's not very funny. Don't they ever stop to think what would happen if there was a real emergency?"

"There's some people out there who just like watching us run around, chasing our tails."

All part of the job, I guess." Captain Harris ran a finger down his clipboard. "We also had two calls yesterday, but there wasn't much to them. We used some CO_2, so it might be a little low."

"I'll take care of it," Caleb said.

"Already done. I e-mailed in a request to fill it up. And the truck's running fine, so you should be good to go." Harris relinquished the clipboard and shook Caleb's hand, effectively passing the baton.

"Thanks, Ken. You guys have a good day. We got it from here."

The two shifts acknowledged each other in passing. Once on their own, A-Shift gathered around their captain.

"All right," Caleb said. "Why don't you guys load your gear on the truck while Lieutenant Simmons whips us up some breakfast?"

"How 'bout some waffles and bacon?" Wayne suggested.

"No, man. I need me an omelet," Terrell said.

"Terrell, didn't we have omelets last time?"

"I'll take either," the rookie said. "I'm not complaining."

"That's the right attitude. You all hear what Eric said?"

In unison: "Yes, Captain."

As the men shuffled out, Wayne cornered Simmons. "Listen, if you do make omelets, you think you could stuff mine with a waffle?"

"A what? Does this look like a restaurant to you?"

"I'm just sayin'—"

"Get outta here."

A tone sounded, followed by a voice through the speaker. "Oh-eight-hundred hours, Albany Fire Department clear."

Caleb and his crew had a long twenty-four hours ahead.

THIRTY MINUTES LATER, Caleb found Simmons straightening the living area, adjusting the matching blue armchairs, setting two-way radios into chargers, picking up magazines. Although Caleb wanted more than ever to be dependable here on the job, he'd been bursting within, hoping to share his newfound faith with the lieutenant.

Caleb was about to speak up when Wayne and Terrell burst through the door from their assigned duties in the bay.

"Waffle time," Wayne exclaimed. He hitched his pants and clapped his hands on his way into the kitchen.

"That boy's about to be severely disappointed," Simmons said.

"*Oatmeal?*" Wayne shouted. "That's just cruel, Lieutenant."

Terrell laughed at the exchange, then scooped himself a large bowl and elbowed into the dining area. Wayne followed, grumbling with each step.

Caleb glanced around, making sure once again that he and

157

Simmons were on their own. He cleared his throat. "Hey, Michael, I'd like to talk to you about something."

"What's that?"

"Well, uh—"

"Hey, Captain." Eric appeared out of nowhere, holding something plastic in his hand. "I think B-Shift's trying to pull a joke on us, man. These salt and pepper shakers won't come apart."

"Hey." Simmons motioned. "Toss 'em over here."

Eric complied.

Simmons studied his superglue artwork, saw that all remained intact, then set it on the end table.

"Thanks, rookie," Caleb said. "Gotta keep an eye out for the jokers around this place. Listen, don't forget to mop the kitchen after breakfast."

"Yes sir."

"And change out the battery on that clock. Looks like it's gone dead."

Eric nodded, then headed off for his food.

Okay, let's try this again.

Caleb tightened his fingers into fists, wondering what his friend and coworker would think of the revelation he was about to make. By confessing his recent decision in the clearing, he would be making himself accountable to it.

Simmons said, "You wanted to tell me something?"

Hands shoved into pockets. A nervous nod.

Simmons waited.

"Uh . . . It's about your faith," Caleb said.

"My faith?"

"Yeah."

"What about it?"

Guess it's time to go public.

158

"Well," Caleb said. "I'm in."

"You're in?"

"Yeah. I'm in."

Simmons's eyes widened. "Now, are you saying that you *wanna* be in?"

"I'm saying, I'm in."

"You're really in?"

"I'm really in."

"'Cause you can't be half in and say you're in. You gotta be all in, brother."

Caleb smiled and dragged his hands from his pockets. He moved forward with a bounce in his step. "I'm saying, I'm *all* in."

"Aww, Caleb." Simmons caught the captain in a sudden back-slapping embrace. "I can't believe it, man. You're my *brother*." He took a step back.

"I'm your brother?"

"Yeah, man. You're my brother from another mother, but now we've got the same Father."

"What?"

"Oh, I'll explain it to you later. Man, this is awesome."

Behind Lieutenant Simmons, fire-hose sizes and pressure regulations were written in dry-erase marker on the board, and Caleb thought it was funny how those figures and algebraic equations made more sense to him right now than the dialogue they'd just shared.

But that didn't dampen his spirits. Something had definitely shifted.

"Does Catherine know?" Simmons asked.

"Uh, no. No, I don't think she'd care right now, to tell you the truth. She hasn't been taking too well to this whole 'love dare' thing." Caleb propped himself on a chair and folded his arms.

"But you're not done yet, right?"

"No, I'm on Day Twenty-one out of forty. But I'll be honest with you, Michael . . . Up to this point, my heart's not been in it."

"Hmm. Well, that's what matters. A woman can tell when you're just going through the motions."

"No kidding. That's absolutely right. So, let me ask you a question: How'd you get off to such a good start with Tina? Why is it so easy for you two?"

"It's not always been easy," Simmons said. "Marriage takes work. Tina is an incredible wife, but we've learned a lot of lessons the hard way."

"Well, at least you haven't had to face divorce."

Simmons turned his gaze toward the floor. He stood and circled the chair, moving away from the captain as though distancing himself from something disturbing. "I wish that were true."

"What does that mean? You and Tina have been struggling that much?"

"Not me and Tina. But I did with my first wife."

"*What?*" Caleb's eyes darted back over his shoulder, verifying they were on their own in here, then his hands shifted to his hips. "You were married to someone before Tina?"

"For one horrible year. I got married for the wrong reasons, then I turned around and got a divorce for the wrong reasons. Man, I thought I was just following my heart."

"Michael, I have worked with you for five years. You've never told me that."

"Because I'm not proud of it, okay? It was before I gave my life to the Lord, and . . . I was only concerned with *my* rights and *my* needs." He poked himself in the chest with his finger. "I ruined her life. Then, when I gave my life to God, I tried to find her, but she had already remarried. So believe me when I tell you, I've got a big scar."

160

Caleb soaked this in, his bewilderment knocked aside by the poignancy in Simmons's words. He'd thought that his friend had the perfect relationship, and yet he, too, had gone through tough times.

Guess I'm not as alone as I thought.

"Listen, Caleb." Simmons held up the joined salt and pepper shakers. "God meant marriage to be for life. That's why you gotta keep your vows to Catherine. You've gotta beg God to teach you how to be a good husband. And don't just follow your heart, 'cause your heart can be deceived."

"Yeah, tell me about it."

"You've gotta *lead* your heart."

Simmons's words seeped down through Caleb's defenses. He'd been twisted this way and that by the fluctuations of the past few months, letting his wife's moods dictate his reactions. His heart had been wandering off in all sorts of directions.

Yes, it was time to start leading instead.

His mind turned to the image of that cross in the clearing. Now that he'd found One to follow, an example, he knew he would have to die to his own desires before there would be any hope of resurrecting his marriage.

So, Caleb—you think you're such a hero?

Time to put that to the test.

CHAPTER 24

On the outdoor patio of the hospital food court, between vibrant shrubbery and colorful blooms, Catherine sat beside Dr. Gavin Keller at a black wrought-iron table. He was in a light blue shirt with a diagonally striped tie, comfortable in his formal attire. She couldn't help but admire that. Her husband rarely wore a tie, and when he did he looked like he was about to choke.

I try to be in style. Is it wrong for me to want that from the man I married?

Catherine brushed back her hair. She wore a red silk blouse beneath a charcoal gray jacket.

"You seem a little down today," Gavin noted.

He was right. He seemed so in tune with her emotions, and that only underlined her resentment toward Caleb.

She poked at her salad and pushed her roll to the side of the plate. "It's just been hard for me, you know."

"Why's that?" Empathy filled Gavin's voice.

"I saw my parents again yesterday, and my mom's not doing too well. It's amazing how much a stroke can affect somebody's life. I just . . . I feel like she's trapped. And Dad does his best to communicate, but it's hard for him, too."

"Catherine, I'm so sorry. You seem very close to them."

"I am." She raised her cup of juice and thought of her mother, stuck in that generic wheelchair, her pressure sores in constant need of cleansing. "They had me late in life, so it was almost like growing up with grandparents."

"I see," Gavin said. "So they spoiled you."

"Hey, now. I think they did a pretty good job."

"They did. They should be very proud."

"You know what?" Catherine lowered her cup and gave him a tender glance. "You're kind of sweet when you wanna be."

"Kind of?"

"Well, with some training, I think you could be a fine gentleman."

"Why? Are you offering lessons?"

Their eyes locked, and then Catherine broke into a wide grin. She looked down, embarrassed by her girlish response.

"So, what does your mom need?"

Catherine sighed. "Well, a better wheelchair and hospital bed would be at the top of the list. I've been working with RMS Medical Supplies to get them, but it's so expensive."

"You can't put a price on helping your mom."

Try telling that to my husband.

"That's right," Catherine said. "I mean, it's worth the sacrifice. I'm actually hoping to have a down payment on the equipment soon, but it's hard with my own bills and everything."

"I'm sure your mom understands."

"That doesn't make it any easier. I do have a little surprise for her, though. I mean, it might not work out. But if it does, it's going to make her so happy."

"You know," Gavin said, catching her eyes once more. "They're lucky to have you for a daughter."

Catherine gazed at him, then turned away just before *that moment* when two people look at each other long enough to know there's something that might happen. Here she was, scraping through the ashes of a fizzling marriage, and Gavin took the time to listen to her personal gripes. Although he'd never even met her parents, he was here, without complaint, to help her shoulder this burden.

"ROOKIE, DON'T LOOK at me like that. I'm tryin' to help you out."

From around the corner, the sound of Terrell's chastisement put a grin on Caleb's face as he entered the station's sleeping quarters. It was mid-afternoon and the men were supposed to have their personal areas straightened.

"Why does it matter," Eric said, "what my bed looks like? I'm the one that's gotta sleep in it."

"Man, what if Chief Hatcher walks through here?" Terrell fired back.

Caleb rounded the fire pole to view for himself the state of the rookie's area. Sure enough, the blankets were wrinkled, and his nightstand was crowded with magazines and discarded candy wrappers. Not even close to the military precision with which Terrell's bed was made.

And Terrell knew it.

"My bed says I take my job seriously. Your bed says your mama didn't drop by to help you make it up this morning."

"You teaching another rookie how to make his bed?" Caleb said.

Terrell sneered. "Somebody's got to."

Eric was the picture of concentration now, slicing his hand along the mattress to smooth his covers.

"You know," Caleb said, nudging Terrell, "his looks as bad as yours did when I taught *you*. I remember—"

The alarm tone stopped him mid-sentence. He waited along with the others to see if the bell rang, thus indicating this one was theirs.

Brrrngg!

They bolted in unison. All three men rushed to the fire poles, hands squeaking on brass as they plunged to the bays at ground level. Lieutenant Simmons dashed in from the kitchen area, and Wayne was already beside his truck. It was second nature, part of their training, to catch the dispatcher's instructions through the speakers while gearing up.

A female voice: "Engine Two, Engine One, Aerial One, Battalion One—respond to 209 Eleventh Avenue. Structure fire. Residence. Time out, 15:32."

They had a hot one ahead of them.

Terrell pulled a Nomex hood over his shaved black head, just in case. Caleb stepped into his boots and adjusted suspenders over his shoulders. Behind him, Wayne and Eric were yanking on heavy brush coats with yellow stripes and silver reflective strips.

Caleb grabbed a handhold to pull himself up into the cab of Engine One. "Michael," he yelled, "you got that?"

"Got it."

"Wayne?"

"Got it."

"Let's roll."

Horns blared and sirens called out in warning. The aerial ladder truck led the way onto Albany's traffic grid, emergency lights

165

splashing the trees and buildings along the way with bright yellow and red. In the back of the engine's cab, Eric looked less nervous than last time around. He was still a bit awkward on the job, but Caleb figured he'd be okay with a little more experience.

Caleb reported into his radio: "Engine One is en route to 209 Eleventh Avenue. Structure fire."

"Ten-four, Engine One."

"Aerial One is en route . . ."

"Ten-four, Aerial One."

"Engine Two is en route . . ."

"Ten-four, Engine Two. Public safety, to all vehicles—be advised, we've received numerous calls regarding this structure fire."

Caleb turned to Eric in the back. "All right, that means there's something to this one, Eric. Make sure you tighten up."

The rookie adjusted his hood, snapped his coat.

The parade of emergency vehicles passed by Phoebe Putney Memorial, and Caleb had a sudden image of burn victims in hospital beds. How many times over the years had he seen people here, with third-degree burns, seared lungs, or severe poisoning due to smoke inhalation?

He exhaled, pushing those thoughts from his head. Best to stay focused. In the moment.

"Remember your training," he told Eric. "Stay with your partner."

"Yes, sir."

An askew column of smoke marked their destination minutes before arrival. The truck rounded a corner and approached clusters of neighbors on the lawn and sidewalk. The structure in question appeared to be a small home with bars on the windows—not the safest area of town. Curling along the front porch and the roof, billows of gray-black smoke tried to flee the lashing flames at the windows.

"Engine One is Ten-twenty-three," Caleb informed dispatch. He leaned out the window as Wayne brought them to the curb. "We have a single-story brick residence, thirty percent involved. We'll be using a one-inch-and-three-quarters for rescue. We'll be Eleventh Avenue Command. Engine Two, bring me a line."

The fire crackled with new ferocity within the structure, as though enraged by their appearance. Glass panes split and shattered, punched out by the heat.

"Be advised," Caleb said, "there is a hydrant right next to Engine One."

"Ten-four."

Eric was already out of the cab, stepping up to the rear of the truck to take hold of the line. Good. He'd been listening. The kid turned and stretched the hose toward the house.

"Let's go, baby," Terrell said to him. "Let's *go*."

Caleb carried his composite oxygen tank on his back. Daylight was already dimmed by the smoke that wafted through the trees. He approached a heavyset African-American couple on the front lawn. "You live here? Is everyone outta the house?"

"Yeah, look, my daughter's in the neighbor's house."

"All right."

"But listen . . ." The man grabbed Caleb's arm and pointed. "*Please*, this is our home. You gotta put that fire out."

"We will. Just stay clear."

The wife had her hands atop her head, her face engraved with fear. Groups of onlookers were standing far back, put off by the growing inferno.

"*Please*," the owner said.

"Hurry up, hurry up." Lieutenant Simmons was waving at Eric.

Caleb knew the damage to this residence was already extensive, probably nearing the point of total loss, but he and his crew would do their best to keep it from spreading to other homes or climbing into overhanging branches. This was where the training kicked in, and as fires went, it was pretty straightforward.

In a flash, that all changed.

"Oh no. No! *Nooo!*" A young white girl darted up to the captain. She was frantic, her ponytail whipping round as she turned toward the fire.

"Megan? Megan?" the homeowner said. "Where's Lacey?"

"She went *home* already."

Caleb came to attention. "What?"

"What're you tellin' us, Megan?" the owner's wife said. "She's not at your house?"

"No! I was talkin' to her on the phone. She said she was makin' toast and forgot all about it. She thought she smelled something burning."

Caleb processed this, realizing a rescue might become necessary—and quickly. Beside him, the owners faced their burning house. The father's face said it all. His daughter was in there, trapped by those flames, maybe knocked out by the smoke, and in danger of dying if he didn't do something quickly.

Burly and determined, the father sprinted toward the front steps.

Behind him, his wife's shrill wail tore through any sense of calm and order that had existed. It was the cry of a mother in distress.

"Lacey!"

168

CHAPTER 25

Caleb knew Lieutenant Simmons had seen just about everything, yet he was still impressed by the tall, wiry black man's instant reaction. Simmons shrugged free of his helmet in a fluid motion and angled ahead in five rapid steps, intercepting the much-heavier owner, dragging him to the grass before he could do anything that would endanger more lives.

The distraught father squirmed to get free.

"No!" Simmons held him down. "No, you can't go in there."

"Get off me! My daughter's in there . . . Lacey!"

With Simmons attending to that situation, Caleb ran back to the truck, dropped his radio into a storage bin, and grabbed hold of a red-bladed ax. "Let's go," he said to Eric and Terrell. "We've got someone inside. Let's go, let's go."

"C'mon." Simmons beckoned from one knee on the grass.

"Lacey, my *baby*!" The mother was sobbing now.

At her side, young Megan was shaking her head and covering her mouth.

169

Caleb removed his helmet, pulled on his protective head covering and face mask, then put the helmet back on. He adjusted his breathing apparatus, while Eric and Terrell stretched out the hose to take inside. Although protocol said to follow the hose, there was a little girl in those flames. All bets were off. Wayne was alongside the truck, monitoring dials, pressurizing tanks, urging them to hurry.

Captain Caleb Holt broke for the front door, ax in hand. He hesitated for one moment to confirm that the glass was already broken, thus allowing the fire to breathe. It needed oxygen. Without it, the flames would be gasping for air like a monstrous set of lungs, and the moment they found an opening they would erupt with new life in a violent back draft.

Behind Caleb, the hose was charging, and the guys readied their grip to pound a steady stream of water into the heart of the house.

He yanked open the screen door, then aimed the butt of the ax at the entry door's catch. He swung with all his might, busting through.

The blast was intense.

Raking over his gear, the temperature made Caleb feel as though he'd lifted the lid on a volcanic crater. Flakes of paint and ash spiraled past his face mask, carried on visible waves of heat.

He dropped to his knees. Crawled forward, as he'd been taught.

"Lacey. Lacey!"

He was already breathing heavier, and he tried to tame the panic that bucked in his chest. He wanted to stand up and hurry forward. Or retreat. Neither would do him any good.

One room at a time. Stay under the smoke.

All around, the fire bellowed. It burned orange and hot, slithering along the baseboards and blackening the walls.

The heat was unbelievable, even here at ground level. Caleb felt as though he'd been plunged into the belly of hell, with the demons all around, mocking him. Somewhere, a little girl was in danger, held hostage by these cackling fiends, and their intent was no different than their fallen lord's.

"... to steal and kill and destroy."

Hadn't Caleb read those words in his father's notebook? Or maybe John had quoted the Scripture to him during their long talk in the clearing.

"Jesus, help me," he mumbled into his mask. Again, he shouted: "Lacey?"

Rolls of smoke writhed along the hall between the rooms. He edged through the first door to his right, but saw nothing through the blackness.

"Lacey?"

No response.

He hung a door tag to mark that the room had been checked, then crawled toward the next doorway. "Lacey! Where are you?"

Still nothing. Only flame-licked chairs and a sofa.

"Lacey. Lacey!"

He pushed through the next burning door with his thick Shelby gloves, ran his gaze beneath the coiling smoke, and spotted the girl. She was curled on the floor, on her side. He yelled out her name again, but she didn't move, didn't say a word.

LIEUTENANT SIMMONS TOOK charge now that their captain had gone inside. He'd convinced the frantic father to stand back, to trust Albany's trained firefighters. He barked instructions to Terrell and Eric, and they dragged the hose up the steps through the entryway. If they fanned out a blanket of water, they might give Caleb a chance to rescue the girl. They could also clear his return escape route. He would be toting anywhere from sixty to a hundred pounds through the blaze, and that was no easy task in full gear.

"Wayne."

"Lieutenant?"

"Talk to the owner there. Find out if there's a breaker box we can access from outside. Shut everything down."

"Yes, sir."

Where was Caleb in this mess? Had he found little Lacey yet?

The growl of a downshifting motor sounded from Simmons's right, and he turned to see Engine Two rolling into view. And a good thing, too. They needed all the help they could get.

"Lieutenant!" Wayne's eyes were wide with fear. "Sir, we got ourselves a problem. The owner says their stove stopped working last year, and they've been cooking on a propane grill."

"What're you saying? Where?"

"In *there*." The driver jabbed a finger. "There's a full tank in the kitchen."

"LACEY!"

Caleb hurried on his knees over the wood floor. There wasn't much in the room, other than an old fireplace and a collapsible baby stroller. Judging by what he'd seen, this family was low-income, with not much to their name. He hoped they were current on their insurance, because this place was going to be unsalvageable.

Nevertheless, he had a chance to give them something far more valuable: their daughter's life.

"Lacey," he said, touching her arm.

She showed no reaction to his presence. She was a beautiful girl, in jeans and a red sweatshirt with tiny flowers on it. Her hair was in cornrows, pulled back into beaded braids. The smoke had knocked her out, but she was still breathing.

Thank God for that.

Caleb knelt down, slid both arms beneath her small frame, then lifted her in a single motion by using his legs to alleviate the strain. He was up. He had her. He was going to get her out of here alive.

ERIC WAS MORE scared than he'd ever been in his life. This was nothing like their training. This was the real deal, with no guarantees.

He jammed a chock beneath the entry door to keep it from closing and pinching the hose behind him. He inched farther into the house, hefting the one-inch-and-three-quarters with Terrell's assistance a few feet back.

He heard creaks and groans and the high-pitched hiss of flames on dry wood. He was scared, but this was what he had dreamed of—the chance to save lives, to put himself at risk for the sake of others.

"Move, rookie," Terrell urged. "Keep going."

Eric was about to rise into a stabilized crouch, a position from which he could control the torrent of water through the hose. He looked back at his partner, thinking of the captain's admonishment to stick together. Despite the constant pranks and the ribbing about his bed, he knew that Terrell had his back.

He turned again to face the flames.

And that's when his world exploded.

A BONE-JARRING blast rocked the brick structure, shaking rafters loose. In the hallway, the ceiling caved in and deposited splintered shafts of wood onto the floor in front of Caleb. Smoke and fire billowed.

That route was blocked.

Caleb stumbled back from the doorway, the girl still cradled in his arms. He hoped the wave of concussive heat hadn't reached down her throat and sucked the last bit of life from her chest.

Carbon monoxide was the greatest danger here. It inhibited the blood's ability to carry oxygen through the body, and a minuscule amount could do quick damage. The percentages were all there in his head, from years of training:

.04% . . . Headache after one to two hours of exposure.

.32% . . . Dizziness, nausea after five to ten minutes; unconsciousness after thirty.

1.23% . . . Instant unconsciousness; death in one to three minutes.

Judging by Lacey's current condition, Caleb knew he was working with a very short fuse.

IN THE AFTERMATH of the explosion, a fireball leaped into the sky and belched a plume of black smoke. Simmons watched it from the front lawn. Through the front door, he saw chunks of wood drop onto Eric's helmet, saw flames wrap themselves around the kid's breathing apparatus and tank.

"Back out, back out, back *out!*"

Simmons wheeled away from the house, helping draw out the charged hose. For the first time ever in his years of working with Caleb, he felt the heart-dropping conviction that his captain was gone. That thought sapped his mental strength and left his arms and legs feeling momentarily numb.

174

Had Caleb survived that explosion? Was he trapped beneath a beam?

Simmons had no doubt about his friend's eternal future—they had the same Father now, right?—but that gave him no desire to see Caleb's life stolen away.

Not while Catherine's heart was still up for grabs.

And not today. Not on the lieutenant's shift.

Simmons told himself to keep moving, to ignore that dread in his chest. He had to clear his head and stay sharp if there was to be any hope of salvaging a horrible situation.

His own words came back to him: *"You have to lead your heart . . ."*

CALEB SLAMMED THE door to the room with a backward kick of his boot, set Lacey on the floor, then took up his ax. They had to escape this place, and that meant he'd have to go through the lone window.

But the bars . . .

These cross sections of iron, meant to keep intruders from getting in, now hindered him from getting out.

He knocked out the glass with the ax, took hold of the metal, and rattled with all his might—finding no give, no indication of a breach. He knew there was little chance of breaking through in the time allotted, and yet the way he had entered was cut off from him.

"Over here!" he yelled through his mask.

He shook the bars. Reached out a hand. Waved for someone, anyone, to notice. Most likely, he was out of sight on this back corner of the house. The crew's visibility was hampered by the black haze and waves of heat.

"Over here," he cried again. "Over *here*!"

No one came.

AT THE CURB, Engine Two was now braking to a halt. Four firefighters jumped from the vehicle, ready to battle this thing, and Simmons rushed forward to enlist the aid of their solidly built leader. Captain Loudenbarger had come over from Station Six to fill a temporary vacancy at Station Two. Though he was new to this crew, he wasn't new to the job, and Simmons could think of no one he'd want here more in this moment.

"There's a hydrant right over there," Loudenbarger directed his men. "Give me one supply line to Engine One."

They rushed off.

"Sir," Simmons said. "We've got two people inside. We need you."

"Hey," Loudenbarger called out. "Hurry up with that supply line, and pull a second inch-and-three-quarters. We've got somebody inside!"

Simmons thanked his fellow officer, then reclaimed a section of the fire hose by corralling it in his arms. "All right. Get back in there, Eric. Let's *go*."

"Where's Captain Holt?" Loudenbarger said Simmons.

"He's trapped in that house."

The moment Simmons spoke the words, the front windows spit out a shower of sparks as another rafter crashed down like a guillotine. The structure's wood sections were coming apart, and it was only a matter of time before the bricks began to dislodge from their places in the crumbling mortar.

"Let's get him on the radio, Lieutenant."

"Yes, sir." Simmons raised the two-way to his mouth and tried

176

to reach Caleb. "Captain, you've gotta get out of that house. The roof is about to give."

Where was he? Why wasn't he responding?

Simmons held the receiver to his ear, hoping for even a faint voice, but there was not a sound. An ambulance rolled up from Phoebe Putney, but it would do them no good if they couldn't find Caleb and Lacey.

He shoved aside his doubts and tried again. "Captain, do you read me? Do you read me? You've gotta get out!"

Simmons did actually hear something now. Could that be—?

Wait. It was his own voice, in a half-second delay.

He turned, still shouting into the two-way, and located the source of the discombobulated echo. There, in an open storage bin of Engine One, sat Caleb's radio, abandoned in the midst of the action.

CALEB PEELED OFF his air mask and snugged it over the girl's petite face. He rested the tank beside her unconscious form. "Breathe," he pleaded. "Breathe, Lacey. I need you to breathe for me, baby."

He wrapped her in his fire-resistant brush coat. Looked around for a way out. Already, fumes were sucking raspy coughs from his lungs.

"God, get me outta here. Get us outta here!"

Claws of flame pried at the edges of the closed door, probing at the keyhole, and sliding along the gap at the floor.

For a split second, his thoughts turned to his mentor, his father-in-law, retired Captain Campbell. What would *he* do in this situation? He could almost hear the man's voice telling him to reject the window and the door, to think creatively. This room was a cube. What did it matter if only a few sides of the box were barricaded?

Overhead, the ceiling was already compromised.

That left the floor.

Choking, Caleb fumbled for his ax. Then he saw it. The air vent near the wall. He lifted the ax handle and slammed it into the vent cover, then pulled it off in one motion. He brought down the handle again to dislodge the ductwork just below the surface. The small hole in the floor had to be larger for them to escape to the crawl space beneath, and the flames beating at the door gave him little time.

Chop fast, Caleb!

He brought down the weighted blade on tongue-and-groove wood. He pulled back a jagged chunk of flooring, dipped his face to the hole, and drew stale but clean air from the space beneath the house.

This could work. It would have to.

He chopped again. Swung a third time with all his strength. He gritted his teeth as he lifted the ax a fourth time over his head, then let out a roar. He was falling into a rhythm now.

Heave-growl-chopppp . . . Heave-growl-choppp . . .

Splinters flew. The hole widened with each blow.

Choppp . . . Choppp . . .

The blade caught. He grunted and tore it loose. Over his shoulder, he saw the fire stretching murderous talons along the door's upper seam. Golden and hot, the conflagration was toying with him. Embers spilled from the ceiling and scattered across the floor.

He gasped for air as the smoke attacked his lungs. He grabbed the air mask and took a deep breath, then placed it back over Lacey's mouth.

Beep-beep-beep-beep-beep-beep—

The warning chime on his SCBA told Caleb this whole scenario was about over. His oxygen reserves were almost gone, and if he didn't hurry, he and young Lacey would be gone for good.

Choppp, choppp, choppp . . .

The opening would have to do.

With quick movements, he tore away exposed spikes of wood, then removed the mask from Lacey's face and shoved aside the expended tank. He took the girl in his arms again. He lowered her through the gap in the floor, easing her onto clods of dirt a few feet below. Still wrapped in his jacket, she was safe for the moment.

From above, the roof gave a loud groan.

Caleb's turn to go down.

He ignored a thick splinter that jabbed through his white shirt, pulled it from his skin in a spray of blood, and shoved himself face-first through the hole.

CHAPTER 26

The house was about to collapse around him. Only seconds to go. Caleb caught his weight with planted hands, then wormed down into the crawl space without landing on top of Lacey. He rolled onto his side, giving no time to aches and pains, no attention to scurrying spiders.

He looped his left arm around the girl's back, hooking a hand under her arm, then searched for the best way out of this disaster area.

A waft of fresh air, from about twenty feet away . . .

A ventilation grate.

He dragged himself forward a half-foot at a time, with his right elbow wedged into the ground and boots scrambling against compact earth. From the room above, beams and drywall crumbled in burning sections and came after him through the hole he'd created.

"Aaarrrggh."

He snatched his legs from the glowing heat and pressed onward, keeping the grate in view. That was his goal. Nothing would stop him.

His muscles protested with each elbow-shredding advance through the dirt. The smoke was thickening. All around, flames flared as they gnawed through the subflooring and rode charred timber to the ground. The structure was caving in.

LIEUTENANT SIMMONS HAD seen few houses conquered so quickly. He wanted to rush into that inferno himself, but the place was about to go. If the captain was in there, passed out, or trapped beneath a fallen beam, or—

In a great whoosh of sparks and eye-watering smoke, the roof crumbled inward and fed the mouth of the volcano. The blaze roared with new intensity, seeming to sense victory.

"Here." Simmons passed off the hose to a fellow firefighter.

"I got it, Lieutenant."

Simmons started a perimeter search of the property. *Don't trust your feelings or your fear*, he reminded himself. *Lead your heart. Lead!*

"Caleb!" he yelled. "Caleb, can you hear me?"

CALEB PULLED HIMSELF another foot closer to the metal grate, glimpsing tiny squares of daylight and grass, of life and hope. Ash and dirt swirled in his eyes and clung to his sweat. He was losing his grip on Lacey, and he tossed the bulky coat aside. Moments ago there had been an enormous crash, and he assumed the roof was coming down. If he didn't get her out of here in the next few seconds, they'd both be crushed by a pancake collapse of the floor.

Another half-foot. Another layer of skin peeled from his elbow.

181

Caleb pushed on.

And on.

Why was he so willing to put it all on the line for a stranger? Yes, he'd been trained for this. Yes, he'd put some experience under his belt. Where, though, had that determination gone in regard to his marriage? Why had he stopped fighting for his wife's heart?

As he threaded between embers and blackened boards, he told himself that if he got out of this alive, he would start loving Catherine with this same gritty, no-backing-down resolve. If there was anything to be gained here, that was it.

Please, God—just get us outta here.

A burning girder tumbled onto his forearm.

"Agghhh."

His flesh sizzled, and Caleb hefted the encumbrance aside with a scream. He crawled faster, calling out: "Jesus, *help* me. Jesus, *please!*"

As the house began collapsing around him, he reached the ventilation grate.

He leaned back, spun his legs around, and kicked out with all his might. His boots clanged against the metal, and he detected little give. Was the thing nailed into place, a guard against rodents and small animals?

He pulled his feet toward his chest. Drove them into the metal a second time.

Nothing.

Caleb screamed in desperate anger. He drove his boots repeatedly against the grate, dislodging dust and pebbles with each attempt. It was starting to move. But so was the floor above. Fire and debris came crashing down around them, and fragments of wood rolled off of his arms and chest. He could feel the blaze inches behind them, and more of the house began to fall.

I don't want to die!

The heat was intense. His mind became a blur of fear and energy. He kicked again at the grate.

This time the force sent the framed impediment cartwheeling across the baked lawn.

His heart pounded in his chest as he pushed the unconscious girl ahead through the opening, expending the last of his reserves. He could hardly breathe, but she would be safe. He had done his job.

Beyond her slumped form, he saw life-giving, beautiful sun, but he was depleted. Done. His lungs felt like lumps of soot, and it was all he could do to draw oxygen across his charcoal-parched tongue one last time, before collapsing on his face in the dirt beneath the blazing residence.

SIMMONS ROUNDED THE back corner of the house, calling the captain's name. He saw movement.

From ground level, a ventilation grate came flying across the lawn.

Caleb?

Simmons bent down and saw a limp form rising from the darkness beneath the house. It was the girl, and that meant Caleb must be down there. Alive.

"There, there!"

Simmons pointed, calling for others to come help. He charged to the opening and cupped his hands beneath little Lacey's armpits. He spotted another body prostrate in the crawl space. From Simmons's right, a fireman from Station Two hurried forward to offer assistance.

"I got the girl. I got the girl," Simmons said. "Grab the captain there."

Fireman Ribolla waited for an opening, then took hold of Capt. Caleb Holt and dragged him from the narrow hole to a tree about thirty feet away.

"Medic. Medic!"

EMS and other personnel gathered around to resuscitate Lacey. A female rescue worker knelt beside Caleb with portable oxygen. He was panting, incoherent, his eyes ringed with soot and white with fear.

"You made it out," Simmons told Caleb. "You're safe."

"The girl . . . Is the girl okay, is the girl okay?"

"We got her, Captain. They're working on her."

"Okay." Caleb gritted his teeth in pain.

"Calm down now," Simmons said. "Calm down."

"My arm . . ." Caleb lifted it. "My arm is burned."

"Yeah, we see it, Captain. We see it."

Caleb coughed. Through his pain, he growled: "Did you get the girl? Did you get the girl outta the house?"

"Yes, we got her."

"Is she . . . okay? Is Lacey okay?"

"She's out, Captain. You saved her. She's okay."

"My arm."

Simmons noticed Caleb's pale expression, and realized his senior officer was experiencing shock. Caleb's mind was a transmission slipping out of gear and grinding, grinding, at the same questions.

Beside them, the EMS lady unwrapped the oxygen mask.

Caleb tried to lift his arm again. "I . . . need something. My arm, my arm is burned." His feet pawed at the ground. "You sure the girl's okay?"

The mask came on, and still the captain demanded answers.

"What about . . . Where's Catherine? Is Catherine okay?"

"Catherine?"

"Tell me she's okay."

"Captain, listen to me. Yes, your wife is okay. You did great. You got everyone outta that house."

"The girl? Is she safe?"

"She's fine. Caleb, the girl's gonna be okay."

"Catherine?"

"She's okay, and you're gonna be okay. I just need you to calm down. Breathe with me. Just take a sec, and breathe with me."

Caleb's expression began to relax as he drew in fresh oxygen.

"Breathe, breathe. I repeat: Everyone is okay, Captain."

Caleb closed his eyes.

"I'm here with you," Simmons said. "I'm right here."

CHAPTER 27

Catherine Holt punched the automatic door opener and marched down the hospital corridor. Her husband, they told her, was being treated after a touch-and-go encounter at a residential fire.

Though she felt some relief that he was safe, her emotions were on a seesaw. She'd seen a marked change in Caleb the past few days, but she needed more than that to wipe out the effects of the past few years.

Was the transformation real? Could he keep up the facade?

She had serious doubts.

On clicking heels, she passed a young patient in a wheelchair and found the alcove where a sooty, sweaty, shoeless man sat slouched on an adjustable bed. It was Caleb, sporting a stained white T-shirt. He smelled like a campfire. At his side, a nurse in a blue tunic and latex gloves was wrapping gauze around his severe arm burns.

Catherine folded one hand across her stomach and gripped

her necklace with the other. Why was she so rankled by his presence here? It was unfair to him, yet there was no denying the annoyance she felt.

"You look terrible," she said.

Caleb's chin lifted toward her. "I . . . I feel terrible."

He had gorgeous eyes. She had to admit that much. Smudges on both his cheeks, and his brow served to intensify those deep green irises.

"You gonna be okay?"

The nurse turned toward her. "Well, he's sustained some first-degree burns, but he should be fine."

Catherine noticed his wedding ring was off, lying next to him on the table. His hand was coated with medicated burn cream.

The nurse addressed a doctor seated in the corner. "Looks like he's left with a partial thickness burn to the left arm."

The doctor made a note of it on his clipboard.

"So, this is your husband?" the nurse asked.

Catherine folded both her arms, knowing what was coming next and why his being here irritated her so. She cast a sideways glance at the doctor.

Dr. Gavin Keller's eyes widened in apparent betrayal.

"Uh." She looked down. "Yes."

"Well," the nurse said, "it looks like you've got a hero on your hands."

There it was. That was the problem. By playing courageous fireman, Caleb had immunized himself against ridicule or gossip. How could Catherine turn her back on him now? It would be so much easier if he were an obvious greaseball, a real scum.

Gavin swiveled in his chair toward her, then shifted his attention to Caleb—the competition. Could Catherine blame Gavin for feeling somewhat betrayed? For weeks now she had gone without her ring, and the doctor had assumed she was fair game. She'd certainly given no indication otherwise.

Quite the opposite, actually.

You've got yourself in a mess now, Cat. Way to go.

Caleb sat there on the bed, oblivious. He was listening to the nurse's instructions to keep the arm elevated for the next twenty-four hours to help the swelling go down. In forty-eight, he was supposed to return for reevaluation.

Gavin and Caleb in the same space?

This was more than Catherine had bargained for, and she knew it could only lead to trouble. Tension hammered at her temples. She was almost shaking.

"Well," she told the nurse. "Let me get outta your way."

"Oh, you're not in our way. You can stay."

"No," Catherine said. "It's all right. I'll, uh . . . I'll let you do your job."

CALEB WATCHED HIS wife go. Though he'd hoped for some sympathy—one soft touch, or even a supportive smile—he had expected nothing of the sort. Still, there was something not quite right about her reaction.

The nurse, too, seemed puzzled by Catherine's uneasiness. She flashed a weak grin. "Sir, I'm gonna go get you some more gauze to take home with you."

"Sure."

"And we'll fill that prescription for your pain, okay?"

Caleb nodded, and the nurse departed. Alone now with the doctor, he took a moment to examine the reddened skin of his shoulder. He could deal with these burns. It was the other pain that cut deep.

He thought back to those intense moments beneath the burning house. He had decided to fight for his wife, hadn't he? To put his very life on the line?

On the table, his wedding band gleamed. Caleb picked it up, started working it down over the sensitive skin of his finger. He flashed to those desperate moments beneath the house, when he'd sensed that someone was trying to cut short his escape. Had it been his imagination? The effects of the carbon monoxide? All he knew was that life was tenuous, and there would always be obstacles out there.

Caleb no longer cared how many days were left in *The Love Dare*, or if there was anything in there about slipping rings over serious burns. He was putting this thing on, regardless. It was no longer an option.

The doctor glanced up. "I, uh, wouldn't put that ring back on till your hand has had a chance to heal."

Caleb eyed the man. Who did this bozo think he was? Sure, the doctor was tall and educated, handsome in that straitlaced, Ivy League, boring sort of way—but that gave him no right to interfere with a patient's personal decision.

"Sorry." Caleb wiggled the band all the way down. "But my hand's gonna have to heal with this ring on my finger."

The doctor gave no further objection.

At that moment, a large black woman rounded the corner. She stared at Caleb, eyes filling with tears. He recalled her face from the scene of the fire—Lacey's mother.

"Captain Holt?"

"Yes?"

"I'm Mrs. Turner. You saved my little . . ." Her voice faltered.

"Is she okay?" Caleb made eye contact. "Is Lacey doing all right?"

Mrs. Turner closed the gap between them, her chest beginning to heave. She reached up, wiping drops from her cheeks, then placed both hands on Caleb's face. He could smell the residual smoke, feel the moisture of her tears. He sensed, from the corner, the doctor observing this exchange.

"Thank you, Captain," she whispered. "Thank you for . . ."

Caleb swallowed.

"For . . ."

Mrs. Turner's wide forehead furrowed and her chin trembled. Through those glistening oval eyes she managed to express all the thanks he would ever need. Then, shaking her head, she bit her lip and backed away.

Caleb blinked as she disappeared. He looked down at his ring. He'd put his life on the line for little Lacey, willing to do whatever it took. Catherine, too, had been a girl once. She'd dreamed of a husband who would put it all on the line for her.

Was that really too much for any woman to ask?

CATHERINE CAUGHT THE evening news from a corner table in the cafeteria. The drama of her husband's day played out on the TV screen. She was getting the opportunity to see him on the job, while he had no clue as to the cozying up she'd been doing at work.

A blonde reporter, WALB's Stephanie Ward, said, "It was a day of sadness and joy for Mr. and Mrs. James Turner of Eleventh Avenue, as they watched their home nearly burn to the ground . . ."

The camera panned to ruins of brick and wood, where emergency personnel continued to battle the blaze.

"The fire," Ms. Ward said, "is believed to have started in a toaster and a faulty electrical outlet, and it spread quickly through the house. The Turners escaped, not knowing that their seven-year-old daughter, Lacey, was still inside."

The scene shifted to an interview with the emotionally wrung-out mother. "Lacey was at a friend's house," said Mrs. Turner, "but came home early through the back door, and we didn't even know it. We . . ." She bit back tears. "We almost lost her today."

"The Albany Fire Department arrived within minutes," the report continued, showing an oxygen tank on the ground, a splintered ax, and toys blackened by the fire. "They made a daring rescue of young Lacey, who had already passed out from smoke inhalation. Captain Caleb Holt used an ax to cut through the floor, where they made a daring escape beneath the structure."

An eyewitness, holding her pet dog, described the scene in shaky tones: "I saw him run into the house, and then watched the roof collapse. I just *knew* they were dead."

"We live across the street," said another, identified as Benny Murphy. "And you could feel the flames. That heat, it was real intense. We're just so excited the little girl got out okay. I mean, that fire was *unreal*."

A school photo of Lacey Turner dominated the television, tugging at viewers' heartstrings with her darling image.

"Lacey," the reporter said, "is now resting at a family member's home and is expected to make a full recovery. The family has extended their deepest thanks to the Albany Fire Department."

"You know, we practice for these things all the time, but every fire is different." The face of Chief Carl Hatcher replaced Lacey's, his name and job description shown below in a horizontal color bar. "I'm just glad everyone got out alive."

The segment drew to a close with the female reporter's voice lilting in professional empathy. "Chief Hatcher plans to visit Lacey soon, and to meet with the team that made the rescue. He says if his firefighters are given a choice between saving a home or saving a life . . . they'll choose a life every time. For WALB News, I'm Stephanie Ward."

PART FOUR

FIRE

JUNE 2008

CHAPTER 28

M om, it'll be fine."
"Honey, I just worry about you. I saw the pictures on the news, and—"

"It's gonna heal up in a coupla weeks, okay? Just think of it as a bad sunburn." Caleb had his cell phone to his ear, seated in jeans and a sweatshirt on the couch. His left sleeve was pulled up so he could air the tender skin on his forearm. Beside him, *The Love Dare* notebook remained unopened.

"Are you sleeping all right? Do you have any pain pills or—"

"Yes. I've got medicine for it."

"Don't let it come in contact with—"

"Yes, I know, I know. Listen, I've got it wrapped up right now." Caleb knew he would scream if he didn't bail on this conversation quickly. Why did he let her get under his skin like this? Why did he feel like a little boy again, being babied when all he really wanted was to be treated like a man?

"Caleb, I—"

"Could I speak with Dad, please?"

"Don't be upset, honey. I'm just—"

"Okay, Mom. I got it. Now, would you please hand the phone to Dad?"

"Here he is."

"*Thank* you." He sighed in frustration.

John came on the line. "Hello, son."

"Dad, would you please ask Mom to cut me some slack? I'm a fireman. I'm gonna be around fires."

"You know, she'll always be your mother. You can't change that any more than she can."

"I know."

"It's just her way of showing love."

"I know, Dad. I just don't like getting grilled every time she picks up the phone."

"I understand. So, are you using your paid leave to recuperate?"

"I've got two days off, then I'll be back."

"Well," John said, "I'm sure you'll use the time wisely. I guess you'll have the opportunity to give more attention to *The Love Dare*."

"Uh, yeah."

"What day are you on?"

"Today?" Caleb had to think. "Uh, Day Twenty-three. But it was hard this morning. You know, the newspaper called me twice wanting an interview. It seems I'm a hero with everybody in the world except my wife."

"You're not quitting, are you?"

"No. No, I'm not giving up."

"Good. Our prayers are with you on this."

"Thanks, Dad."

"In fact, your mother and I were just heading over to our weekly Bible study. I'd best not keep your mother waiting."

"All right. I'll talk to you later."

"You call anytime, son. Good-bye."

196

"Bye."

Caleb closed the phone, pulled his hands back through his hair, then felt his eyes drawn to the computer desk in the corner. He knew the temptations it presented, and he decided to work on a crossword puzzle instead.

That occupied him until he came to the clue for *5 Down*.

He knew the answer without even thinking—the name of a curvaceous celebrity—and it stirred thoughts that would only lead to trouble.

No, Caleb. Not today.

To be an honorable man was his goal—honoring God, and his wife.

He tapped the cover of *The Love Dare*, knowing he had work to do, but first he would grab a drink from the kitchen. He'd come back to this in a bit.

A few minutes later, with a glass of ice water at his side, he tackled a stack of bills while propped on the edge of the couch. There was the electric, the water, cable and Internet, vehicles and insurance, the mortgage. Although he and Catherine had received an economic stimulus check from the IRS a few weeks back, that money had gone right back into their account to cover his mother-in-law's most recent therapy.

So much for a boat anytime soon. Every dime went to other things, it seemed. Despite Caleb's earnest savings attempts in the last four or five years, he figured he had another two or three before getting the cabin cruiser he wanted.

He tucked the last check and bill into an envelope, sealed it, and stood.

Now what?

Time to go dream a little. Nothing wrong with that.

At the computer, he logged on to the Internet and went to a

few of the boat Web sites he'd been checking out. He'd been considering twenty-four-footers, loaded with 375 horsepower. Aside from the basic necessities, there were so many other options—onboard surround sound; transom showers; sonar and GPS systems; ladders and slides; and wakeboard towers.

Each site featured photos of vessels gliding through the waters of the Gulf, or sports fishermen pulling marlins out of the Atlantic. Each one represented a vision of something he didn't have.

They looked so good. So close he could touch them. Glimmering hulls and polished rails. Sails unfurled and gusting in the breeze.

Ahh, to live out that fantasy.

Of course, the reality of the seas included sudden squalls, stinging salt water in your eyes, and shoals to avoid. While on a friend's boat down in Tampa, he'd almost gotten sick from diesel fumes as they chugged back into the harbor. And that didn't even count the joys of emptying a gray-water tank.

No doubt about it: the entire experience looked so much more glamorous in pictures, casual and carefree.

Speaking of which . . .

A video-cam box popped up on the screen, featuring a woman's sultry smile and two small words full of boundless possibility: "Wanna See?"

His pulse picked up.

Yes, of course he wanted to see. What man wouldn't? Hadn't God created the male species to be visually oriented?

For some reason, though, that excuse failed to work, even in his distracted mind. Such justification would be like Catherine saying that she simply had to eat chocolate whenever she saw it, because it triggered helpful female hormones. Wasn't the truth that each person had to show some self-control? It was a key to society's survival. What gave him the right to point fingers at the gluttonous, when he lacked control of his own desires?

The male side of his brain understood this logic, but none of it—not one little bit—changed what he was feeling at the moment.

"Wanna See?"

He stiffened in his chair. His hand rested on the mouse, nudging the cursor toward the Click Here button.

No.

An honorable man.

He froze, then let go of the mouse. His eyes stayed glued to the video-cam box. He told himself he was only looking at the sleek boats behind the box, but those, too, represented glossed-over realities.

The woman's face was still staring at him.

His hand returned to the mouse and his finger lifted over the button, ready to tap down, to obey the blinking command. No one was watching.

Click Here, Click Here, Click Here . . .

So easy.

Groaning in frustration, he shook his head and lifted his gaze. There on the wall, the dark wood panel hung as a reminder of his grandfather's care and devotion. At this very moment, his father and mother were shouldering his burdens at a Bible study.

"Caleb, what're you doing?" he whispered.

He stood and turned his back on the desk. From across the room, he swiveled to see those sultry lips still teasing, teasing.

"Wanna See?"

He sighed, leaned his arms on the fireplace mantel, and fought with his desire. This desire, this sinful nature—it had been crucified on the cross; taken upon Jesus' flayed back.

I'm dead to sin, he reminded himself. *And alive in Christ.*

He turned his eyes and peered at the still-lingering image. He dropped his head, let out a loud sigh, then looked at the family Bible propped here on the mantel where it had gathered dust since its arrival as a wedding gift.

His father had warned him that he would have to die to his fleshly desires each day, but that sounded almost unreal—until faced with the reality.

Click Here, Click Here . . .

"God," Caleb grumbled, "why is this so hard?"

The sound of his palm striking the mantel echoed in the empty living room. Caleb cast a hard glare at the computer and dropped onto the love seat, arms crossed. He stretched his legs, trying to relax. He decided now was as good a time as any to get this day back on track.

He picked up the notebook from the coffee table and began reading.

Day 23

Watch out for parasites! A parasite is anything that latches on to you or your partner and sucks the life out of your marriage. They're usually in the form of addictions, like gambling, drugs, or pornography.

They promise pleasure, but grow like a disease and consume more and more of your thoughts, time, and money. They steal away your loyalty and heart from those you love.

Marriages rarely survive if parasites are present. If you love your wife, you must destroy any addiction that has your heart. If you don't, it will destroy you.

"If the Son sets you free, you will be free indeed" (John 8:36).

Caleb eyed the computer across the room.

For twenty-three days now, he had dared to love Catherine—or tried to, anyway. He wanted to love her freely, no holds barred. But these images, these addictions . . .

They were parasites out to destroy him.

Resolve burned in his eyes. His pulse raced, but with new conviction. He stood, with shoulders pulled back, and stomped across the room to the computer that had been an unguarded gateway into his home, into his very heart and soul.

"No more!"

He ripped the cables from the back of the monitor and tore the power cords from the wall. This was insane, what he was doing. He knew it was over-the-top. And he just didn't care, didn't care one bit. He was *done* with this. If it meant protecting his marriage and his soul, he wasn't going to let an inanimate object stand in the way. He would fight for this.

Monitor and keyboard, first.

He marched the items through the side door, out of the garage to the driveway. He set them in the sunlight on the patio table. He picked up his aluminum bat.

Oh, *yeah*.

Oh, you better *believe* he was going through with this.

With determination feeding adrenaline through his muscles, he took up his stance and furrowed his brow. "Okay, Lord . . ." The long bat lifted in his hands. "No more addictions."

He swung.

The monitor shattered with a gratifying burst of plastic and glass. It flew from the table and thudded upside down on the grass. Demolished and useless, it would never again feed him those tawdry images.

The computer tower was next.

Forget about the money. Why, an ugly divorce settlement would cost him a lot more than this. His marriage was worth it.

He set his jaw and prepared for swing number two.

Then he saw them . . .

The Rudolphs, as a couple, were fixed like statues on their back patio. Dressed in plaid shorts, cowboy boots with no socks, sunglasses, and a straw hat, Mr. Rudolph dangled a watering hose from his hand. Mrs. Rudolph stood by with a watering can and a garden trowel.

They were both staring in his direction.

He lowered the bat. "Mr. Rudolph."

"Caleb."

"You doin' okay today?"

The elderly neighbor showed no emotion. "No," he said. "Not really." He released the hose nozzle and turned away from the disturbing property damage taking place only yards away.

Caleb winced. Could he blame the man?

Well, no use explaining. Some things just had to be done, regardless of who was watching and what they might think.

Caleb swung again, rocketing the computer tower from the table.

He tracked it down.

Swung again.

Watched it crack open. Saw the CD/DVD tray splinter.

Another swing. Another. And one last time.

That's right. You see that! This love is worth fighting for.

He pressed his mouth into a grim line, lifted the bat, and dropped it in disdainful victory onto the wreckage. Brushing off his hands, he headed toward his truck. He had an idea, a little something for Catherine. Except this time, he wouldn't go cheap.

As he walked off, he overheard Mr. Rudolph's gruff voice.

"Irma, I don't want you talking to that guy. He is *weird*."

The old woman muttered back, "Takes one to know one."

CHAPTER 29

Catherine parked in the garage and stepped from the air-conditioned car. At work earlier, she'd received a number of compliments on her pleated gray skirt and jacket, but the attire was stifling in this weather. Dougherty County was fairly flat, blanketed with fields and orchards, and the summer humidity hovered, as though too lazy to get up off the couch and go to bed.

What was that near the trash container?

Despite the heat, she had to see this for herself. She strolled to the mouth of the garage and contemplated the busted computer pieces poking from the garbage.

Okay, Caleb. What's this all about?

She thought of their confrontation a few days back, of her livid accusations about his online distractions. Maybe this was his way of striking back at her, like a child breaking a toy that he had been told to put away.

Well, that wouldn't surprise her. Guys could be so juvenile.

In fact, men in general were not high on her list right now. She'd tried to join Gavin at lunch today, hoping to explain why she wore no wedding ring, but he'd left in a hurry with some excuse about being late for his rounds. They hadn't spoken much since the scenario with Caleb in the hospital alcove, and the doctor probably thought she had been messing with his heart.

Maybe Gavin had never had those feelings for her anyway. Maybe it was all part of some fantasy she'd been courting in her own head.

Tomorrow, she would talk to him and determine where they stood.

Turning her back on the destroyed computer parts, Catherine strolled into the house and set down her keys.

No sign of her husband.

Except for his half-empty water glass on the coffee table.

She started toward it, to clean up—again—after this man she lived with, but then the cleared computer desk across the living room snagged her attention. It wasn't the absence of machinery that made an impression so much as the handwritten note beside a fluted vase of a dozen red roses.

Her favorite.

Were they for her? They had to be. She picked up the note.

In Caleb's handwriting, the note read, "I love you more."

A warm sensation moved from her fingers up through her arms and into her chest. She caught her breath. Caleb had made a choice today, and this was what remained: fragrant flowers in place of his computer.

CALEB, SWEATING AWAY any extra calories, was on the final stretch of his late-afternoon jog. He kicked it into another gear as he neared the house, spurred on by the sight of the white Camry in the garage.

She was home.

She should've found the bouquet by now.

The first time he'd given Catherine a dozen roses was on their third date, Valentine's Day of 2000. That's when he had known he was in love with her.

Of course, it'd all started that first day in the bay. The chemistry was instant, but he had waited a full year before acting on that attraction. He saw her occasionally around the station, was invited to barbecues at the Campbell home, and wooed her slowly. They were fierce combatants in the volleyball sandpits at the park, and she shared his love for Georgia-based rock bands.

Their first date was ice-cream cones and a walk along the Flint River. The second was a Third Day concert in Atlanta. Then came Valentine's Day, with roses and dinner and a first kiss.

Twelve months later, they had tied the knot—*"for better or for worse."*

So how could it be they were now teetering on the brink of divorce?

He walked through the front door into the kitchen for some ice water. No sign of Catherine. He ducked into the living room and saw the roses still on the desk. His note was moved from its original position, indicating she'd given it a glance.

He moved toward the master bedroom and almost knocked on the closed door. But no, that seemed too invasive. Too pushy. He'd made his gesture, and it would be best to wait for her reaction.

For now, it looked like another night alone in the spare bedroom.

At his bedside, he prayed, "Lord, whatever it takes. I want the chance to love my wife again—body, soul, and mind. Please, I need You to show me how."

DAYLIGHT WORKED ITS way through the window and woke him up. Caleb lifted his head, saw that the bedside clock read 6:47 a.m. He sat up in his T-shirt and pajama bottoms, listening for the sounds of his wife—showering, cooking, humming.

There was nothing.

He used the bathroom, brushed his teeth, then applied new gauze to his arm. On his way down the hall, he noted the open master door.

"Catherine?"

He tried two more times, but she was gone. Maybe she had a morning work meeting. That happened sometimes.

The flowers and note were still on the desk, and he smiled at the thought of her discovering them yesterday. Surprises had always been special to her, and he was trying to demonstrate love in ways that were meaningful to her.

On the table, beside a bowl of fruit, an envelope bore his name.

A slight smile tugged at his lips. So, she *had* been thinking of him.

He lifted the envelope and pulled out the contents. He imagined, briefly, that she had written him a full confession of her feelings. Would she mention that it was his recent thoughtfulness and dedication that had won back her heart?

Instead, he found a several-page legal document titled "Petition for Dissolution of Marriage."

"*What?*"

He flipped to the second page, then the third.

It was all right here, a request for a divorce, notarized and stamped with an official seal. He gasped, shaking his head. He couldn't breathe. He stood stunned, blinking against emotions of denial and knee-buckling grief.

Why was she doing this? Why now?

"No, Lord. *Nooo.*"

He backed away from the table, tears flowing as he slid down the wall. The papers dropped from his hand and scattered across the floor.

JOHN HOLT PRESSED the End button on the cordless phone and leaned forward in the cushioned armchair. Though the sun was already warming up here in Savannah, spreading an amber glow through the sheer curtains over the window, he felt nothing but heaviness.

Cheryl was seated across from him. She rubbed his arm.

"She's filed the papers," John said.

"How's Caleb taking it?"

"He could barely even talk."

"Oh, honey."

John cupped a hand around his chin, the prayers in his head finding it difficult to make it all the way down to his mouth.

STREET SIGNAGE ADVERTISED RMS Homecare, as well as Bobby Lee Duke's Lollipop Shop and the Biscuit Barn. Though the pairing of these storefront properties seemed odd, Catherine often found herself stopping in for a watermelon lollipop after the gloomy financial situations she faced in RMS. She couldn't deny that the brief sugar rush helped.

The Lollipop Shop also featured framed news articles about local football teams, which she thought gave the place a homier, more personal flavor—forgive the pun.

And the owner? He was a stocky man with a crew cut, a former high school coach who always sported a lollipop of his own.

As for the Biscuit Barn, they served some of the best breakfast around, even if they did wear goofy biscuit-shaped hats. A few years back, she'd bought a run-down Hyundai coupe from the assistant manager, but he was no longer in the used-car business.

Catherine stared through her windshield at the RMS entryway. She knew there'd be no goodies or biscuits for her today. She'd left the papers for Caleb, then left the house early so that she'd have time, on her way to work, to make another payment on her mother's home-care supplies and physical therapy.

She strolled into the building, past walking aids and motorized wheelchairs. At the corridor's end, she propped her purse on the counter. This was where she paid in person each month, and the staff knew her by name.

"Good morning, Mrs. Holt."

"Hi, Mrs. Evans. How are you?" After greetings, Catherine said, "I wanted to come and talk to you about some of the equipment we've been looking at."

"Oh," Mrs. Evans replied. "I'm so glad you had picked some stuff out."

"Well, it might be a while before—"

"No, it shouldn't be long at all, Mrs. Holt."

"Excuse me?"

"I bet your parents are excited. When a patient gets the right wheelchair, it can make such a difference."

"I'm sorry. What?"

"I'm talking about the bed and wheelchair being delivered to your parents this morning."

Catherine was confused. "To *my* parents?"

"Yes. It should've been delivered by now."

"But I . . . I haven't paid for anything yet."

"Uh, it's actually already been paid for," Mrs. Evans said with genuine pleasure. "A gentleman called and said that he wanted to pay for all that you'd picked out. He covered everything, plus some accessories."

Catherine felt overwhelmed. How could this be? Did this mean her mother would actually have a comfortable bed and fully functional chair—at last?

This was . . . this was too much. And all because of one man's generosity.

"Did, uh, this gentleman tell you his name?" she inquired.

"Actually," Mrs. Evans said, checking a note in a file, "he said he wanted it to be anonymous. But I think you . . ."

Catherine had already turned, hurrying back down the hall. She could hardly believe this. He had *paid* for her mother's equipment. How could she have ever doubted him?

"Uh, Mrs. Holt?"

Catherine ignored the receptionist's voice and shoved through the door. She had an apology to give, as well as a very big thank-you.

CHAPTER 30

"Man, you were hammering those weights this morning. What's going on, Caleb?"

"Nothing."

"Nothing?"

"Nothing I wanna talk about."

"Sure," Simmons said. "I understand. Just remember what I told you, though . . ."

"What's that?"

"We're brothers. You got something you need to get off your chest, you can talk to me. It ain't going nowhere."

"Thanks, Michael."

Caleb hit his turn signal, steering the big red pickup down East Lullwater Road to drop off the lieutenant on his way home. They'd put in a good workout at the station, and now Caleb had a long, lonely day ahead—hour upon hour to think about the impending divorce. Sure, Simmons was a good friend and listener, but this was too close to the heart. As a man, Caleb wasn't certain he could risk opening this sort of wound.

Medically, he knew things worked just the opposite. A wound had to be opened, cleansed, and tended to. Ignoring such things only made them fester.

Here goes, Lord. Give me strength . . .

"You know, Michael," he said, "you can just pray for us."

"You and Catherine?"

Caleb nodded, flicking his eyes between the road and his mirrors.

Simmons said, "I can do that, man."

Rearview, side view . . . all clear. Caleb pulled into a cul-de-sac and edged into his friend's driveway.

"Hey," Simmons said as he grabbed his bag and stepped down from the cab. "Don't forget there's another enemy out there who's just as determined to tear you down, by hook or by crook."

"What do you mean?"

"The enemy of your soul."

Caleb stared forward, his arm draped over the truck's steering wheel.

"You hear what I'm saying, Caleb?"

"I grew up in the South. Believe me, I've heard my share of hellfire and brimstone."

"True." Simmons gave a wry grin. "Well, I'm not saying you need to live in fear, but to stay alert. To be ready when the fire comes."

"And how do I do that, Michael?"

"You remember the story in the book of Daniel, about the three guys in the fiery furnace? They walked through the flames without even a singe. Right there in the middle of it all, God stood with them."

"Then why didn't He stop *this*?" Caleb wiggled his bandaged arm.

"You're alive, aren't you? I'd say He was with you in that house."

"Yeah, I think you're right."

"So, then, stop whining about a minor flesh wound."

"*Flesh* wound? Oh, thanks, man. Thanks for the sympathy."

They shared a short laugh.

"I better get inside and say hi to Tina," Simmons said. "I appreciate the ride, Caleb. I know you got a lot on your mind, but don't you forget—I got your back. That's what brothers are for."

A PAIR OF white-jacketed RMS Homecare technicians were in the front room at Catherine's parents' place. She stepped through the open front door, dodging a bed rail that was being carted inside. Her eyes took in this top-of-the-line equipment that would simplify and stabilize everyday life for her mom and dad.

Mrs. Campbell was already propped up in her new chair, while the tech squatted to attach a cable between the motor and armrest controls.

Catherine felt tears well in her eyes. This was too much.

Her mom was fiddling with the touch-panel, familiarizing herself. Her father was watching every move as the other tech attached a rail to the adjustable bed.

"Hi, Dad."

Retired Captain Campbell looked up and drew her into a bear hug. "Hi, sweetheart. How are you?" Though not as fit as he had once been, he was still strong and warm, and he made her feel secure in his arms.

"Doing great."

"Isn't this wonderful?"

"It's amazing." Catherine kneeled beside the shiny new chair and rubbed her mother's hand. "Hi, Mama. Are you happy?"

Joy Campbell gave a gentle smile.

"You look good in it. Can you believe this? We'll have to get you all dolled up and take you out. I bet you'd like that, huh?"

Her mom's eyes glowed.

"Plus, I've got a surprise of my own for you, and we'll need you looking your best so you can make a good impression."

Eyebrows pushed together in curiosity.

"Don't worry, Mama. I guarantee you're gonna love it."

Her mom scrawled a quick note on her portable chalkboard: A CAT?

Catherine shook her head.

NEW BATHROBE?

"Not quite. Here, I'll give you a clue." She turned the board around and held it up, hidden while she created a fill-in-the-blank message. "There. Figure out the puzzle, and that'll give you an idea."

"What've you got up your sleeve?" Mr. Campbell said.

"I'm gonna need your help, Dad. But the hardest part'll be up to Mama."

Her mother was already pondering the board on her lap. It read: R_ _DY TO GO F_R A SP_N?

DR. GAVIN KELLER stood at the counter, marking a check sheet after doing his rounds. "Tasha, do you think you could file this for me?"

"Sure, Doctor. Just leave it on the desk."

"If you can wait a few seconds, I'm just about done."

"Sorry, gotta run. I'm already late for the nurses' staff meeting." Tasha was petite, but with permed hair combed back from her face, she had the look of a lioness as she hurried off in her dark blue smock.

Gavin kept his eyes down. He'd made a flirtatious remark to

the young black nurse one time—and that was the last time. Her eyes showed strength and a no-nonsense attitude that were sure to blow up in his face.

As for Catherine? She was more vulnerable.

She confused him, now that he'd met her husband, the local hero. What was wrong between them—two successful, attractive people? He'd have to tiptoe carefully. If things continued to fall apart, though, he'd be more than willing to pick up the pieces.

Still standing at the counter, he caught a whiff of her perfume. It sent a tingle through his limbs, but he didn't look up. He'd let her initiate the contact.

Sure enough, Catherine moved closer from his right and propped an elbow on the counter beside him.

She said, "Has anyone ever told you that you're wonderful?"

"Maybe." He gave her a bashful grin. "But not today."

"Gavin, you didn't have to do that."

"Do what?"

"Giving money to help my parents." She fiddled with a button of her blouse and locked soft brown eyes on his. "That was *so* thoughtful. Thank you."

He felt a burst of satisfaction. He hadn't meant it as any grand gesture, but after Catherine's account of her parents' medical and financial woes, he'd felt compelled to act. She'd mentioned RMS Homecare, and so he'd gone in and discussed setting up a fund in the name of Catherine's mother. He'd drawn from his own savings to get things rolling in the right direction.

"You're welcome," he said. "Catherine, you had a need that I could help with. It was the least I could do."

"You didn't even tell me."

"I wish there was more I could do, but it's a start."

"A start? It's more than a *start*, Gavin." She slipped her hand into his and squeezed. "Do you have lunch plans?"

"I do now."

When she smiled in response, it worked like sunlight, warming him from head to toe.

CALEB TOOK A solitary stroll through the woods behind the house. He felt drawn to the rugged simplicity of that cross in the clearing, to the grace and strength and hope it represented.

He needed all three of those right now. He felt so weak.

Sure, he'd criticized others in the past for needing the crutch of religion, yet now he saw it differently. He wasn't turning to a set of rules and moral codes. It was more than that, much more. His dad had helped him understand the deeper possibilities of a restored relationship with God.

A crutch? Some might think so.

But Caleb now realized he was choosing to lean on the Lord.

"Jesus, I need You," he whispered. "You did not give up on me, so I'm not giving up on Catherine. Would You save my wife, Lord? If You need to take me out of the way to do that, then do it. I know I can't do this on my own. I'm giving You everything."

There was no audible reply, no booming voice from the pale Georgia sky. Caleb did, however, feel a slow spread of calm through his chest and new clarity in his thoughts.

The next morning that all changed.

He was emptying trash cans around the house as part of his commitment to Catherine, when he happened upon a love note addressed to his wife in another man's handwriting.

CHAPTER 31

He'd been avoiding the master bedroom, so he felt almost awkward as he entered. Aside from a pair of Catherine's heels next to the closet door, the space was tidy. The bed was made, the comforter pulled up over the pillows against the mahogany headboard. It was a reminder of her rejection of him, of the good times once shared and now left to rot in their past.

"Petition for Dissolution of Marriage . . ."

Those words were daggers, stabbing at any hope of reconciliation, yet Caleb had already decided to see this thing through to the end. He stepped into the room. He would have to leave shortly for his own shift, and he was in here only for the purpose of collecting the garbage in a plastic sack, for tomorrow's curbside service.

He spotted bottled water on the dresser. He shook the container. It was room temperature and half-full. Into the bag it went.

Then the Hallmark envelope caught his eye.

He lifted it from its place against a vase and saw Catherine's name on it. Well, this was his bedroom, too, wasn't it? He paused no more than a second before deciding to see what was inside. The card was pastel and pretty. He opened it and read the words aloud, feeling them burn into his mind and set off an alarm that had been silent for far too long.

Dear Catherine,
I can't tell you how much I've enjoyed getting to know you.
I find myself thinking about you often, and I look forward to seeing you every day. Let me get you lunch any day this week.
Love, Gavin.

"Gavin?"

Caleb couldn't pretend this was casual. This was his marriage on the line, and there was *nothing* casual about another man getting cozy with his wife.

He dumped the garbage sack, then paced the dining room with the phone pressed to his ear. "Um, yeah," he said. "I need to know if there's a Gavin that works there at the hospital. Uh, no . . . No, I just have a first name."

Twenty-five minutes later, in his captain's uniform and coat, he brushed through the doors at Phoebe Putney Memorial. He took the elevator up, asked directions from a male surgical nurse in the hall, then marched on.

Yes, indeed . . .

He had an ailment, and he was going to find just the man for the cure.

GAVIN SAT BEHIND the desk in his office, a white jacket over his shirt and tie. It was a small space, and during his short tenure here in Albany he'd done no more than hang his diplomas and a few animal prints on the walls. He'd come on short notice, and he was still unknown to half the staff—though he liked to think that he'd already made a favorable impression on the ladies in the building.

His door was open this morning, yet he was still surprised to hear an unannounced visitor enter the room.

"Dr. Keller?"

The voice was steady, but bordered on anger.

Gavin lifted his gaze from his paperwork, annoyed by this intrusion. He made no move to rise or shake a hand. He recognized this intruder as the firefighter he'd treated with the first-degree burns.

Catherine's husband.

Gavin turned up a palm and said, in a tone that indicated he was busy and wished to be left alone, "Yes?"

"Caleb Holt. I need a word with you, please."

"Look, it's really not a good time. I'm just about to make my rounds and—"

"I think you need to make time. This is concerning Catherine." Caleb hovered over the desk. "My *wife*."

"All right. What can I do for you?"

Caleb pointed a finger, his voice low and icy. "I know what you're doing. And I have no intention of stepping aside as you try to steal my wife's heart. I've made some mistakes, but I still love her. So just know, I am going after her, too." He arched an eyebrow. "And since I'm married to her, I'd say I've got a head start."

Gavin squirmed beneath the cold glare.

"By the way . . ." Caleb lifted his left hand.

The doctor leaned back, wondering what would come next.

"Thanks for helping me with my hand. My ring finger's feeling a *whole* lot better." Caleb curled his fingers into a solid fist, showing his wedding band. He stared hard and long, then turned back the way he had come.

Gavin's heart was in his throat. He remained frozen for a moment, and he noticed Deidra just outside his door, her mouth gaping.

Wonderful. Now the whole staff would hear about this.

As the short black nurse took off on stubby legs, armed with her juicy gossip, Gavin pulled out his top desk drawer. He sifted through Post-it Notes and paper clips.

There it was. His own wedding band.

Okay, so he hadn't exactly made his marital status public. He liked to keep his options open, and his wife was a saleswoman who spent a lot of time on the road. Surely she had her little dalliances, and he had his. No one got hurt.

Really, Doctor? Are you so sure about that?

He imagined the look that would cross Catherine's face if she were to see him sporting this ring. Not only would she erupt in tears or shouts, she would sever any connection they had made to this point. He was only fooling himself if he thought otherwise.

Still, he decided, it was best to keep his options open.

He shook his head and pushed the ring back down beneath the jumble of office supplies.

"Y'ALL, I JUST saw Caleb and Dr. Keller goin' *at* each other." With breathless whispers, Deidra gathered the others at the nurses' station—Tasha, Ashley, and Robin. "He had his fist all up in Dr. Keller's face."

"Uh-uhhh."

"Are you serious?"

"Mmm, I ain't lyin'. He said if he—"

"Shhh, shhh, shhh," Robin said. "Here she comes."

219

Catherine's heels announced her approach. She slid a hand onto the counter, parting their huddled heads. "What're you all talking about?"

Ashley made a quick exit.

"Hey, Cat," Deidra said. "How ya doin', girl?"

"Fine. But it sure got quiet really fast."

"Well, that's just because we decided to stop talkin'."

Tasha and Robin exchanged a brief glance. Avoiding Catherine's probing glances, they left Deidra to cover the awkwardness. Which was just fine with Deidra. She was an old pro at this sort of thing.

"Wassup?" she said in a singsong voice.

Catherine looked at her watch. "Well, I'm setting up an interview in about ten minutes. I was wondering if you guys have seen Dr. Keller this morning."

"Umm. I think he was doin' rounds. He may be on the eighth floor."

"Okay." Catherine patted the counter. "Guess I'll see you all later."

Tugging at the stethoscope around her neck, Deidra watched Catherine prance off on those long, tapered legs till she was out of earshot. In a flash, Ashley reappeared from her busywork, and the others closed in to hear the lowdown.

"Why didn't you tell her?" Robin asked Deidra.

"'Cause it ain't none of our business."

"You told all of *us*."

"But," Deidra said, waving her hand, "I don't want her to know that *her* business is *our* business, if it ain't none of our business."

"Ohhh," the ladies said in unison.

They scattered back to their individual tasks.

220

CHAPTER 32

Catherine was flying high with the recent blessings that had come her parents' way, and with the unexpected generosity of a certain single doctor. She found him in the hallway, coming toward her in his white jacket and fine clothes, and she admired once again his clean-cut appearance. She'd smelled enough smoke on men's clothing to give her a pair of blackened lungs.

No more of that, thank you.

Beaming, she said, "Hey, how are you?"

Gavin's eyes swept the hallway in both directions, his demeanor distracted and detached. "Uh, hey, Catherine."

"How's the good doctor today?" She placed a finger on the edge of his clipboard.

"Uhh. Pretty busy, actually."

"Are we still on for lunch?"

"Well . . ."

"You did make the offer in your card, remember?"

"You know, I feel like there's a few things I need to catch up on. I've gotten a little behind lately."

"Okay." She tried not to read too much into his cool response. "Well, um, maybe we could talk later."

"That'd be good."

"All right. I'll see you around."

"See you."

She watched him lower his head and continue down the hall. That made two strange interactions in a row, with different sets of coworkers. Somewhere, it seemed, she had been left out of the loop. Baffled, yet trying not to let it get her down, she headed for the cafeteria alone.

CATHERINE STABBED AT the lettuce on her plate and chased a cherry tomato around the edge. There was a fresh carnation on the table, the same table she'd first shared with Gavin, and that realization only intensified her isolation amid the other chattering diners.

"Hello, Catherine."

She looked up to see a silver-haired nurse in a colorful top. Her tray was full, and she seemed to be seeking a place to sit. Although Catherine wasn't in a social mood, she knew she could trust this woman. Anna had always avoided the hospital rumormongering, sticking to her job and its details.

"Oh, hi, Anna. How are you?"

"I'm doing well. And you?"

Catherine pasted a smile over her true emotions. "I'm okay, I guess. Do you wanna sit down?"

"I'd love to, if I'm not disturbing you."

"Not at all."

Anna settled across the table. "So," she said cheerily, "what's been going on in your life? We haven't talked in a while."

"Well, it's . . . It's been one of those years."

"Oh? Good or bad?"

"You know, I hate to say it . . . but mostly bad."

Anna's eyes filled with concern.

Catherine went back to poking at her plate. "You know, when you get to a fork in the road, and you know that either way you go is gonna change your life."

"Life does give you some of those. Excuse me just a minute." Anna bowed her head in prayer. A moment later, she looked back up. "So, have you decided which path to take?"

"Umm, I think so. It's just hard not to second-guess yourself."

"Pardon me. I don't mean to pry, but does this concern relationships?"

Catherine smiled, almost glad to get on a subject she enjoyed. "It does."

"Well, having lived as long as I have, I'd say relationships pretty much determine your quality of life. Did you know that recent studies show married people are more successful in their careers? They also live longer and claim to lead happier lives."

"So then, ending a relationship that's been a burden would be a good thing, right?"

"I suppose that depends on the nature of the relationship. Some are worth fighting for, even if they seem difficult. Others may seem interesting but are *not* healthy. You know, forty percent of marriages these days end in divorce, but sixty percent of second marriages have the same fate."

"Sixty?"

"It's even worse for third marriages."

Catherine wasn't sure she liked this turn in the conversation. She and Gavin had a spark, a sense of chemistry and intrigue, and she had no intention of letting a middle-aged lady—even a nice one like Anna—tear that hope away from her.

"Well," she said, "my husband and I aren't getting along anymore."

"Oh?"

"It's been seven years, and I'd say the last four or five have been headed downhill. I don't even know why we're still putting each other through this. I think we'd both be happier with someone else."

"You know, it often seems that way, doesn't it? Catherine, you're so young. I would encourage you to make your choices carefully."

"I'm trying to." She closed her eyes, then leaned forward and gave her lunch guest an honest confession. "I'm also tired of feeling empty. Anna, it's *so* nice to have someone treat you like they really care about you."

"Forgive me, but you're talking about a certain young doctor, aren't you?"

"I suppose it's no secret, as much as he and I talk."

"I couldn't help but notice how you act around each other, but I also wonder how your husband would feel."

Catherine stiffened, sitting straighter in her seat. "My husband has had his chance. Dr. Keller is a good man, and he treats me better than my husband has in years. He listens to me and makes me feel important. I haven't felt that way in a very long time."

"It's always good to have that. But, sweetheart, if this doctor is trying to woo you while you're still married, what makes you think he won't do that with someone else?"

She cleared her throat. "I don't think I wanna talk about this, Anna. We're getting a little personal."

"Oh, Catherine, I'm sorry. I didn't mean to overstep my bounds."

"I need to go. It was good to see you, Anna."

She snatched up her tray and, fighting her fitted tan skirt every step of the way, marched to the trash can where she dumped her stuff. Anna meant well, but she wasn't the one stuck in a miserable marriage.

Catherine quivered with sudden indignation.

This was *her* life. And no one else was going to tell her how to live it.

THE DOZEN RED roses were wilting in their vase, where the ill-fated computer used to sit. Caleb couldn't bring himself to throw them out, even now, after eight days had gone by. To do so would feel like an act of defeat, tossing the last vestiges of hope he had for this marriage.

Another weekend came and went, during which he and Catherine moved past each other like water around rocks in a stream.

She refused to budge . . . and so he drove off to work for another twenty-four-hour shift, with barely a glance from his wife to acknowledge his departure.

He stood waiting in the mornings . . . and she hurried right on by, heading for the hospital and that smug Dr. Keller.

The routine of their lives became a numbing salve during these final days between Mr. and Mrs. Caleb Holt. Soon, he knew, she would go back to being Catherine Campbell, taking once again her father's last name. For Caleb, it would be tearing away a part of him—like an arm, or a rib.

Over the next week he spent a number of afternoons alone at their dining table, and he found himself thinking of her here at the same table, with her dinner plate, making one of her lists of things to do.

Always something to do. Always on the move.

He admired that about her, actually—the way she had put

herself through college and refused to be sidetracked. Once she set her mind to something, she was a hard person to dissuade.

Just his luck.

And so, the numbness kept seeping deeper into his skin, down into the chambers of his heart and soul, but Caleb knew—he knew with every molecule of his being—that nothing could deaden the pain that was to come.

One afternoon he crawled up onto the aerial ladder truck, away from the other men. He understood why animals sometimes crawled away to die on their own. He didn't want to be seen in this condition.

He twisted the ring on his finger and ran back through his early days with Catherine. He had done everything to win her heart, then backed off once she'd surrendered to him. In the old story-books, though, wasn't that how it happened? The knight fought for the fair maiden. He won her favor. And the credits rolled as the lights came up.

Real life was so much more complicated.

With feet dangling over the truck's edge, he leaned his head back and prayed for the strength to keep fighting: *Lord, I'm trying to be patient here. I'm waiting on You. It just seems like nothing I do is working.*

He'd done everything in his father's notebook—the kind words, the flowers, taking out the garbage, sweeping floors, and mowing the lawn. But it went beyond all that. He wanted to come up with his own gestures, ones not included in the book. Catherine didn't fit any particular mold. He wanted to love *her*, in ways *she* would understand.

In so doing, he would pray for her heart to melt again. Or, he would turn wrinkled and gray in the process.

Either way, if he was going to die, why not do so for the woman he loved?

CHAPTER 33

"E ric, name at least three types of Class B fires."

"Gasoline. Oil. And, uh . . . mineral spirits."

"Good," Caleb said. "And what's the correct form of suppression?"

"Umm . . ."

Terrell sneered. "C'mon, rook. You oughta know this in your sleep."

Eric's mouth wrinkled at first as he searched his brain for an answer, then the light came on in his eyes. "Oxygen exclusion," he said.

"Bingo."

"Give the boy a gold star," Terrell said.

"Your turn, Terrell."

"I'm ready, Cap'n. I done studied *my* stuff."

"Now you sound like Wayne."

"I heard that." The driver swaggered into the firehouse dining room, bearing bags of foot-long Subway sandwiches that a friend had dropped off. He handed Lieutenant Simmons the change and a receipt, then divvied the bags around the table, checking the name on each one. "Talkin' behind my back again, huh?"

"Nothing we wouldn't say to your face."

Terrell nudged Caleb's arm in agreement. "That's right. Man, *some*one's gotta cut down that ego of his. You know whatchu need, Wayne?"

"A raise?"

"Don't even ask," Caleb said.

"You need a wife."

"What?" Wayne plopped into his chair. "So I can be miserable like you?"

Terrell kicked at him. "Man, that ain't even funny. Ask the captain or the lieutenant here. They can tell you, it ain't no cakewalk."

"It's a lotta hard work," Simmons said. "But I think that goes both ways."

Caleb had nothing to add that wouldn't feel like sandpaper being rubbed on his burn wounds. He quietly lowered his head, said a prayer for his meal, then peeled back the paper on his sandwich and took a bite.

As the others dug into their lunches, Wayne used the opportunity to sound off yet again. "I'm not knockin' any of you, but believe me—*I'll* be the one who wears the pants in my house. Oh yeah. When the time comes, all I gotta do is *snap*"—he demonstrated twice, quickly—"and she'll come running."

"Hmm." Terrell cupped a hand to his ear. "I hear footsteps, all right . . . But they're running *away*."

Caleb decided this had gone far enough. They had mandatory testing coming up in a few days, and he would lead by example. Not to mention if he wanted to be a battalion chief in the future, wearing three trumpets on his collar, he needed to stay on the cutting edge of technology and techniques.

228

"Okay, okay. While we eat, let's do some more studying and—"

A sudden flare of heat set Caleb's tongue ablaze. Taste buds sent urgent signals to his brain, while his vision wavered and his throat clenched down on the words he'd been trying to speak.

"You okay?"

Caleb blinked and looked up. Across the table, Wayne's eyes were wide and innocent. Everyone else seemed intent on their own food.

"Sure hope I got your order right, Captain."

"Mine's good," Eric said.

Beads of sweat popped out along Caleb's hairline. He swiped a hand across his head and gripped his glass of water. No, that would be like pouring water on an electrical fire, simply feeding the flames. This was habanero sauce, and the damage was already done. He knew the taste—oh yeah, he'd tried it years ago and sworn to never do that again.

"Cold drinks, anyone?"

"No, thanks," Caleb said through gritted teeth. "I'm good, Wayne."

"Really? You sound kinda . . . choked up."

"Think I just swallowed wrong."

"You sure?"

"Yeah." He cleared his throat. "Yeah, yeah, I'm good. I think it's just this sauce. It's kinda bland, actually."

"Bland?" Wayne looked confused.

"Yeah. I mean, it tastes just like tomato juice."

"Tomato ju—"

"Wayne," Terrell barked. "Man, would you let us eat in peace?"

Head down, Caleb took another bite. He imagined the enemy of his soul, the one Simmons had warned about, trying to humiliate him. He refused to show any sign of surrender or defeat, and he certainly didn't want Wayne to get any satisfaction out of this. Ignoring the heat, he pressed on.

He was only halfway through when, thankfully, the station alarm sounded.

THE ALARM LED them to an industrial building near the Cooper Tire plant. After a thorough inspection, they found nothing and headed back to Station One. Caleb and Terrell were stepping out of their turnout gear, ready to head in and get some more exam preparation under their belts, when the bells clanged again.

Caleb hesitated. Was this—?

Yep, this call was also theirs.

He stretched his suspenders back over his shoulders and grabbed his brush coat.

Upon arrival at the dispatched location, they were greeted by the battalion chief and his field testers, stern-looking men with clipboards and stopwatches. Captain Holt and his team had been clocked on the earlier run, and now that they'd shown themselves fast and fit, they would face nine PAT—physical ability test—components.

Caleb welcomed the challenge. He liked to prove to his guys that seniority was no excuse for complacency. He would never ask them to do something he was unwilling to do or incapable of doing himself.

Hydrant opening in seventeen turns? *Check.*

Victim rescue, with a 165-pound dummy bag? *Check.*

Stair climbs in full equipment with a standpipe rack? *Check.*

For Eric, the young rookie, it was all on the line. Still in a probationary period, his future hinged on his ability to successfully complete all nine components. Even one miscue could derail his career.

Eric moved through the equipment tests with relative ease, stretching hose lines, performing solo ladder carries, and fumbling through each twist of the huge wrench used for opening hydrant caps. Wayne and Simmons chuckled at his efforts, but clapped him on the back when he managed to meet the standards.

Later, he demonstrated his skills with a ceiling pole. Oftentimes a fire's pressure could be released by using this tool or an ax to tear a hole in the ceiling, thus venting the heat.

Overall, Caleb thought, the rookie was doing well.

"You think I'm gonna make it, Captain?" Eric asked on the way back to the station. "Those testers didn't look happy out there."

"They've been too close to too many fires," Wayne said from the driver's seat. "All that heat's made their lips pucker. Not to mention—"

"Okay, Wayne. We got it. Listen, Eric, you did fine today, but you've got another day ahead. Rest up. Relax. And just do as you've been taught. You'll be a firefighter yet."

"Yes sir."

"And don't even worry about the aerial ladder climb," Wayne said. "Man, that's the easy part."

"Really?"

"Oh yeah."

"Is there some secret to it?"

"Secret? Nahhh. It's like climbing a set of stairs. Just watch each step so that you don't slip, and you'll be up and down like a yo-yo."

Caleb grinned. Ah, the joys of being a rookie. Soon enough, Eric's fear of heights would be put to the test.

CATHERINE PROPPED HERSELF on a stone bench and stared into the fountain's dancing waters. She'd joined Gavin here in the hospital gardens not so long ago and blossomed beneath his gaze. What had she been thinking? She was an educated, self-reliant woman, and she'd let some white-jacketed wannabe Prince Charming make her weak-kneed with a glance.

A few years ago she would have scoffed at the thought.

Recently, the doctor's demeanor had changed. Gavin was friendly still, as he would be to any other staff member, but the warmth in his voice and the brazen glances were gone.

Catherine took a sip of her lukewarm vanilla latte. The taste wasn't the same as that day when Gavin brought her one.

Seemed everything had gone flat. Not just the coffee.

Her days were blending one into the next, and she'd completely forgotten a few of her appointments at work. She'd heard how emotional stress could wreak havoc on the mental processes, but this was the first time she'd experienced it herself. At times, she questioned if she was losing touch.

She kept her smile on, nonetheless—she was, after all, the public relations manager—and kept herself outfitted in the latest fashions. So what if that meant racking up a few more charges on the credit cards? Maybe she'd be able to split the debt in a settlement.

Was that remotely fair to Caleb, though?

Her husband was so confusing. Though these past few weeks he had shown a whole different side, she wasn't convinced that it would last. Sure, he'd been sharing the chores around the house. Yes, he'd tried to show a little romance—the way it had once been between the two of them.

But was it worth taking a chance again?

No, she didn't dare go there. She couldn't. For the time being, it was all she could do to survive beneath a veneer of normalcy.

Lives changed, and marriages didn't always work out.

People fell in and out of love.

To move on *was* the new normal.

She took one more sip of her latte, then dumped the remains into the low shrubs behind her. Despite the personal pep talk, she felt more disengaged and out of place than ever.

CALEB JOGGED ALONG the trails behind his property, pushing past his muscles' protests and the tightening in his lungs. His churning legs parted swarms of gnats. He ran with endurance, locking the pain away in a corner of his mind while he concentrated on his reading of the most recent entry from *The Love Dare.*

The words were from 1 Corinthians 13.

Love . . . always protects, always trusts, always hopes, always perseveres. Love never fails . . . And now these three remain: faith, hope and love. But the greatest of these is love.

When it came to protecting, he considered himself far above average. His entire job revolved around that very thing. He wasn't as great in the trust department—particularly after finding that Hallmark card on the dresser.

Wiping sweat from his eyes, he ran on.

When he slipped through the side door forty minutes later, Catherine's car was already cooling in the garage. The sight triggered an unexpected flashback to their first year of marriage, when he had come home from a workout to find her waiting with grilled-cheese sandwiches and a tall glass of sweet tea.

For just a moment, a flicker, he allowed himself to hope.

Love . . . always hopes . . .

And then that silly notion faded as he realized she was already locked away in the master bedroom. He went to tap on the door. Maybe she'd join him for dinner, even if it was nothing more than microwave entrées.

He lifted his hand to knock. Hesitated.

Why even risk it?

He turned and hit the hall lights. She had gone into hiding for a reason, and he would only stir her resentment against him if he interrupted her time alone. It was easier to not knock at all than to endure a flat-out rejection.

In his own room, he knelt to pray. Not because he had it all together—just the opposite. He felt like he was coming apart at the seams, like all his attempts had been for nothing. On his own, he was lost.

On his knees, he knew he was found.

CHAPTER 34

The next day there was a slight shift in the routine. Caleb handed Catherine her coffee as she jetted out the door, and she accepted it this time, with a mumbled thanks.

He held on to that moment for hours. In the woods, awash in a golden afternoon haze, he balanced himself on a wide mossy branch and thought:

She actually let me serve her.

As dusk settled, he found his way to the camp circle and faced the familiar symbol of love and sacrifice. Silently, he prayed: *God, help me know how to obey and be patient. I'm just a man. Please, help me.*

THE FIELD TESTERS were on duty again, ready to gauge Station One's capabilities by yards, inches, and seconds. Caleb understood the purpose of these drills, yet nothing mattered as much as a person's actions in the face of real danger.

With a hand motion from the battalion chief, the ladder truck's hydraulic outriggers extended on one side, then lowered until the vehicle was firmly braced on the passenger side.

"Rookie Eric Harmon," said the tester with crew-cut gray hair.

"Sir?"

"You're goin' up."

Caleb and the others let their gazes follow the hundred-foot aerial ladder into a cerulean, cloud-dotted sky. With nothing to lean against, the rungs seemed to disappear into thin air, rising high above the Georgia pines that guarded the lot. Memories of this test caused nerves to flutter in Caleb's stomach.

"C'mon, rookie," he said. "You can do this."

Eric, in full gear, bit his lip and nodded.

"You'll have all the time you need," the tester said, "but if you fail to reach the top, you will be disqualified. Is that clear?"

"Yes, sir."

Wayne patted him on the back. "It's not as scary as it looks. Get about fifty feet up there, let the breeze blow you around a little, and you'll see there ain't nothing to it. My rookie season, I didn't even get sweaty palms."

"Man," Terrell said, "you froze at the top, like a penguin in an ice storm."

"Penguins don't freeze, Terrell."

"You don't know that."

Wayne's eyes narrowed. "I know my stuff, okay. I watch Animal Planet."

Caleb couldn't resist ribbing his driver. "Then how come those penguins all stand together huddled like that? I thought it was better to keep moving when you're cold."

"Oh, that's easy to explain," Terrell butted in. "It's because, just like Wayne here, they can't dance."

Caleb threw Lieutenant Simmons a smile, and even Eric managed a grin.

The field testers were not amused.

"You're cleared to go," said Mr. Crew Cut.

Eric started climbing. His boots clunked against each step, moving slower as his elevation increased. He looked back over his shoulder, saw Simmons backing him up the first twenty feet or so, and then he was stepping higher and higher, with no one there but the doubts and fears that Caleb knew from experience came whispering in your ears.

Two-thirds of the way up, the rookie stopped. With gloves clamped onto the sides, he ventured a look down through the rungs.

Bad idea. That was enough to flip your gut and twist it twice.

"Look up!" Caleb yelled. "You gotta trust the ladder to hold you."

The rookie's legs were visibly trembling.

With the wind buffeting the skies, it was doubtful Caleb's cries could be heard, but he called out again anyway. "Don't quit now, Eric! Don't *quit*!"

One stiff step.

"You got it!" Simmons joined in.

The others formed a chorus, the brotherhood coming together for one of their own. "You got it, Eric! Keep *going*. You got it!"

Eric took another step. And another. Eventually, he gripped the top rung, nearly ten stories in the air and dangling over nothing but hard earth far below. He lifted his free hand a few inches in nervous victory, and the crew on the ground high-fived in celebration.

One more had been added to their ranks.

And that meant there was a final gesture to be made, to let him know he was in.

It happened two hours later, back at the firehouse. The rookie was polishing the brass fire poles, as instructed, when Terrell and Simmons edged to the opening above with tin kettles full of cold water. If you were going to be a firefighter, you wanted to keep yourself immune to the heat and the flames, wasn't that right?

Eric never saw the deluge coming. He froze in place at the bottom of the pole as a shower of ice-cold water soaked every thread on his uniform.

Caleb walked past, showing impeccable timing, and handed the kid a mop without saying a word.

THE TESTING CAME to an end, only to be supplanted by the real deal. A warehouse on the east side of town was burning in the wake of a chemical explosion, and the blaze was already jumping through the treetops to nearby buildings. The night dragged on with multiple fire stations involved, engines and ladders positioned so that crews on the ground could attack from the bottom, while men aimed down torrents of water from the aerials above.

Eric was up there, steady as a rock.

Others entered burning structures in search of victims— wielding axes, sucking air through smudged masks.

By early morning, they had wrestled down the fiery beast and stamped it into ash and dirt.

It would be back, though. Captain Caleb Holt knew that as a fact. In some other location, with other lives and buildings at stake, it would rise up again with a vengeance and use orange-red talons to tear at wood, metal, and brick. Fire prevention and education were much-needed values, but they would never negate the need for competent, fearless fire suppression.

And that was done by those who stood against the flames.

He arrived home the next morning. Showered. Did Catherine's dishes from the night before. Took a mind-clearing walk through the woods to shed the last lingering tendrils of smoke from his hair and skin.

CHAPTER 35

When Caleb woke up, the house was quiet. He rubbed his eyes, pushed aside the covers, and found himself still clothed in sweatpants and a T-shirt. His watch told him it was eleven thirty a.m. No wonder he felt so groggy.

He walked into the living room and was perplexed by the sight of Catherine's purse and keys on the love seat. She was a reliable employee who never called in sick. And she never got home this early.

Was something wrong?

He tiptoed to her door, knocked gently. When there was no answer, he cracked open the door and saw his wife on her side in their king-size bed.

"Catherine? Are you okay?"

She kept her back to him. She sniffed. "I'm fine."

He noted the wadded tissue on the nightstand. "Aren't you going to work?"

"No."

Caleb took a few hesitant steps into the room. "Are you sick?"

"I'll be *fine.*"

He knew he should turn and leave before incurring her wrath, but he was held in place by his concerns for her health. This just wasn't like her. Though he'd have to deal with the consequences later, he had to know what was bothering her.

"Is it your allergies?" he asked in a soft voice.

She turned. Her eyes were puffy, her face pale. "I said I'll be fine. Don't worry about me." She sounded more tired than upset.

Caleb figured he could press a little further. As she rolled over again, he said, "Because if you need something, I can run to the store."

"No, I'm okay." A weary tone. A sniffle. "You can go."

He weighed his options and decided he had pressed as far as he should. A part of him wanted to lie down and curl up beside her, to hold her in his arms and keep her warm.

That was out of the question, of course. She wanted no such thing.

"Okay," he said.

He left the room, treading quietly down the hall.

CATHERINE WAITED TILL he was gone, then turned onto her back and stared at the empty doorway. She knew his departure should come as no surprise. Despite his efforts around the house, this was the same old Caleb—the one who had spent most years of their marriage focused on his own sense of valor, on his dreams of a boat, on his camaraderie with his coworkers that so often left her feeling out of the loop. No wonder nearly 70 percent of firefighters divorced.

She rubbed at her eyes and pressed a hand against her forehead. She felt feverish. She heard his Sierra start up and pull down the street.

Off he went, again.

"Go on," she muttered. "Go play the hero to some stranger out there."

So much for playing hero to your own wife.

Even with these musings, she was too tired to feel anything hostile toward him. Just as had happened during her foot-stomping tirades as a child, her anger was running out of steam, leaving an ache that throbbed in her chest. She closed her eyes and faded into restless sleep.

When she awakened again, she wasn't sure how much time had passed. A door clicked. With one hand clutched around her pillow, she opened her eyes.

"Hi," Caleb whispered.

What did he want now?

She turned and saw her husband approach the bedside with a Chick-fil-A bag in one hand, and a to-go cup in the other. He opened the bag and set its contents on the nightstand.

"Uh, can you sit up for me?"

"Yeah."

She watched his movements with sleepy eyes, trying to convey annoyance, but not putting much effort into it. She heard concern in his voice, and the truth was, his attention felt good. It fed something in her that had been dying.

She pulled herself up, supported by the pillows. Her hair was back in a ponytail, a few stray strands in her face, and she hadn't touched up her makeup since yesterday.

So, it all came down to him just doing his job—"*in sickness and in health.*"

Still, it felt nice.

Catherine gazed up, expecting to see a dull sense of duty in Caleb's green eyes. As she did, he leaned over and touched her forehead with the back of his hand. Their eyes met—truly met—for the first time in weeks. He wasn't looking past her, or simply at her . . .

He was peering *into* her, with an adoration she'd forgotten existed.

"You've got a fever," he said.

He was right. Her head was on fire, and she felt light-headed and flushed. He left the room, and she heard water running in the bathroom. As she waited, she noted the thick and creamy chicken noodle soup he had bought her, along with the cold drink, pile of napkins, and box of cold medicine.

She sat up a little straighter, fiddling with her Kleenex. Caleb returned with a washcloth. He propped himself on the edge of the bed and reached forward. She lifted her hands to take the cloth from him, to see to this herself, but he was already pressing it lightly against her forehead.

The cool dampness soothed her. She relaxed, just a bit.

"Here." Caleb opened the medicine. "You think you can take this?" He set two tablets in her palm, then passed over the drink.

She washed them down with lemonade through the straw, while he peeled back the plastic lid on the soup. The aroma of chicken broth and light seasoning wafted into the air, promising relief to her stomach and throat.

"Why're you doing this?" she said.

"I have learned . . ." He stretched his neck, then looked up at her. "You never leave your partner, especially in a fire."

Her eyes narrowed. "Caleb, what's happened to you?"

He licked his lips and paused, as though mulling the best way

243

to say this. She gave him no easy way out. She wanted him to tell her, in his own words, what had changed—if anything.

"Dad asked me," he said, "if there was anything in me that wanted to save our marriage. And then he gave me something . . . I, uh, I could let you read it."

Catherine reached beneath the covers and lifted into view a leather-bound notebook she'd seen in his room the day before. She hadn't been trying to be nosy, but it had caught her eye tucked between his bed and the nightstand, almost as though he didn't want anyone to find it. "Was it this?"

He blinked in surprise. "How long have you known?"

"I found it yesterday. So what day are you on?"

"Uhh . . ."

"What day, Caleb?" She should've known. His hesitation confirmed what she had suspected. Most likely, this was nothing to him but some silly exercise.

"Forty-three," he said.

"Forty-three?"

He nodded, his eyes locked on hers.

"But there's only forty."

"Well." He shrugged. "Who says I have to stop?"

Those words seeped into her like water into parched ground. She pushed a quivering hand across her brow, covering eyes that were turning watery against her wishes. Why should *she* be the vulnerable one? He was the man. Let him make that first step.

And, the thing was, she really wanted him to.

Despite her hesitation and chilly exterior, despite everything they'd said and done to tear each other to shreds, she realized she wanted this more than anything—to see him lower his guard in her presence and prove just what sort of man he could be.

"So, you've actually done all these things?"

"I've tried," he said.

She brushed her fingers over *The Love Dare*, then fixed him again in a flinty stare. "Hmm. I guess I see it all now, looking back. But . . . Caleb, I don't know how to process this. This is not normal for you."

"Welcome to the *new* normal."

The new normal?

How ironic. Just a few days ago, she'd been thinking about divorce and its acceptability, its normalcy, in today's culture. Now here was her husband, describing the exact opposite.

CALEB HAD HOPED his words would bring about a change. He meant what he had said with his whole heart, and yet Catherine sat two feet from him with the notebook clutched to her stomach and her eyes still darkened by suspicion.

She said, "You didn't want to do this at first, did you?"

"No," he admitted.

"I didn't think so."

"But halfway through, I realized that I did not understand what love was. And once I understood that, I *wanted* to do it."

"Caleb, I *want* to believe that this is real, but I am *not* ready to say that I trust you again."

"I . . . I understand that. But whether you ever reach that point or not, I need you to understand something."

Her mouth was set, her eyes questioning.

Caleb eased from the bed and slipped down to his knees. He didn't know what to say. He was a man, after all. He had nothing rehearsed.

This was unfamiliar territory and the idea of stepping out from behind his protective layers scared him in ways he could not

245

describe. He would rather strip away every layer of fire gear and apparatus and go dashing into a blazing building than expose the things inside him.

He would rather die.

Sometimes, though, wasn't that what it took? It was time to put it all on the line. What were the words he'd just told her?

"You never leave your partner . . ."

"Catherine, I am *sorry*." He took a deep breath to steady the trembling of his voice. He looked up into her eyes. "I have been *so* selfish. For the past seven years I have trampled on you with my words and my actions." He could barely hold her gaze, overwhelmed by the depth of the damage he had caused.

His wife's hands were clasped in her lap. Silently, she began to weep.

He felt drops stream down his own cheeks. "I have . . ." He had to finish this, had to say it all now or never. He spoke each word with husky determination. "I loved other things when I should've loved *you*. In the last few weeks, God has given me a love for you that I've never had before. I have asked Him to forgive me, and I am hoping—and *praying*—that somehow you would be able to forgive me, too."

It killed him to see those hot streaks on his wife's face. Each one represented pain he had inflicted upon this woman he'd sworn to cherish.

God, show me mercy.

"Catherine," he whispered, barely able to get out the words, "I do *not* want to live the rest of my life without you."

HEART READY TO burst, Catherine soaked in her husband's confession. There was no doubting his sincerity, and even though she

246

hadn't paid much attention to spiritual things since her senior year in high school and that one really bad relationship, she'd seen God's hand move in other people's lives.

Maybe, now, even in her husband's.

That did not, however, erase their history of harsh words and distrust. Some things simply didn't wash away in a bucketful of tears.

"Caleb." She brushed her hair back over her ear. "I'm supposed to give those divorce papers to my lawyer next week. I just, um . . ." She turned away, then decided it was best to look him in the eye, since he had been willing to afford her that courtesy. "I need some time to . . . time to think."

Behind a brave smile, he nodded. "You can have all the time you need."

Catherine watched him retreat down the hall, out of sight. She was on her own, with the midday sun coming through the blinds and splashing across her arm, with the aroma of the soup promising to make her feel better in no time.

She wanted to believe. She really did.

Weeks earlier, though, she had made a decision to move on, and she refused to go stumbling back into the past without a good reason. If Caleb's sincerity proved to be short-lived, she would have only herself to blame. She needed to know—*really* know— that his heart was in this for the long haul.

She wiped the moisture from her face and touched the cover of the leather notebook. He had done everything in here, and still she was not convinced.

PART FIVE

FLAMES

JULY–AUGUST 2008

CHAPTER 36

Caleb sat on his bed in Station One's sleeping quarters, the bedside lamp aimed at the Bible opened in his lap. Though he didn't like to make a show of his new reading habits, neither did he try to hide them.

Terrell trudged into view, his mouth turned down. "Cap'n?"

"Hey, Terrell."

"You got a moment?"

"Sure."

Terrell perched on the next bed with a sheepish look. "I've been talking to Michael over the last coupla shifts about my, uh . . . It's about a personal issue. He said maybe I should just come see you."

"Okay."

"I never even wanted to say anything around the guys, but, um . . ." Terrell pursed his lips and looked off at the wall clock. "Man, it's been tough. Lauren moved out, and I just don't know what I need to do."

Caleb nodded in thought.

251

"It won't affect my work, though, Cap'n. I promise you."

"I know that, Terrell. I've always been able to count on you."

The stocky black man waved a dismissive hand. "You know, I shouldn't even have brought this up. Forget about it."

"No. No, that's not gonna help, is it? I've been in the same boat with *my* wife recently, and I've been learning a lot through the process."

"Yeah, Michael said that."

"What?" Caleb acted upset. "You guys're talking behind my back again?"

"Well, I'd be lyin' if I said I hadn't noticed something different about you."

"I guess I'm glad *somebody* noticed."

"Yeah, man." Terrell folded his arms. "I hear what you're sayin'. When it comes to me and Lauren, I tried, but she ain't interested in makin' this thing work. Tells me she's done."

Caleb held up both hands. "Listen, it sounds like you and Lauren have been going through the same stuff we have."

"You and Catherine?"

Caleb shrugged. "I've made some mistakes."

"But . . . You two?"

"Yeah. Well."

"Guess there ain't no one that's safe."

"Terrell, how much are you willing to work on your marriage?"

"Whatever it takes."

"All right." The captain slid the Bible onto his bed and reached for the nightstand drawer. His hand closed around the journal's worn leather. "I, uh . . . I've got something that may help you. It's nothing magical, no quick cure or anything. I mean, Catherine's still not even sure she wants to be with me."

"Hate to hear that, man. I'm sorry."

"The thing is, this is more about *you*. I've changed because of doing this—for the better, I hope. You and Michael seem to think so, anyway."

"So what is it?"

"I'll tell you," Caleb said, "but you're not gonna like it at first."

"Why would you say that?"

"Well, it involves God."

"What? Man, I've been an atheist all my life."

"I'd be an atheist, too—if it wasn't for God." Caleb wore a wry grin. "Seriously, though, if you're not even open to the possibility, Terrell, then what I have really won't help you much."

Terrell weighed that. "Well, I'm . . . *open* to the possibility."

"I'm not guaranteeing it'll fix your marriage. Life's not that simple. But the real question is, how far will you go to work on it?"

"With God?"

Caleb shrugged. "That's sorta the key to it all."

"Hey, man . . . I, uh . . . Sure, whatever it takes." Terrell's eyes snapped to the left and the right. "Just don't tell Michael."

"Okay."

"Or Wayne."

"If you say so, Terrell. I'm not trying to twist your arm or anything."

"Okay, okay. So, just tell me what the deal is."

"It's not a deal, really," Caleb said. He pulled the notebook from the drawer and handed it over. "It's more like a dare."

CATHERINE COULD JUST imagine the look of delight on her mother's face. She had been planning this surprise for months, and now at last she would be able to divulge the secret. Joy Campbell would beam through her speechless lips. Her eyes would dance with pleasure.

First, however, Catherine had to be sure that her mom was outfitted with all the necessities for the trip.

She approached the receptionist's desk at RMS Homecare. Her steps were bouncy, and her brunette hair bobbed on her shoulders with new honey highlights. She'd determined to set aside her temporary confusion caused by Caleb's transformation and to move ahead. She found herself warming up to him, but fear was keeping her heart at arm's length. She was staying focused on her career—simpler that way, uncluttered.

"Hello, Mrs. Holt," the receptionist said. "How're you today?"

"Fine, thanks."

"I hope your parents are doing well."

"I'll tell you what, Mrs. Evans—that new wheelchair and bed are certainly helping."

"I'm so glad. Now, what can I do for you?"

"Well, I'm gonna be taking my mom on a short trip—and then, hopefully, a longer one after that."

"Oh?" Mrs. Evans said. "Sounds like fun."

"That's the plan. Are you a *Wheel of Fortune* fan?"

"The game show? I love it. But I don't usually get home till it's over, and anyway I'm no good at those puzzles. My mind just doesn't work that way."

"That's the thing. My mom's a whiz at it."

"Mrs. Campbell's a sharp cookie, all right. Many people assume that if someone can't talk, they must not be too bright. You know, my grandma used to tell me it was the other way around. She said it was right there in the Bible somewhere—Proverbs, I think— that a person of few words is wise."

"Well, it's true in my mom's case." Catherine propped her purse on the counter. "I can't wait to tell her about the surprise. See, I signed her up for the Wheelmobile that travels around. It's gonna be in Atlanta soon, and they use it to let contestants audition for the show."

"But I heard they have lines out the door. Are you sure you—"

"She's gonna get a chance. Guaranteed."

"Oh, you don't want to get her hopes up, Catherine."

"It's guaranteed," Catherine repeated. "As manager of PR at Phoebe Putney, I was able to get ahold of one of the show's associate producers. I pitched an idea for a segment featuring physically handicapped patients from around the country, and he loved it."

"They're gonna do it?"

Catherine smiled. "It's airing in two months."

"Oh my goodness."

"The best thing is that they're gonna match the contestants' earnings with donations to their chosen charities."

"That's wonderful."

"My mom will have to go through the preliminary steps like any other contestant, but her application's already on the short list for Atlanta. She's gonna get her big chance, spelling out guesses on her chalkboard."

"Well, this *is* exciting news." Mrs. Evans patted Catherine's hand. "Let's get her all stocked up for the trip, shall we? But, of course, that's why you're here."

"You know, all I really need are a few more linens to fit her hospital bed."

"Sure. We have some in stock."

"It's about the only thing that wasn't covered by the doctor when he purchased that bed and wheelchair."

"The doctor?"

"Yes. Dr. Keller, our secret philanthropist."

"Uh, I don't think Dr. Keller covered those things."

"No, I'm sure he did. I spoke with him about it."

Mrs. Evans thumbed through her files. She removed a receipt and looked it over. "Mrs. Holt, if I remember correctly, twenty-four thousand three hundred dollars was given for the bed and wheelchair, but Dr. Keller was not the main giver."

"What? What do you mean?"

"Oh yes, his initial donation was used to *start* the fund in your mother's name, but of the amount given, Dr. Keller gave just three hundred dollars."

Catherine took a step back. She was shaking her head, going down a mental list of the few others who even knew of her mother's specific medical needs. This couldn't be right. She had thanked the doctor. He had accepted that thanks.

"Then who gave the other?"

By Mrs. Evans's expression, it was clear she thought Catherine should already know. "Your husband," she said. "Caleb."

Catherine exhaled. Her fingers went numb as she took the paper and verified the information for herself.

Caleb?

"He came in about two weeks ago and paid for everything," the receptionist assured her. "I assumed you knew."

"Two *weeks* ago?"

"Yes. He told me not to tell anyone, but I didn't think that included you. It was the Tuesday before last. He called and asked what the price of a particular bed and wheelchair were, so I looked it up and . . ."

Catherine had turned and started walking. She was stunned.

"Mrs. Holt?"

Catherine could not speak. She pulled a hand to her chest.

256

"Are you okay?"

Catherine kept going, her chin quivering, as she pulled both hands over her mouth and her vision blurred behind a veil of tears.

SHE WAS SURPRISED to make it home without a major collision. She couldn't stop the tears from flowing, and her cheeks burned with the stains that now also marked her blouse. Afraid of running over Caleb's mountain bike or driving straight through the garage wall, she braked hard in the driveway.

The truck was gone. Caleb was on duty right now.

"Good," she blubbered. "I can't let him see me, not like this."

Catherine dumped her purse on the kitchen counter and found her gaze drawn to their wedding photos in the hallway. Seven years ago, Caleb Holt had declared his love for her, but in the time that'd elapsed, things had faded—just like these pictures would fade; just like she and her husband would wrinkle with age.

Something had happened, though. Caleb had changed.

The old Caleb would've made some snide remark about how her fever would go away if she just got out of bed.

The old Caleb would've stormed from the room after she told him she needed time.

The old Caleb would've never depleted his entire savings to buy medical equipment for his mother-in-law.

She found herself reflecting over the past forty-five days. His sarcasm had vanished, and kindness and helpfulness had taken its place. The computer that she had grown to hate so much had been destroyed. He'd even kept on his ring while his hand healed from a burn. But this . . . this was unmistakable.

He had sacrificed his money. His boat. His dream.

257

For her.

Catherine wondered if she, too, could change. She wanted to. Desperately.

Reining back her sobs to mere whimpers, she stumbled across the carpet to her room—*their* room. She opened the top right dresser drawer and fumbled through her clothing. In her mind, she could hear her husband's voice on their wedding day, his vows washing her in promises that sounded heartfelt. She thought she'd found Prince Charming, but it turned out he was just a regular guy.

And wasn't that all she really wanted?

Someone to have and to hold. A man, a lover, and a friend.

Someone who knew her inside and out, strengths and weaknesses—and loved her anyway.

Caleb was that man. He had kneeled at the edge of their bed only days ago and shown renewed faithfulness to her. In his patience and brokenness, he had demonstrated manliness beyond anything a silly dress shirt and tie could do.

She slammed the drawer shut.

"Oh, where *is* it?"

She snatched open the left drawer. It had to be here. Her fingers slid along the bottom edges, brushing aside garments, and—

There . . .

Her wedding ring.

She took it in her hand and eased it over her finger. She was shaking. Each tear caused new sparkles to radiate from the diamond's princess cut. It fit as it always had, and she crossed her hands over her chest, overwhelmed by waves of sudden joy and regret.

Oh, Caleb—will you still take me?

She brushed her hair back past her earrings and stared into

the mirror at her tear-streaked face. She was a mess. She smiled at the ring glistening on her finger, and she wanted to shout her love for her husband from the rooftops, but how could she do so looking like this?

Of course, that realization sent her spiraling into another whirlpool of weeping. What was *wrong* with her?

Laughing? Sobbing? Happy? And sad?

A total mess.

"Ohhh, stop crying," she scolded herself out loud. She pulled a brush through her hair. Tried to apply fresh makeup. What a catastrophe this was. "Stop it," she told herself again. "Stop! You can't . . . keep . . . crying . . . like this."

CHAPTER 37

A pot of water simmered on the kitchen stove, while a jar of spaghetti sauce waited on the counter. Lunch was on the way. In the meantime, Caleb insisted they spend a few minutes around the table, going over the material for their upcoming written exams. Sure, the physical testing was behind them, but the mental challenges could be equally taxing.

"We're gonna nail this," he told the guys. "Okay, Eric, you ready?"

"Ready."

"Explain RECEO."

"Uh-oh," Wayne said.

Terrell covered the study book with both hands. "He ain't gonna get it."

"RECEO: Rescue, Exposure, Containment, Extinguish, and—"

"Captain."

Caleb turned at Lieutenant Simmons's strident tone. Between the exams and the continual array of possible emergencies throughout the city, he felt his pulse spiking.

"Yes?"

"Can I see you for a minute?"

"Right now, Michael?"

"Yes, sir."

Caleb pushed away from the table, leaving the books to the boys. He approached his lieutenant and tried to quell the worry in his voice. "Is something wrong?"

Simmons squared his shoulders. He said, "Catherine's in the bay."

"*My* Catherine?"

"Yes, sir."

Caleb's eyebrows knotted as he studied Simmons's face for a clue or an explanation. The lieutenant remained stoic, nearly motionless. Caleb would have to investigate this on his own. He brushed past and exited through the side door. He walked down the hall toward the bay entrance, his mind racing.

Was this a bad thing? Catherine had stopped coming to see him here years ago.

But maybe . . .

Caleb pulled open the door to the bay and entered. He was standing at the edge of the vast room, his eyes blinded momentarily by sunrays streaming from his left. As his pupils adjusted to the interplay of shadow and light, he saw a silhouette.

A moment of déjà vu.

Standing thirty feet away, his wife was a vision in a necklace and a red summer dress.

The dress.

Tied at the waist, her mini-sweater was the same one she'd worn ten years earlier, the day they'd first met here at this same spot.

His heart lurched.

"Catherine?"

She stood wringing her hands, rocking slightly on her feet in a pair of simple flats. Gone was the corporate fashion. This was the woman he had first fallen in love with—not that he minded her professional air, but she'd often held that up as a shield between them.

The shield was down.

Through watery eyes, she said, "Caleb, if I haven't told you that you are a good man . . . you are."

What? Did she just say what I think she said?

Wearing a tender, humbled expression, she continued. "If I haven't told you that I've forgiven you . . . I have."

Caleb felt his heart tremble within. Could this really be happening?

She took cautious steps toward him, and he followed suit, closing the gap to twenty feet. But she wasn't done.

"And," she said, "if I haven't told you that I love you . . . I do."

The words sank deep inside him, and his throat tightened.

"Something has changed in you," she continued, her voice fragile and soft. "And I want what happened to you to happen to me."

He found himself drawing closer. Only ten feet apart.

"It can," he answered tenderly.

"Is it too late . . . ?" Catherine held up her hand, revealing her wedding ring. "To ask you to grow old with me?"

He filled his lungs, about ready to explode. His heart seemed to shout: *Go to her, Caleb!* He could wait no longer, and he ran to join her in the middle of the bay, embracing her small waist and lifting her on tiptoes. She wrapped her arms around his neck, and she felt so warm and smelled so good he wondered why he'd ever thought he could belong anywhere else.

With the sun carving out their joined forms, Caleb looked down into her deep brown eyes and felt himself falling in love all over again, falling deeper than before, with a love built on something stronger than both of them.

And he kissed her.

Catherine responded with a soft purr, the one she shared only with him, and kissed back with lips even softer than he remembered.

LIEUTENANT SIMMONS HAD witnessed many wondrous things in his life. He'd watched a miraculous rescue on a battlefield in Iraq. He'd seen the sun set over three different oceans, not to mention various towering mountain ranges. He knew beauty when he saw it, and he tried his best to give God the glory.

As for what was happening in the bay . . .

Now, *that* was beautiful.

Simmons stood at the side door, peering through the narrow glass panel and feeling his mouth widen into a huge smile. He threw both hands up in a cheer. "Yes! *Yes!*"

"Hey, man," Eric said, coming up from behind.

"Lieutenant," Wayne joined in. "Whatchu lookin' at?"

Simmons spun around and blocked the windowpane with his body. "Hey, back up. Back up. There ain't nothing to see here."

Terrell came forward with a knowing grin. As for the two white boys? They looked completely mystified. Wayne was craning for a glance, but got rebuffed. Eric kept asking what was going on out there.

Simmons remained steadfast, nudging them from the door. "Go on back to your business. Caleb's just in there starting a fire."

"What?" Wayne demanded. "What's he startin' a fire in the bay for?"

"It's not *that* kinda fire. Now, go. Back to your business. Hey!" He corralled Terrell. "Don't be thinking you get a peek. Man, I'll put you on cleanup duty."

CHAPTER 38

This was pure torture. A fireman on duty could not leave work except to handle official department matters, and now, after experiencing the most powerful moment in his married life, Caleb had to watch his precious wife head home while he finished his shift.

He stared at the clock in the meeting room, desperately hoping for the hours to pass quickly. He wanted to see her. Talk with her. Be with her.

"Captain?"

Caleb turned toward Lieutenant Simmons, who displayed a sympathetic grin.

"You're gonna stare a hole through that clock if you're not careful."

Had it been that obvious? They had finished their duties for the day, and now their downtime seemed to tick by in painful slow motion.

"I can hardly stand it," Caleb admitted. "It's killing me. I've never wanted to get outta here so badly in my life."

Simmons looked around the station to make sure they were out of earshot, then turned toward his captain with a serious expression. "Sir, that's why I came to talk with you. With all due respect, you need to tend to your illness and head home for the night. I can take responsibility for the remainder of the shift."

Caleb stared. "What are you talking about?"

"I'm talking about Proverbs 13:12, 'Hope deferred makes the heart sick, but desire fulfilled is a tree of life.' I'd say you need to go tend to your sickness, 'cause your symptoms are showin' all over your face."

Caleb wasn't quite sure how to take this. Part of him wanted to find an excuse, *any* excuse, to go to his love. Was Simmons messing with him?

"Michael," he said, trying to keep his tone balanced. "You know I can't do that. This may be a huge deal to me, but leaving for a reason like that would have to be cleared by the chief. I wouldn't know how to explain it to him."

A big smile spread across Michael's face. "That's why I called him for you."

"You did what?"

"I told him that you were showing signs of emotional distress, and that I believed an extra day off would do you some good. He agreed."

In normal circumstances Caleb would've asked for more details, but at the moment nothing was more important than getting home.

"One more thing," Simmons said. "I called Catherine, too, and told her I was covering your shift."

265

As Caleb shot up out of the chair, he made eye contact with his lieutenant. "You are a true friend."

Simmons waved him off. "Stop talking and get outta here. I got this."

That was all Caleb needed.

CATHERINE'S CAMRY WAS in the garage when Caleb pulled up. He grabbed his duffel bag and found himself running toward the door.

Take it easy, he scolded himself. *Be cool.*

He took a deep breath and paused just outside the garage door, with the day's events still pouring through his mind. Catherine had come back to him. Not only that, she had seen a true change— a change he could've never made on his own.

Now she wanted it, too.

Thank You, Jesus. Thank You, Lord.

He reached for the doorknob and stepped inside. The first thing that hit him was the scent of her perfume. He'd been aware of it as they embraced in the bay, but now she had obviously sprayed it about their home.

The next thing was the music.

Soft, romantic, and calming.

With his interest piqued, he rounded the corner to the living room where a few candles provided the only light in the house, and scattered rose pedals formed a walkway to the master bedroom. It'd been years since Caleb experienced chills, but now they were racing over his arms, up his back, and across his neck. His heart rate kicked up a notch.

On the coffee table, a simple note sat next to their small kitchen fire extinguisher.

For my wonderful husband,
Use this if things get out of hand.
Love, Catherine

His bag thudded from his hand onto the floor. For a moment, his legs weakened. Not only had he tried to win his wife's heart back, but she was now taking care of his.

And apparently, she was enjoying it.

He followed the path of petals to the bedroom. *Their* bedroom. That's when he saw her.

Many images in his life had permanently imprinted themselves in Caleb's mind—some good, and some bad. But a new one now took the top spot.

Catherine was beautiful. She stood by the bed with a soft yet hopeful smile, wearing the same garments she'd worn the first night of their honeymoon. They were his favorite. From the nightstand and dresser top, the light of seven candles caressed her skin. Her hair was in his preferred style, flowing down, resting lightly on her smooth shoulders. Her makeup was perfect.

The covers of their bed had been carefully folded back and the last few rose pedals adorned the pillows.

"Welcome home, my husband," she said with a loving smile.

He tried to catch his breath.

Catherine walked up and wrapped her arms around his neck, kissing him gently on the lips, then on each cheek. As she gazed into his eyes, something happened that Caleb did not expect.

He began to cry.

It wasn't only that he was here with his wife, or that he now had a right relationship with God. Or that he'd experienced a much deeper understanding of what love really was. It was all of that—every lesson, every truth, every experience.

267

He had embraced these things with the same passion he now used to embrace his precious wife.

"Caleb, are you okay?" she said.

He smiled at her through his tears, wanting her to know his every thought, to know how overwhelmed he felt at this moment.

"I've never been better in my life," he said. Then, he reached down and picked her up. "It was a good idea having that fire extinguisher ready. We might need it."

"My thoughts exactly," she cooed with a sparkle in her eye.

He carried his bride to the bed that was theirs again. He set her down gently and began kissing her with tender passion.

THEY HAD BREAKFAST together for the first time in months. Caleb had learned from Simmons at the station how to make some mean French toast, and Catherine seemed impressed.

After the meal, Catherine sat staring at him as if it were their first date.

"Tell me what happened to you, Caleb. I want to know everything."

The door was wide open. He had prayed for such an opportunity to share his new faith with her, the same faith that had changed his father and mother, and his friend, Lt. Michael Simmons.

"Come with me." He stood and reached for her hand. "I want to show you something."

They strolled into the woods, Caleb sharing what had happened to him over the past few months. Morning rays gilded draperies of moss in gold and danced across the lake as Caleb and Catherine approached the cross together.

Hand in hand. Step for step. Husband and wife.

BACK INSIDE, SAFE from the bugs and the growing darkness, Caleb settled into the couch, with one foot propped on the coffee table. He could hardly contain himself. So much had happened in the last few months, and he needed time to let this day's events sink in.

First, though, Caleb knew there were two phone calls he had to make.

"Captain Campbell?"

"Caleb, is that you?"

"Yes, sir."

"How's my favorite son-in-law doing?"

Caleb's foot was bouncing on the edge of the table. He had great respect for this man who had gone before him not only as an officer with the Albany Fire Department, but also as the father of an intelligent and strong-willed young lady.

"Good," he said. "Doing really good, actually. But, uh, I need to ask you something, Captain."

"I'm all ears."

"Well, I guess for a while there I got a little offtrack as a husband."

"We all make mistakes," Mr. Campbell said. "You might recall my own little detour in a fire, following a pipeline into the heart of danger."

"I'll never forget it."

"So what're you getting at?"

"Sir, I wanna ask for your forgiveness."

"Forgiveness?"

"Yes sir. I made a promise to love and cherish your daughter, but for the last few years I've not done a good job of it. That's changing, and I want you to know that she has become more precious to me than ever."

269

"Caleb Holt, I've trusted you since that day you pulled me to safety. Just recently here you've played a big role in helping my wife with her medical equipment, and I thank you for that. For what it's worth, you're forgiven. Now, take care of my daughter with that same kind of intensity."

"Thank you, sir."

The retired captain gave a hearty chuckle. "Just don't forget the things I taught you on your way to earning your trumpets."

"'Course not. You taught me everything you know."

"Whoa. Hold on now, Caleb. That's not quite accurate."

"What? But you promised—"

"Oh, I did teach you everything *you* know. I just didn't teach you everything *I* know."

JOHN HOLT SAT at the desk in his book-lined study, the setting sun's warmth oozing in through thick curtains. He drew a breath as he answered the phone. He wanted to believe the best, but he knew a long journey still lay ahead.

"Hello, son."

"Dad, it happened."

"What happened?"

"We're back together. And what's even better, Catherine has given her heart to Christ."

The news was like a shot of adrenaline to John's body, and he stood up from his desk chair. "When?"

"This morning. We went to the clearing and I led her in prayer. It was incredible."

John turned and motioned to his wife. "Cheryl, Catherine gave her heart to the Lord this morning."

Cheryl brought both hands over her mouth in amazement, then embraced her husband as they shared the phone between them.

"She and I are doing this together," Caleb went on. "Dad, I know we still have lots to learn, but at least we're walking the same path."

"That's right."

"When it was all done, I got down on my knees and asked her if she would marry me all over again. We're gonna renew our vows to each other, before God and man, there in that very spot where you and I talked."

"I do hope your mother and I are invited."

"Of course," Caleb said. "Dad, I want you to help me write new vows."

John felt simultaneously humbled and proud. He pulled Cheryl closer. "I could do that, son. Why, yes, I could."

THE NEIGHBORS WERE coming out of their house. Yep, here they came, through the garage. They always came that way, and Mr. Rudolph had to wonder whatever had happened to using the blasted front door. Just didn't seem practical to build things you had no intention of using.

From his patio swing, he watched the Holts' every move.

Caleb was holding the car door for that pretty wife of his, and she slipped into the passenger seat. Caleb looked over and caught Mr. Rudolph's eye.

Mr. Rudolph didn't even flinch. No, sirree. He'd lived here longer than any of these young whippersnappers, and he wasn't going to let them run him off. With his Sunday paper in his lap, and his wife beside him in hair curlers, he had every right to sit and watch the happenings up and down this street.

And Caleb Holt was as strange as they came—shattered computers, baseball bats, smashed garbage cans. And now, behind a great big smile, that young man was waving a Bible.

"Good morning, Mr. and Mrs. Rudolph."

"Caleb," Mr. Rudoph replied.

He and Irma raised their right hands in synchronized greeting. No smiles. No emotion. No reason to get too chummy with the neighbors.

Caleb climbed into the car and backed out of the driveway. The Holts were on the way to church, judging by their clothes, their Bibles, and this time of morning on a Sunday. Well, that was a new twist in the unfolding drama next door.

"Irma, I don't understand that boy," Mr. Rudolph said.

She turned toward him on the swing. "After forty-eight years, I still don't understand *you*."

"Hummph."

He worked hard at maintaining his stoic demeanor, and his wife's remark made him want to smile in a show of victory. But, no sir, he had his image to protect, and he went right back to wearing his long-faced scowl.

CHAPTER 39

There were still two surprises to come. Reflecting back, Caleb knew he should've seen these things coming, but he had let his own assumptions blind him to the truth.

Wasn't that how it usually worked?

Nearly six weeks had passed, and Catherine and Caleb's reaffirmation ceremony was only a day away.

John and Cheryl Holt arrived for an extended visit, with plans to house-sit while the younger Holts spent a second honeymoon on Saint Simons Island, along the Georgia coast. In their car, they had brought floral arrangements and a rented ivory archway that would be assembled at the clearing.

Others would provide folding chairs. The lieutenant's wife, Tina Simmons, was making the cake. All parties involved had agreed to keep the focus on the couple's commitment instead of racking up years of additional debt and stress through purchasing "all the trimmings" that some felt must accompany a wedding ceremony.

"Why do so many marriages start that way?" Caleb inquired as they helped his parents unpack the car.

"All part of the fairy tale," Catherine said. "For us girls, it's constantly being pushed on us—the style of our dress, the bridesmaids' gowns, the photographer and videographer. The list goes on."

"And it all costs a fortune. Seems like starting a marathon with a pair of lead boots."

She shot him a look. "Nice, Caleb. Way to make it sound romantic."

"What? You'd look cute in lead boots."

Another shot.

"Would it help if they were pink?" he said.

"Son, you oughta be thankful she's got her arms full," John said. "Or I think you'd be in trouble."

Catherine nudged by Caleb, a twinkle in her eye, and whispered: "Pink with black soles. Otherwise, no way."

WITH CATHERINE AND Cheryl in the house preparing lunch and catching up on recent events, father and son headed for the now familiar wooded trail. Caleb figured they could spend a few minutes fine-tuning the vows his dad had written.

He found out John Holt had something else in mind.

"I'm getting to where I know this trail pretty well," John said.

"You're welcome to walk it anytime, Dad."

"I just might. I love Savannah, but we sure enjoy seeing you. And we're still praying for grandkids."

"All right, all right. I get the message."

"You're not getting any younger."

"Hey, take it easy on me. Anyway, God knew we needed to get some things in order before going down that path."

"You may be right." Shrugging, John slipped his hands into his pockets. "But your mother made me promise that I'd try."

Caleb rolled his eyes. "Figures."

He wondered if her hounding would ever end. He could recall being a little boy, trying to chop wood on his own—to be a man, to do it just the way Dad did it. His mom had rushed out and snatched the ax away, frantic with worry. Since then, her every cautionary word and prying question had stirred that same irritation in him. Throughout high school, in particular, he'd lashed back every time she tried to butt in. Couldn't she just let him be his own person?

His father, on the other hand, had always known when to help or back off.

"I wanna thank you, Dad. *The Love Dare* has changed my life."

"God's changed your life. *The Love Dare* was just a tool He used."

"You know," Caleb said, "I've already given it to one of my firemen."

"Good. It's meant to be passed on."

Caleb could only imagine the burden the forty-day challenge must've been for his parents. Whereas he and Catherine had only seven years of bad habits to unwind, John and Cheryl had incurred decades. The yelling. The silent treatment. It must've been daily torture to forge ahead with that much baggage.

"I, uh, I just can't tell you how grateful I am that you didn't give up on me, Dad. Or on Mom for that matter."

John stopped walking and looked down. When he lifted his gaze again through his glasses, there was something purposeful there. "Caleb, I wanna be a godly man, and I'm learning so much. But there's something I haven't told you."

Caleb tilted his head. Where was this going?

"I wrote that notebook in my own handwriting," his father said, "because I knew you'd accept it from me. But I didn't do *The Love Dare* on your mother. She did it to me."

"What?"

"Son, *I* was the one who wanted to leave."

Caleb winced. This wasn't possible. His father was the one who had held this thing together and been the good guy throughout.

John said, "God got ahold of your mother, and she prayed and loved me unconditionally. It was through *her* example that I came to Christ."

Caleb took a gulp of air and glanced away. This changed everything. This upended the assumptions that had leveraged him against his own mother. "*Mom* did this?" He could hardly pose the question as his eyes began to swim.

"She did. She's such a blessing to me, and she's grown so much. I love her with all my heart."

Tears pricked the corners of Caleb's eyes. "Dad, I . . . I have treated her so *wrong*."

"Caleb, she deserves your respect."

He knew his father was right. He'd heard the words before, yet this time he viewed them in a different light. How could he have acted toward her the way he had? He turned his gaze back up the trail, toward the house. How could he face her, knowing how far he'd veered from what was fair and right?

How could he *not*?

John gave him an affirmative nod, as though reading his thoughts.

Without another word, Caleb strode back the way he had come, kicking through the leaves and ground cover. He broke into a run.

CHERYL HOLT STOOD in black slacks, a mint-green sweater, and an onyx necklace. She folded a napkin and set it beside her son's plate. Across the table, Catherine was setting down iced drinks and a plate of deviled eggs.

Cheryl heard footsteps from the hall, but she was focused on her task and moved to the next place setting.

The footsteps neared.

Someone was running. In the house?

Suddenly, she recognized that rhythm: it was the cadence of Caleb's feet that had warmed her heart every school day when he got home, and struck terror into her every time he came in from the backyard—had he hurt himself, cut himself, or broken an arm?

Cheryl stopped what she was doing now. All those maternal fears came coursing through her, but—as always, as every mother must do—she turned.

Her son was crying.

Oh, Lord, what has gone wrong?

There was no sign of physical pain in Caleb's wet eyes, though—only tenderness like she hadn't seen in ages. And then he rushed to her, enveloping her in an embrace.

"Mom . . . Mom, I'm so sorry."

She soaked it in, uncertain where this was coming from but not pushing it away. Not after all these years. "It's all right, son."

"I didn't know," he mumbled into her ear. "I didn't know."

But she did. Now she understood. She rubbed his back and felt her own eyes moistening behind her glasses. "It's all right." Her voice quavered with emotion. "It's okay. It's all right."

"Mom." He backed away to look at her, cupping her face with both his hands. "Please forgive me."

"I do, Caleb. You're forgiven. I love you."

He pulled her close again. "I love you, too, Mom. I love you so much."

CATHERINE WATCHED THE reconciliation between her husband and mother-in-law, sensing that it was a vital step in the healing of her own marriage. As the afternoon bore on, she didn't press Caleb for any explanations. She was learning that sometimes a man needed time to process things. And while women wanted face-to-face communication, men preferred side-by-side.

"Well, I s'pose you two lovebirds could use some time to yourselves," John offered. "Cheryl, how 'bout joining me for a walk?"

She nodded. "Let's go enjoy the last of the daylight."

"Just be back by seven," Catherine said.

"What's at seven?" Caleb asked.

"You'll see. But none of you'll wanna miss it."

"Well, we'll be here then." Cheryl turned on her way out.

"And not a minute sooner," John added with a wink.

Caleb slipped an arm around Catherine's waist, and she leaned back into him. He pointed out they had an hour to themselves. She shrugged and pretended there was nothing to do.

The pretending didn't last for long.

WITH THE TELEVISION tuned to WSWG Channel 44, Caleb and his parents waited on the couch. The onscreen guide told him they were about to watch a game show, but he had no idea why.

"Here we go," Catherine said. "Turn it up."

Caleb notched the volume in time to hear a studio audience cheer out:

"Wheel . . . of . . . Fortune!"

"It's Wonders in Wheelchairs Week," the MC announced, "featuring men and women who would not let fate keep them from *our* Wheel." The camera panned over three contestants, seated at their podiums on specially built platforms, smiling wide and ready to play. The MC continued, "Ladies and gentlemen: Pat Sajak and Vanna White."

"Hey, did I just see your *mom*?" Caleb said to Catherine. "She passed the audition?"

"With flying colors."

"I can't believe this. You acted like she didn't make it."

John and Cheryl were listening in, elated at this revelation.

"Is she there right now?" Caleb asked.

"It was filmed weeks ago. Dad went with her to L.A. for the taping."

"So, does she win anything?"

"Shhh," Catherine said. "I'm trying to watch the show. Look, there she is."

Mrs. Campbell appeared comfortable and confident, in a lavender blouse, with *Joy* on her name tag. Her hair was styled and colored, her eyes alive with wonder. By the first commercial, she had won $2,000 in a toss-up round. By the second, she'd taken a commanding lead with two puzzles solved and $8,600 in total earnings.

"Isn't she darling?" Cheryl asked as the last commercial came on. "I'm so happy for her. She looks like she's having the time of her life."

"Oh," Catherine said. "Definitely."

"Look at her smile," Caleb said. "And your dad looks so proud."

"That was part of the deal, that he would spin the wheel for her."

"She's done good so far."

"It's not over yet." Catherine squeezed his hand. "Just keep watching."

By the game show's third commercial, Mrs. Campbell had steamrolled the competition and earned a total of $14,900. She was wheeled forward in the finale, as the bonus-round contestant who now had a shot at the big prize—as yet undisclosed.

279

The puzzle was *a thing*. It was two words.

Joy chose her three free consonants and a vowel—*F, K, M,* and *A*—to be added to the supplied *R, S, T, L, N,* and *E*. She was left with:

_ _ _ KST_RE _AFE

Using the electronic chalkboard provided by the show, she wrote two wild speculations, then, with only seconds left, made her final guess: BOOKSTORE CAFE.

"That's correct!" Pat Sajak said.

The audience went wild and Mrs. Campbell lit up.

Pat waited for the cheers to quiet. "Well, let's see what you've won." He opened the envelope in hand to reveal the prize. "A new boat!" he exclaimed.

The screen filled with the image of an impressive thirty-two-foot cabin cruiser. It was amazing. Caleb's eyes widened in appreciation of such a fine vessel. Then, as the camera returned to the winner and her reaction, Mrs. Campbell surprised everyone by spelling out a final message with her electronic stylus. She held it up for all to see:

4 U CALEB

CHAPTER 40

They were all here at the campsite clearing. Catherine stood on the grass in comfortable flats, glowing in a shimmery gold dress with a matching shawl that draped her thin arms. She ran her gaze over the small, formally dressed group of friends and family, those who'd come to witness her and Caleb's special day.

This was really happening. A fresh start.

There were her parents, and Mr. and Mrs. Holt. Some of her coworkers were present—Tasha and Robin, Anna and Ashley. Farther back, the nurse who had treated Caleb's burns had made it, too.

Near the front, Caleb's crew sat tall and proud—Terrell, Eric, and Wayne, as well as Michael and Tina Simmons. Earlier, Catherine had been introduced to a tall man, a Marine, who had put himself on the line at the train tracks a few months ago. He was in the crowd now. And was that Chief Hatcher?

Nothing could keep her from smiling ear to ear as she faced the tan-suited man before her. Caleb was older now, with even a few hints of gray at his temples, but he looked more handsome than ever. Above his gold tie, green eyes were peaceful, filled with a love deeper than those first giddy moments of infatuation in a firehouse bay ten years ago.

Sparks were nice. No doubt about that.

But these flames between them now burned longer, hotter, richer.

"We've gathered here today," the minister was saying, "to celebrate the reaffirmation of vows with Caleb and Catherine. And whereas this may be the second time they've made a commitment to this marriage, it is the first time they have done so upon a foundation of faith in Jesus Christ . . ."

Behind the minister, the moss-draped cross stood tall against the sun.

"It is the desire of Catherine and Caleb that their vows, from this point on, be a covenant and not a contract. For marriage is a sacred institution established by God, and one that is meant to last for life."

A cool breeze swept up from the pond, rustling the leaves in the majestic pecan trees and stately oaks. Catherine couldn't imagine a more beautiful day.

She caught the minister's slight nod.

This was it. Time to seal this before all present.

She and Caleb stepped in unison toward each other. She wondered, for just a moment, if her hair was still in place and if she'd used the right color of lipstick for this setting—and then that all floated away as she locked eyes with her husband.

"Caleb," the minister said, "in the presence of God and these witnesses, do you come today to freely and unconditionally commit to this covenant marriage to Catherine?"

"I do."

"And, Catherine, do you come today to freely and unconditionally commit to this covenant marriage to Caleb?"

"I do." She gave a bashful smile. "With all my heart."

"Genesis 2:24 says, 'For this reason a man will leave his father and mother and be united to his wife, and they will become one flesh . . .'"

CAPTAIN CALEB HOLT liked the idea of becoming one flesh. He couldn't wait for their four-day, three-night stay at Saint Simons. Against his every compunction, he hadn't even asked about getting his new thirty-two-footer docked there somehow.

When it came to love, there were some things you just didn't dare.

The minister continued with the vows, and the gathering remained polite until the words Caleb had waited for: "You may kiss the bride."

Catherine lifted her face to his. Willing and waiting.

Nothing had ever sent his heart into somersaults quite like that.

Down the grassy aisle they paraded, grinning amid the crowd's jubilation. They moved beneath the ornate ivory archway, past flowers on short pillars, to tables in the back of the clearing.

A punch bowl waited on one.

Good. Caleb was thirsty out here in the August heat.

On the other table, beside the guestbook, a picture of him and his wife showed them squeezing a stuffed, oversized Dalmatian between them. Towering over the display, a resplendent cake with buttercream icing waited for the first cut from bride and groom. Tina Simmons had done an amazing job on this. Even Caleb, a rookie in the ways of baking, marveled at the delicate rose petals carved into the frosting, interspersed by actual deep-red rosebuds.

And it looked like Lieutenant Simmons had added a touch of his own.

Caleb laughed out loud.

Crystal salt and pepper shakers stood atop the confectionary work of art, one wearing a black top hat, and the other a tiny white veil.

God demonstrates his own love for us in this:
While we were still sinners,
Christ died for us.

—ROMANS 5:8

ACKNOWLEDGMENTS
From Alex Kendrick and Stephen Kendrick

Eric Wilson (writer)—once again you've captured the story and presented it in a way that engrossed even our imaginations. You are a gift to us! Well done.

Larry and Rhonwyn Kendrick (Dad and Mom)—your witness of faith and love continue to minister to so many. You are our godly heritage. We love you!

Christina and Jill (our wives)—you took a dare to love us and to walk this path with us. Your encouragement and support have fueled our desire to tell these stories. We are more than blessed! We love you and thank God for you.

Joshua, Anna, Catherine, Joy, Caleb, Grant, Cohen, and Karis (our kids)—may your growing faith draw you close to Jesus. His love for you is fireproof!

ACKNOWLEDGMENTS

Allen Arnold and Amanda Bostic (publisher and editor)—thank you for your work, encouragement, and flexibility. We've enjoyed the journey. May God bless you!

Michael Catt and Jim McBride (pastors)—we are so honored to be on the team with you, in life, in ministry, in friendship. We remain overwhelmed! Keep going!

Albany Fire Department (friends and consultants)—may God guide and protect you as you protect us. We are grateful and proud of you!

Sherwood Baptist Church (home base)—thank you for your consistent prayer, support, and amazing heart for the Lord. He shines through you!

ACKNOWLEDGMENTS
From Eric Wilson

Alex and Stephen Kendrick (directors, producers, and friends)—may God continue filling your hearts and minds with His artistry, passion, and joy.

Carole Hall Collins and Ron Collins (the Kendricks' aunt and uncle)—may the hospitality you showed me continue to spread through others to every continent.

Amanda Bostic (editor and friend)—may you experience the same grace you extended when I goofed on my deadline. You forgive me?

Allen Arnold, Jennifer Deshler, Deborah Wiseman, and the Thomas Nelson Crew (publisher, publicist, and editors)—may you find continued creativity, discernment, and grace under fire. You're my heroes!

ACKNOWLEDGMENTS

David Robie and BigScore Productions (literary agent)—may your perseverance pay off, and may we have many more projects together.

Cassie and Jackie Wilson (my incredible daughters)—may you both find husbands who love you as Christ loves His bride, the church. I'm a lucky dad!

Mark Wilson (father)—may all your patience with my computer ignorance pay off on a trip together, just you and me, through some remote Oregon woods.

Linda Wilson (mother)—may your never-ending love and support come back to you from others, and may we share more adventures overseas.

The Council of Four and my Nashville Nucleus (writers and friends)—may you grow in wisdom, skill, and the ability to enjoy life to its fullest. What would I do without you guys?

Captain Kenny Loudenbarger (Albany Fire Department)—may you stay safe on the job and find the few hours it takes to read a book. Maybe even this one?

Scott Bach, Jake Chism, Laurel Cockrell, Todd Michael Greene, Lauren Howell, Wolfe Moffatt, James Nichols, Pat Porter, and Melissa Willis (bloggers, reviewers, and fans)—may you be encouraged as you spread the news and wrestle with the written word. You've blessed my socks off!

Warren Barfield, Casting Crowns, Greg Holiday, Leeland, Third Day, John Waller, Webster County, and Mark Willard (musicians

ACKNOWLEDGMENTS

and artists)—may the songs you added to this story touch others as they did me while I worked on the manuscript. Keep rockin'!

Dear Readers—Thank you for joining me on this journey of danger and bravery, of faith, hope, and love.

Feel free to visit my Web site: www.WilsonWriter.com
or e-mail: WilsonWriter@hotmail.com

A PERSONAL MESSAGE FROM THE KENDRICK BROTHERS

Thank you for reading *Fireproof*! We hope you thoroughly enjoyed Caleb and Catherine's journey. Now that you have read the novel, we want to boldly challenge you in your own spiritual journey. How will the story of *Fireproof* influence you? Will you allow the message of faith and love to penetrate beyond the pages of this book?

If you do not have a relationship with Jesus Christ, we want you to know that He is the Real Deal. We're not talking about religion . . . but a *relationship* with Jesus. He alone has proven to be the missing link to God that people are longing for . . . and desperately need. One that you need.

His entire life demonstrates His uniqueness as God in the flesh. His virgin birth, sinless life, powerful teachings, amazing miracles, unconditional love, sacrificial death, miraculous resurrection, and impact on the world are all unique to Jesus Christ alone. Try reading Matthew, Mark, Luke, and John in the Bible and see for yourself what those who were with Him witnessed firsthand. He not only is qualified to forgive your sin, but He can change your heart and make it pleasing toward a holy God. It is foolish to trust in your own goodness to get into heaven. Only God can make us clean through Jesus Christ.

The Scriptures say that all of us have fallen short of God's righteousness (Romans 3). We've all broken His commands. Each of us has lied, lusted, and hated. That's why we could never stand before Him. We are guilty of many sins. He requires righteousness to enter heaven.

That's why He lovingly sent Jesus. His death on the cross was necessary to make things right between us and a holy God. He didn't have to do that. That's just love in action . . . personified.

Regardless of where you are, let us encourage and challenge you, on behalf of Christ, to do what Caleb and Catherine Holt did, and surrender your heart afresh to God. Romans 10:9 says that if you confess with your mouth that Jesus is your Lord (Master or Boss), and you believe in your heart that God has raised Him from the dead, then you will be saved.

If you are already an obedient follower of Christ, then we want to encourage you further in your spiritual journey. We challenge you to let the faith and integrity that Christ brings influence your relationships, children, daily habits, and work environments. Do you model honesty and the golden rule in how you treat others? Have you dedicated your personal ethics and work environment to God? Are there people you need to get right with that you have wronged in the past? Don't wait any longer. Do it!

We encourage you to refocus your passions toward the higher purpose of glorifying God and not living for your own temporary fulfillment in this life. Start your days in the Word of God and in prayer. Pray that people will be "wowed" by the changes that Christ has made in you. And let your commitment be independent of others. People will fail you, reject you, and let you down. But don't be discouraged. Don't let anything or anyone cause you to stop loving Him. Find a group of believers at a local church who share this passion and who will join you in this great adventure! Then let's plan to rejoice together as we watch God glorify Himself through our lives and do more than we can ask or imagine! May your life in Christ be fireproof!

God Bless You!

Alex Kendrick and Stephen Kendrick

FIREPROOF
DISCUSSION QUESTIONS

1. What are the multiple meanings of the word "fireproof" in the story?
2. How did Caleb and Catherine fail each other in their marital roles?
3. Could you relate to either Caleb or Catherine? In what ways?
4. In what ways did Caleb's view of marriage change after he accepted Christ?
5. What was holding Caleb back from trusting in God in the first half of the story?
6. What do the salt and pepper shakers represent?
7. What was the eye-opening moment for Caleb when he realized his hypocrisy?
8. How was John an effective mentor to Caleb?
9. How did Caleb resolve to love his wife in the second half of *Fireproof*?
10. Why did Catherine struggle so much to accept Caleb's demonstrations of love?
11. Why did Michael say it was unwise to always follow your heart?

12. How were Michael and Anna an influence on Caleb and Catherine?
13. In what ways did God prepare Catherine's heart to open up to Caleb?
14. What struggles did Caleb have after accepting Christ?
15. What did John mean when he said, "You can't give her what you don't have"?
16. Has there been a time when you came to a point of total surrender to God? If not, what is holding you back?
17. How is the cross a picture of sacrificial love?
18. What lesson impacted you the most in the story?
19. What did you learn about love and marriage from this book?
20. What commitments do you personally need to make in light of what you've read?

THE MAKING OF *FIREPROOF*

BY STEPHEN KENDRICK

DECEMBER 2005

My brother, Alex, had just finished jogging and called me outside my house to share the news. "I think I've got the storyline for the next movie," he said enthusiastically. At that time, *Facing the Giants* was edited and ramping toward a theatrical release the following September. We didn't know what to expect from it, but had already begun a season of prayer asking God for direction about what should come next.

Lord, what do You *want the next movie to be about? We've got multiple ideas, but Yours are always better. We need* Your *wisdom.*

We began asking specifically for a story that would impact the culture. We had waited and prayed for several months. Now on my driveway, Alex looked at me and declared, "I just got an idea for a movie about marriage."

Marriage?

When you think of movie ideas believers long to see, you imagine a Christian time-travel flick or an end-times thriller about the mark of the beast, loaded with chase scenes and explosions. But when was the last time you saw a movie that honored and tried to rescue marriages? *The Parent Trap*?

That day, Alex began to lay out the initial idea of what he called *The Love Dare*. After listening to him, I said, "I believe this is of God. Married couples desperately need this right now. The body of Christ needs it!" We began to pray for the Lord to develop this very unlikely plot into a screenplay that would please Him. So a new season of focused prayer began . . . for marriages to be impacted through the next movie.

FALL 2006

While developing the storyline, God surprised us with the response to *Facing the Giants*. This $100,000 football drama produced by untrained volunteers from our South Georgia church grossed $10 million in theaters and would become the top-selling DVD in Christian bookstores in 2007. Thousands were reportedly coming to Christ through it, and churches were creating effective ways to utilize the movie for ministry. Our Sherwood church family was thrilled!

SPRING 2007

Over the next several months, the Lord graciously allowed *Giants* to be distributed in thirteen languages on DVD to fifty-six countries, resulting in an international ministry. E-mails started pouring in with unbelievable stories of how this little church-made movie (that openly honors Jesus and the Word of God) was spreading to unlikely places.

International retailers were showing clips in their training classes. A cruise ship was playing it continuously in their cabin rooms. A Turkish airline featured it as their in-flight movie. Teens in China were on YouTube, uploading their own versions of the Death Crawl, and NFL players were distributing it to their teams. The amazing stories of God's goodness were overwhelming. He was doing more than we could ask or imagine.

While movie critics scratched their heads and blogged about it, we shared a sense of awe at the Lord as He continued to glorify Himself through our weakness. No one could take the credit but Him!

Countless scripts and books started landing in our offices at Sherwood Baptist Church with notes that said, "God told me that my story needs to be your next movie." Sports dramas, dark thrillers, and pro-life stories piled up along with my favorite—the kung fu pastor who beats up vampires in Jesus' name.

But our focus shifted to developing "The Love Dare" movie. We believed God was inspiring the idea. Our wives and pastors were supportive and agreed we should move forward. We studied the Scriptures to find that marriage is a huge priority to God. Hebrews 13:4 says that marriage should be honored by all. It was the first human institution established by God, and one that families, children, churches, and governments are built upon. If marriage crumbles, so does everything built on it.

Looking around us, we saw that the need was massive. Our culture has fallen so far from God's design for marriage. It is supposed to be the strongest and safest human relationship. A haven of unconditional love. And most importantly, a picture of Christ and His Bride. (Ephesians 5) We found that 90 percent of Americans get married at some point in their lives, but I'd argue that most of those marriages are not Christ-like.

Statistically, fewer people are valuing marriage. You often hear pop culture stars say statements like, "I don't need a piece of paper to solidify my relationship," revealing they have totally missed its meaning. In addition, young couples are foolishly getting married with no marriage preparation or counseling. Husbands and wives are not seeking or obeying God's Word concerning their roles and responsibilities. We see pornography and divorce destroying families. However, we're also watching God's Word bring liberty, health, and healing to marriages that obey and seek Him.

We began praying that this movie would throw a lifeline to couples considering divorce and that we would also inspire strong marriages toward greater love and intimacy. Ultimately, we hoped to directly affect the rate of divorce in our culture.

SUMMER 2007

After Alex and I developed the plot, my mother-in-law suggested we tell the story through the backdrop of a firefighter. When we thought about it, the parallels between the two worked. Firefighters constantly respond to fires that spark up around them—and so must husbands and wives. Firefighters must communicate well, learn to protect one another, and be willing to lay down their lives for each other—so must husbands for their wives. Firefighters never leave their partner—and neither should couples.

Alex suggested the title *Fireproof* since it carried multiple meanings, both spiritually and literally. I looked up the word in the dictionary to find a unique definition. When something is fireproof, it does not mean it prevents fire, but that it is able to withstand it when it comes. Since all marriages encounter "fires" of some sort, this seemed fitting.

FALL 2007

After our pastors agreed that *Fireproof* would be Sherwood's next production, our church's prayer ministry began praying for the needed resources. God confirmed the direction by delivering in amazing ways! More than twelve hundred people from our community volunteered to serve in some capacity. The Albany fire department offered their stations, equipment, and new trucks for our use. Multiple homes and businesses were opened to us, and a local hospital offered an entire wing for the shoot. Before we knew it, we had all sixteen needed locations available for free.

We prayed for the right people to play the lead roles of Caleb and Catherine Holt, and began the casting process at the church. After pouring through many auditions, a young lady named Erin Bethea was cast as Catherine after grasping the heart of the role and making us cry with her performance. For Caleb, our pastor, Michael Catt, suggested we call Kirk Cameron because of his acting experience and passion for the gospel. Kirk, who is a big *Facing the Giants* fan, quickly caught the vision behind *Fireproof* and volunteered to invest in this ministry. And our friends at Provident Films agreed to distribute the movie before the first frame was shot.

Kirk was blessed to be on a set where daily prayer and encouragement were the norm, not to mention the Southern cheese grits and boiled peanuts he learned to love. We were blessed by his professionalism, and to have him help Alex and me craft the scene where the gospel is presented.

As the production picked up speed, we were amazed at how the church family rallied together in service and prayer. Ministry leaders from around the nation flew in to see part of the production and watched our church members cooking, sewing, building, acting, and praying together. The Lord was showing up daily to enable and provide.

While filming a rescue scene, we needed to place a wrecked car onto train tracks but found it too heavy to move. While our crew stood around staring at it, the man who lives next to the tracks walked out into his front yard and said, "You need a forklift? I've got one in my backyard you can use." He then drove it around his house, picked up the car, and moved it in place. Our director of photography looked at me and said, "Unbelievable! What are the chances that anyone within a hundred-mile radius of where we are has a forklift in their backyard ready to be used?" God is good.

Although we were consistently amazed at answered prayer, the production was not all peaches and cream. Hundreds of people working sixteen-hour days in close quarters for months can be challenging. Equipment failure, personal injury, and family needs are all part of the equation. One Sunday, during church, we received word that one of our cameramen, Robert "Chip" Monk, had flipped his car on the way back to Albany and was tragically killed. The crew was shocked and chose to shut down production for a week to mourn and minister to his pregnant wife. This only drew us closer together and ignited a greater passion for investing in eternal things.

The other dynamic is spiritual warfare. We've found that the enemy knows where to attack based on where God is working and where believers are praying. Satan is always trying to discourage, divide, and distract the body of Christ. We sought to daily guard against this by having morning devotions together and prayer times on the set. Churches from across the nation also began e-mailing us of their corporate prayer support for the project.

We praise God for the way the body of Christ is working together to try to save and fireproof marriages. When the movie was completed, we were thrilled to have more than fifty marriage ministries extend their support for the ministry of the movie.

The more we looked at the dynamic of marriage, the more we saw the fires that could naturally ignite. When a man and woman tie the knot, they are joining their hurts, fears, baggage, and imperfections. They unpleasantly discover how selfish they are and how sinful their spouse is. At the same time, communication barriers, work pressures, health issues, and financial needs usually flare up at some point and add heat to the relationship.

God's Word declares that God is sovereign in the midst of all of this. He created marriage as a good thing. He uses it as a tool to eliminate loneliness, establish families, raise children, and bless us with relational intimacy. Marriage also forces us to grow up and deal with our own issues with the help of a permanent partner. It causes us to die to ourselves in order to love another person unconditionally. Marriage can really test us and purify us by fire! It is a picture of what Jesus does for us.

Through the story of *Fireproof*, we want movie fans and readers to see a marriage go through the fire and then see what happens when God's truth and love get involved. Our hope is to use the art form of movie making and novels to realistically show some of the fights and struggles that married couples experience daily and then hold up the truth of God's Word to deal with those struggles.

Our prayer at Sherwood has been that the Lord would help us take the gospel to the ends of the earth and to help prepare the Bride of Christ for His soon return! May God get the glory!

For more information, visit www.fireproofthemovie.com.

FIREPROOF MOVIE STILLS

1. *Young Catherine gets a kiss from Daddy*

2. *Caleb struggles with temptation*

3. *Caleb surfs the Internet*

1. Catherine vents her marital frustration with friends

2. Caleb complains to his friend Michael
3. Caleb gets a lesson from salt and pepper shakers

1. The train heads for a stranded car

2. Captain Caleb Holt tries to stop the train
3. The firemen attempt to move the car

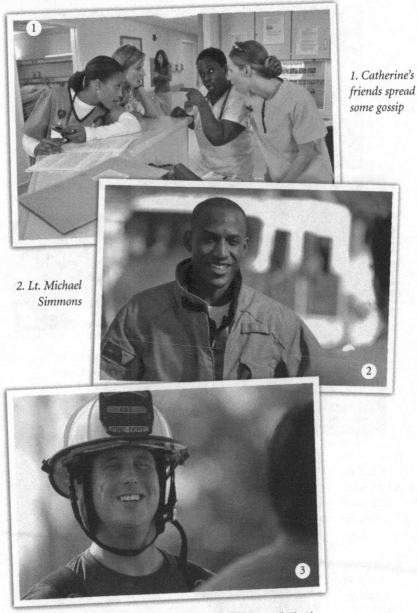

1. Catherine's
friends spread
some gossip

2. Lt. Michael
Simmons

3. Wayne "The Man" Floyd

2. Caleb tries
to save Lacey

3. Caleb attempts
a daring rescue

1. Caleb's
father, John,
discusses
what love
means

4. Catherine
gets an
apology
from Caleb

FIREPROOF PRODUCTION STILLS

1. The Fireproof production slate

2. Producer Stephen Kendrick leads the opening prayer

3. Shooting the Apology Scene with Erin Bethea

4. Director Alex Kendrick discusses a scene with Kirk Cameron

1. Curry Bushnell touches up Erin's makeup

2. Alex Kendrick plans a shot with Bob Scott

3. Assistant director David Nixon calls action

4. Sherwood church members pray for the cast

1. Sound mixer Rob Whitehurst, ready to ride

2. Alex directs the firemen at the house fire set

3. A forklift shows up as an answer to prayer

4. Shooting the train sequence

311

1. Director of photography, Bob Scott, preps a shot

2. Shooting the courtyard scene with Catherine and Gavin

3. Writers Stephen Kendrick and Alex Kendrick

4. The Sherwood Pictures Producer Team, Michael Catt, Alex Kendrick, Jim McBride, and Stephen Kendrick

ALSO AVAILABLE

FROM THE CREATORS OF COURAGEOUS

FACING THE GIANTS

NEVER GIVE UP. NEVER BACK DOWN.
NEVER LOSE FAITH

BASED ON THE MOVIE BY
ALEX KENDRICK
& STEPHEN KENDRICK

NOVELIZATION BY ERIC WILSON

THE CREATORS OF COURAGEOUS

FLYWHEEL

IN EVERY MAN'S LIFE
THERE'S A TURNING POINT

BASED ON THE MOVIE BY
ALEX KENDRICK
& STEPHEN KENDRICK

NOVELIZATION BY ERIC WILSON

ABOUT THE AUTHORS

ALEX KENDRICK and STEPHEN KENDRICK helped Sherwood Baptist establish Sherwood Pictures in 2003. They have co-written *Flywheel*, *Facing the Giants*, *Fireproof*, and the upcoming film *Courageous*. Both live in Albany, Georgia, and serve in leadership positions at the Sherwood Baptist Church; Alex is associate minister, and Stephen is associate teaching pastor.

ERIC WILSON is the *New York Times* best-selling writer of *Fireproof*, the novelization, as well as the novelizations of *Flywheel* and *Facing the Giants*. He lives in Nashville, Tennessee, with his wife and two daughters.